SLEEPING PARTNERS

Martin enjoyed the spectacle of his mother's friend, Joyce, walking up the beach in her wet bathing suit. Every curve of 'Auntie' Joyce's figure was moulded to the sodden material. How it clung to her full breasts, revealing each shapely globe perfectly to his inquisitive eyes. She reached her towel and began to dry herself, unwittingly displaying every luscious inch of her mature frame as she rubbed and stretched. Her broad buttocks and the bulging mound at the join of her thighs were plainly outlined as the soaking costume clung like a second skin to her ample body.

Martin grinned to himself, remembering last night. Now he knew exactly what lay beneath that skintight bathing suit . . .

CW01498981

Sleeping Partners

Lesley Asquith

 HEADLINE DELTA

First published in 1996
by HEADLINE BOOK PUBLISHING

A HEADLINE DELTA paperback

10 9 8 7 6 5 4 3 2 1

ISBN 0 7472 5107 X

Typeset by
Letterpart Limited, Reigate, Surrey

Printed and bound in Great Britain by
Cox & Wyman Ltd, Reading, Berks

HEADLINE BOOK PUBLISHING
A division of Hodder Headline PLC
338 Euston Road
London NW1 3BH

Sleeping Partners

Chapter One

NIGHT GAMES

The single tap at Martin's bedroom door was secretive, gauged not to arouse the other members of the Compton household. Martin was not asleep, but so furtive was the knock that he missed it. As ever on retiring to bed, lewd thoughts intruded to disturb him, lurid imaginings of an ever-randy youthful mind. He pondered all the delightful sexual acts a horny teenager might enjoy with a nubile naked girl in his lonely bed. *Two* girls to romp with, to feel and fondle and fuck, would be even more splendid. His right hand automatically crept down to clasp his responding prick. He had the very two girls in mind as he conjured up a suitably erotic scene.

Haughty Linda Simon was definitely first choice, so ripely endowed with tit and arse for her seventeen years; and Mandy Field, plump, cuddly and reckoned to be hot stuff. Both were Martin's sister Becky's best friends and frequent callers to his home. How enticingly they shaped up that summer! He had ogled girlish breasts in their bikinis, fully rounded out with big nipples projecting; and the bulges behind the triangles of material at their crotches had matured into womanly cunt mounds. He swore to himself he'd have them in time. Before he was much older he would have every female he could, dedicating himself to that ambition. He already had the equipment, fortunately being endowed above average – and Martin was determined to put his advantages to good use.

In every respect a normal youth, he fantasised about his sexual preferences as if in training to experience them. Females were the most delightful creatures, worthy of his desire to provide their pleasure as well as his own. He thought of the curvaceous, barely concealed buttocks he had seen on the beach. Given the chance, he would pay respectful homage to such sweet bottom flesh with kisses. Such bottoms would never be short of a place to sit as long as he had a face. While he was stroking his prick and savouring the thought, the knock at his door was repeated.

Annoyed at the interruption, Martin reluctantly released his cock and sat up to click on the bedside lamp. In its soft glow the face of his Aunt Joyce was revealed, peering around the door. She held a finger to her lips.

'Martin, move over,' she ordered hoarsely. 'Do as I say.' She entered the room and shrugged the dressing gown off her shoulders. It fell to her feet, revealing her naked to his stare. 'Move over, make room,' she repeated urgently. 'Let me get in with you.'

Dumb with surprise, Martin shifted over in the bed to make space. In the fleeting moments before she joined him, he noted the flushed handsome face, her eyes glassily fixed on his bare upper torso. She had loosened her abundant chestnut hair and it fell to her shoulders. He marvelled at the size and fullness of heavy mature breasts thrusting from her chest: a pair of perfectly matching globes with big brownish nipples sprouting from lighter brown aureoles on milk-white skin. Her figure was comely, the ample curves rounded with firm flesh, enticingly ripe in the fashion of older women who retain sexual attractiveness.

She raised a knee to get in beside him. As he drew back

the bedcovers, Martin was given a glimpse between Joyce's sturdy thighs. Nestled there was a plump mound with a thick curling bush of hair surrounding the slit of her sex. To his disappointment she switched off the light, but now her soft warm womanly flesh was pressed to his body. He heard a low groan in her throat as her mouth sought his. Lips parted and tongue probing, he was on the receiving end of a long, passionate kiss. 'Yes, oh *yes*,' she moaned as her open wet mouth parted from his, the sweet aroma of sherry on her breath. 'I *must*, I need to – can't help it—'

Help yourself all you want, Martin thought eagerly, recovered from his surprise and congratulating himself on such a heaven-sent stroke of luck. He was glad he slept nude as they hugged skin to skin, the big pliant mounds of her breasts cleaving to his chest, the taut nipples digging into him. His face, neck and mouth were covered in long suctioning kisses. 'Dear boy, sweet boy,' Joyce muttered repeatedly, making him aware his aunt had lost all control. Was it frustration or drink? Whatever had brought her to his bed, Martin welcomed the fact. In her desperate state, he reasoned, he had a chance to fulfil some of his own wildest fantasies. Some lewd talk to start with, he'd always liked the idea of that. And, as Joyce took the initiative, uncontrollable in her haste to be at him, he would let her have her way. He would enjoy being the helpless subject of female domination, for starters at least.

'Aunt Joyce,' Martin groaned as her hand grasped his stiff cock and he heard her gasp of surprise. 'You made it like that, so big and hard and painful. I can't help it.' Delighted with his cunning, he acted as if he was in the extreme of shocked pleasure. 'It went that way when I saw you without any clothes. Please! Won't you do something to ease it for me, please!'

'It *is* huge and so hard,' he was delighted to hear his bed

3

partner say. She squeezed his cock tightly and stroked it energetically. Then, unable to resist, she gave a heartfelt low moan and threw a leg across his thighs. In the gloom, as his eyes focused, he saw her loom over him, tits bobbing and bouncing. He felt her point his prick, directing it upright. With a grunt she bore down, impaling herself on him to the hilt. Now Martin had his whole length encased in the warm folds of her flesh. Without pause she began working herself up and down on the unbending stalk, muttering her pleasure. She was so well lubricated, Martin exulted in the thought that she had been playing with herself before she had yielded to the temptation and come to his room.

'Oh, aunt, aunt,' he pleaded, determined to make her lapse a memorable one for her, giving up to her driving force. 'Oh, you are fucking me, fucking me – and it's so *nice*!' He chose his words with deliberation, certain that was increasing her pleasure too. But his mounting arousal demanded more of an active part. He reached up, stilling her bouncing tits and capturing them in his grasp. 'Such lovely tits!' he moaned. 'What a cunt you've got, just made to fuck. You're all hot and juicy for it—'

'Shut up, lie still!' Joyce suddenly hissed out as Martin lifted his hips to meet her downward thrusts. 'Don't you dare move – there, there, I'm coming, coming! Lord, Lord, heaven, heaven, I'm C-O-M-I-N-G!'

She certainly was, Martin did not doubt it, as her wild gyrations increased in pace, her large soft buttocks bouncing against his thighs. At last she collapsed over him, her body wracked with spasmodic shudders which decreased until she lay prone. When her breathing finally steadied she rose from him, snatching up her dressing gown and fleeing silently on bare feet from the room. Martin lay back, jubilant. He was amazed that women could desire sex so much, to the point where propriety and inhibitions were cast aside in their need.

4

And Aunt Joyce of all people too, he chuckled. Using him like that! What a fabulous cunt she had. Too fabulous for him not to want to be there again.

And be there again he would, he promised himself as he settled back, resisting the urge to go to her bedroom. In the dying convulsions of her orgasm, several at least he liked to think by her spasms and gasps, he had spunked up her gloriously. It beat the dickens out of any handjob. Now Joyce had revealed her hidden nature, he intended to use the knowledge to satisfy his own desires by fair means or foul. He could appeal to her as the one who had aroused such feelings him and even use a little coercion or blackmail if required. All was fair in love and war. Martin looked forward to seeing Joyce at breakfast.

'Mirror, mirror,' Linda Simon recited proudly to her reflection, 'who has the prettiest tits of all? Me, Mandy, or Becky?' The girl posed, cupping her breasts, lifting them as if on offer. 'No contest!' she announced smugly.

How very much Becky's brother, Martin, would like to see her like this, she considered, standing naked before the full-length mirror on her bedroom wardrobe. It was a game she played nightly. Well aware of the curvaceous allure of her young body, she excited herself with lewd thoughts and desires that readily filled her mind. 'What a randy bitch I really am,' she told herself happily. 'Our secret, isn't it, mirror? Ours and Clifford's, of course.'

Her breasts were rounder, fuller and much bigger than those of her two close friends and she had comelier hips and thighs too. She noted with satisfaction how the fine hair of her pubic bush had thickened and curled over the prominence at the fork of long shapely legs. Pleased with her startling beauty, one cupped palm left her right breast. It travelled sinuously over a silk-smooth stomach to stroke the

5

outer lips of her sex. How they thickened, opening like a flower to the sun when aroused, inner moistness flowing so readily in response. Fondling herself, she stepped back a pace or two until the backs of her legs met the side of her bed. Falling backwards, she lay with widely parted legs hanging over the edge.

In this position she could still admire herself in the mirror. The fingers of one hand continued probing her cleft while the other squeezed each breast, pinching and plucking at the nipples. 'Yes, so *good*,' she murmured, her bottom lifting as the self-pleasuring went on. Again she thought of how Martin could not keep his eyes off her. He'd have his hands all over her if given the chance, which he wouldn't be. That way would keep him drooling around her. She craned her neck the better to watch herself, imagining he could see her now. One day he *would* see her like this, she thought pleasurably, and in even more sexy situations. When they eventually married.

The kind of marital situation Linda envisaged would be freethinking and free loving. She was certain no one man could satisfy her cravings. With her undeniable beauty of face and figure, men would pursue her married or not. She masturbated slower, a finger circling in her saturated inner flesh, stroking lightly at her erect and highly sensitive clitoris as she pondered her future. She would use men as objects of her pleasure and there would be no shortage of willing volunteers. Her body twitched and shuddered but she resisted the final rush of her climax, savouring the delayed pleasure. Martin would be thrilled to have her on her own terms, she considered. He was tall and handsome, almost a man, and she was quite certain he was in awe of her. She saw him as her ideal partner. Therefore his fate was signed and sealed.

Martin would be pliable too, she decided. So infatuated

with his lovely wife as to be her adoring slave. She whimpered softly as her fingers worked sensuously in her quim, the palpitations causing her hips and bottom to writhe. There would be moments like this when Martin would stand watching her, she imagined. Then it would be *his* fingers titillating her; yes, and his tongue. She would make him do that, like it or not. Better still would be his beautiful big prick up there, giving her the poking she craved. Linda had seen him rampant and been more than impressed; the thought of that stout length fucking her made her rub more strenuously at her clitoris. Easy, she warned herself, make it last, *enjoy*.

That afternoon Linda had visited the Compton house with Mandy Field. The girls had tried on each other's clothes and were in their bras and brief panties when they suspected they were being spied on. Becky had yanked open the door to reveal her brother peering in. 'You dirty beast!' his sister had berated him angrily.

With help from Mandy, she had dragged him in and pushed him roughly down on the bed. With his face pressed into the bedcover, he had been cuffed about the head by his indignant sister. He had laughed about it too.

'Whack him like all dirty-minded boys deserve,' Mandy had suddenly cried, always the most forward of the trio. 'Give him a good thrashing. Pull down his jeans, girls, and get his belt. Let's teach him a lesson.'

Linda had stood back as if not wishing to be involved, yet she had watched with interest. She felt her excitement grow as Martin's jeans and underpants were hauled down over his buttocks. It struck her that, despite his loud protests, he did not struggle too much. His belt was drawn from the loops of his jeans by Mandy, who doubled it in her hand. The first crack across his squirming bottom brought forth a loud howl. 'Be quiet and lie still!' Mandy ordered fiercely, her free hand pushing down Martin's neck while poised to deliver a second whack. 'It will be the worse for you if you don't.' Yet from Martin's moans and mumbles as the strapping continued, Linda suspected he enjoyed the humiliation.

He wouldn't have found it so pleasurable had *she* been wielding that belt, Linda recalled grimly, still fingering herself to the edge of a much delayed climax. It had been hard for her to resist taking the belt from Mandy and really laying it on Martin's cheeky arse. Her suspicion had proved correct when the punishment ceased. Rolling over. when released, grinning from ear to ear, Martin had proudly displayed the huge erection he had gained from the treatment. Girlish giggles from her two friends turned to shrieks of outrage at the sight. Linda had been struck dumb by the length and thick girth of the upright stalk, her lower belly and cunt churning. In proportion to his slim body, his rigid cock looked monstrous.

She had remained aloof as Martin was bundled from the room but the memory was impressed in her mind. Linda would ensure that magnificent cock would be all hers. In the meantime, if she played hard to get, not easy like Mandy, it would make him all the more eager to have her. For the present, she reminded herself as her sensuous fingering proceeded, she had a secret life. One that fully satisfied the strong sexual urges so demanding of regular relief. No one suspected, that was the beauty of it. 'You are a wicked horny slut, Linda Simon,' she smugly expressed again, writhing in her self-induced pleasuring.

Her parents were pleased their lovely daughter appeared more interested in scholastic achievement than in boyfriends. She knew her circle regarded her as a prude. Let them; they hadn't a clue as to her true nature. She was a highly sexed young woman with an older lover. It would soon be time to go to Clifford now. Her father had gone to bed after watching the late night news on television. Mrs Simon, the mother from whom she'd inherited her looks and figure, had followed soon after. She had looked in to kiss her daughter goodnight, sure the girl was settled.

Linda was anything but. On her mother's departure the duvet had been thrown back and she had stood naked to begin her ritual before the mirror. First, however, she had tiptoed along the thickly carpeted landing, hearing with amusement the familiar sounds of her parents' lovemaking. Her father was no great lover, she knew, noting the urgent pounding of the bed, the haste employed and the stifled grunts which told of his coming. That Marion, his wife, was left unsatisfied, Linda knew from complaints she had over-heard through the door after such couplings. Perhaps, their daughter thought, mother would lie beside her sleeping husband bringing herself off. As it was, in time all would be quiet and she would be safe to go to her lover. She lustfully anticipated the hours of sex ahead.

The thought of Clifford made her hand slide under her pillows to draw out a long plastic vibrator. It was ridged along its girth, topped by a bulbous crown, jet black in colour and a perfect replica of an engorged penis. Linda pressed it to her lips, kissed it lovingly, licking around the crown before sucking it into her small neat mouth. With-drawn, it gleamed with saliva. A touch at a flat switch in the base made it buzz almost soundlessly, the knob rotating a half-circle and back. She trailed it down between her breasts, thrusting them out, then concen-trated on her nipples. She moaned and sighed, unable to resist further.

Watching her reflection in the mirror, she lowered the object between her parted thighs. Easily inserted in her lubricated state, she fucked herself with it vigorously, buck-ing her pelvis, climaxing in continuing spasms. Sated at last, she lolled back with the long vibrator projecting lewdly. Now her greedy cunt had been readied. She would slip silently out into the night, worked up to receive the real thing for which there was no substitute. 'You're cock-happy,' Clifford had once taunted her. There's many a true word said in jest, she had thought.

Chapter Two

TEACHER'S PET

Linda enjoyed the pressure of the cycle saddle against her swollen and saturated cunt as she pedalled through the night stillness. Though it was risky to sneak out, nothing would stop her going to the man who provided the sex she loved so much. Clifford Maine was a retired academic and writer, who gave private tuition in English and literature. Clifford Maine was a good teacher but even more skilled as a libertine. From their first meeting he had set out to have his new pupil, subtly succeeding in the theft of Linda's virginity.

If only Clifford had known that Linda was as eager as he. With wanton desires engaging her thoughts, Linda regularly fantasised about sexual activities and masturbated over them nightly. Now she had Clifford to make them a reality. He wholly fulfilled her great appetite for sex without her having to resort to the inexpert fumblings of local youths who boasted of their supposed conquests.

Martin Compton would be no different, she assumed. What she learned from Clifford was for his sake too. If she were qualified in every act of sexuality, her inhibitions eliminated, when she and Martin eventually got together surely that would be better than his bedding a shy and shockable girl? One day he'd be delighted to be told how he'd featured in her masturbatory flights of fancy. And as a

11

would-be writer, she considered gaining every experience as vital.

From the start she had done nothing to discourage her tutor. She had revelled in his flattery, savoured his hot breath on her neck as he leaned over her, longed for the touch of his hands on her breasts. Their first kiss had lingered until he'd led Linda to the bedroom of his bungalow, undressed her and initiated her into the glories of fucking.

Clifford opened the door on her arrival dressed in an old comfortable dressing gown. Hanging open to the waist-belt, it revealed a broad chest matted with hair matching the thick growth on his large handsome head. That abundance of hair, she'd learned, curled around heavy balls and surrounded the thick base of a penis that grew huge in length and girth when aroused. Everything about Clifford was big; a well-kept man in his early fifties, his body was solid and without an ounce of fat. Linda wondered how many females his prick had serviced: college girls, married women, virgins like herself on private tuition. She wished he would tell her about them, knowing it would excite her; she wouldn't be jealous but glad to be numbered among them.

He closed the door quickly behind her, leading the way to his book-cluttered study. 'Not again?' he chuckled, shaking his head. 'It seems I've created a monster, a horny little baggage and veritable wanton, with all her ambition centred between her legs. Commendable as that is, young lady, there's more to life than being a receptacle for a stiff prick. I thought you wanted to write as well.'

'You know I do. That's hardly relevant now, is it?' she argued, annoyed at his flippancy. 'When I risk coming to you at night, we both know very well what it's for. To fuck. Fuck the way you've taught me, Clifford. Why are you like this tonight?'

'Guilty conscience perhaps,' he said, still amused as Linda's hand sought between the folds of his dressing gown and grasped his prick. It felt hot and thick with recent tumescence although still soft. He silenced her expression of surprise by lifting a sheaf of papers from his desk. 'Your latest essay, young lady,' he announced, affecting a stern tone. 'You tell me nothing fresh about the works of twentieth-century American novelists in this scrawl. I won't have it. You can write, I know. Your parents pay me good money to tutor you.'

'You've done that in more ways than they've imagined,' Linda reminded him, working his prick slowly and expertly with her forefinger and thumb. 'I will work hard, do extra projects that will please you,' she promised, 'but I'd like you to please *me* now. I've been looking forward to this all day. It's been all I could think of.'

Her admission was all part of a deliberate game Linda had perfected. Playing the pupil to his schoolmaster increased the impropriety of the situation, heightening the lust between them. Despite the now iron-hard stalk throbbing in her hand, Clifford tut-tutted. 'You should concentrate on your work. Instead you tell me coming here was all you thought about,' he admonished her. 'Tell me, Linda, just why was that? I'm curious to know.'

'And you love me to spell it out, don't you, Clifford dear?' the girl answered, sounding sullen on cue. 'You've made me this way, wanting it and liking it too much. Before I came to you I was a virgin. Now I just want you to do things to me.'

'Things?' Clifford laughed. 'You'll have to be more explicit. Otherwise I won't know what it is you expect.'

'If you must make me say it,' Linda began, the excitement making her voice tremble. 'All day I've thought about you playing with my breasts, using them like you do. Fondling them, sucking on my nipples, rubbing your penis between

13

them. Then licking me, feeling me, before you make me suck you. Fucking me when you're hard. Like you are now, Clifford,' she told him. 'You want it as much as I do. I'm going through to your bedroom.'

She stood before him, throwing her coat to the floor, unzipping her dress before unclipping her bra and stepping out of her briefs. A flick with each foot threw off her shoes and she stood naked before him, just as she had posed in her mirror, a cupped hand lifting her lovely breasts, the other stroking the lips of her cunt. Wordlessly she turned and walked off, hearing him laugh delightedly, calling out that there was a little surprise in store for her. Entering the bedroom, Linda stopped in her tracks. On the top of the duvet, stretched out as naked as she herself, lay a woman of mature years who regarded her with a kindly smile.

Linda's sudden halt had Clifford bumping into her rear as he followed. He had cast off his dressing gown and she felt bare skin against her back and bottom, plus the rigid length of his erection pressed to the cleave of her smooth cheeks. Unabashed by the woman on his bed, grinning at her over Linda's shoulder, he slid both arms around to hold the girl steady as she reacted. One large hand circled her breasts, the other cupped the mound at the fork of her thighs, giving suggestive little squeezes.

'Meet my wife, Gaynor,' Clifford announced. 'Gay for short, of course, and well named, it's been known for her to diversify occasionally. You're not averse to making out with another of your sex, are you, my dear? Meet Linda, whom I've the pleasure of tutoring.'

'Undoubtedly a pleasure,' the woman agreed admiringly. 'Such a lovely girl, so pretty and with a gorgeous figure. Bring her closer, so that I can admire her fully without you mauling her. I'm very pleased to meet you, Linda,' she said, smiling sweetly as Clifford led the startled girl to the bed and offering her hand as if meeting on the street. 'Don't look so shocked, dear. Have you never seen another woman naked before?'

'It threw me for a moment,' Linda said, recovering and determined not to be shown up as naive. 'I mean, finding someone else here tonight.'

'I'm not just someone else, I'm this lecherous creature's wife,' said Gaynor teasingly. 'And you're the little treasure he wrote to me about in Ibiza. I thought he was exaggerating, but you're all that he claimed. Young, beautiful, obviously over-sexed. Such lovely big breasts for a slip of a girl, too. Risking slipping out at nights to visit my brute of a husband. I hope he makes that worth your while, Linda?'

'Don't worry, I've fucked her thoroughly,' Clifford chipped in proudly. 'Front, back and sideways. You know me, Gay.'

'I wasn't asking you, Clifford,' his wife said tartly. 'Perhaps Linda thought otherwise. Men have such exalted ideas of their prowess. I want to hear Linda tell me how it was. Don't be shy, dear.'

'Do I look shy?' Linda retorted defiantly. She refused to appear overawed in the presence of two such sexual sophisticates. 'I'm here, aren't I? Your husband has been fucking me for some time. I like it very much.'

Gaynor smiled, releasing Linda's hand and brushing the back of her fingers lightly over the fine growth on the girl's mound. Startled, Linda stood her ground, more than ever determined to match as an equal anything the pair had in mind. 'I'm sure you've learned to like it very much, my dear,' said Gaynor. 'Clifford has that effect on his lovers. He's very good, is he not? I don't blame him having you, such a prize with those nice big breasts. They tempt me, let alone him. And such a pretty little mouth on you too.'

'All the better to suck me with,' Clifford chimed in lewdly, his engorged stalk nestling upright between Linda's bum cheeks. 'Of course I considered it a duty that she be tutored in that art.'

'How selfless you are, dear,' Gaynor said, barely a note of sarcasm in her tone. 'The wonder is these sweet little lips could encompass your brute of a weapon. Or this charming girlish quim, pouting so wickedly for attention.' Her hand turned at the wrist and a curled finger probed to the second knuckle beyond Linda's already swollen sex lips. 'Goodness gracious,' she said in mock surprise. 'The girl is *drenched* in there. Did you fuck her across your desk, Clifford? Someone has been there already tonight.'

'Not guilty, my love,' swore her husband laughing. 'Evidently the little baggage can't leave it alone and has worked her wiles on another partner. Maybe I've taught her too well.'

'There's no one else,' Linda defended herself, her throat dry and hoarse with mounting arousal and finding that a female finger, gently titillating her, excited both mind and body as much as any man's touch. The calm and deliberate salacious talk also increased her fervour. 'If you must know,' she said boldly, deciding she could be as forthright, 'before I came here I masturbated, worked myself up to be ready for *him*.' She gave Clifford a glare. 'Like he advised me to do, so I'd be all the more eager. If you think I've been fucked already tonight then it was with the dildo your dear husband gave me—'

'Not Mr Big, the black one,' Gaynor chuckled. 'No wonder I couldn't find it anywhere! It's had us both then, Linda, for I've resorted to it at times, usually with Clifford enjoying the spectacle. He really has made you wanton, hasn't he? Seduced you and got yet one more of his pupils with a lasting craving for sexual thrills. What a lecherous beast he is.'

16

'And isn't Linda glad of it?' Clifford laughed gruffly, swaying on his toes, methodically sliding his taut length up and down the cleavage of Linda's lovely bottom. 'Note the way she responds to your fingering, dear. How she tries to restrain herself with my prick nestled in her cheeks, or attempts not to give herself over to climaxing with a woman fondling her. I can feel her body like a coiled spring, desperate for release but unsure if she should. She's still not at ease with your presence, Gaynor, but the experience will be good for her. Two's company, but three is more fun, Linda. Come now, my wife wants you too, and I'm certain you'll find it pleasurable. Let yourself go! Work against her hand, that's right! Go, girl, I'll see to this end of you.'

With a low moan Linda began moving her hips to the fingers now expertly swirling and fluttering inside her. Two at least, she felt, probing to make her thrust forward for deeper penetration, then making her shudder violently as they plucked and pulled her clitty. 'Yes, yes, do,' she was mumbling, bucking from the waist down and drawing Gaynor's head to her as the woman sat up on her knees and nuzzled Linda's breasts. She felt a suctioning on a nipple, peering down to see Gaynor's mouth clamped to her, drawing in flesh, sucking avidly. All the while too, the inserted fingers continued their play, driving Linda ever wilder. Her climax came like electric jolts making her cry out, gasp, and continue thrusting against the hand for more of the same. Both her hands were clutched in Gaynor's hair, keeping her to the breast as her other nipple was sucked upon.

Behind Linda, despite her torso gyrating in the throes, Clifford now had strong hands clamped to her buttocks, forcing the rounded cheeks apart. Determined to have his share, he adjusted his stance to direct his prick to his chosen target. The plummy knob, glistening in his

17

aroused state, nudged around in the deep sweat-slippery cleavage, homing in on the puckered anal orifice. With a satisfied grunt he eased forward, the entrance giving way, allowing the head to intrude. He heard Linda give a different cry from that expelled from her by his wife's pleasuring. It was a gasp of shock, amazement, protest, all silenced by a sharp smack delivered to her rear. Mastered, she relaxed for him, allowing his inches to penetrate, aided by her own jerky movements in the continuing spasms of the orgasms pulsating her cunt. Clifford moved faster to match her agitated motions and embedded himself fully, filling her with mass and heat.

The combined assault proved more ecstatically wanton and wholly abandoned than Linda had ever envisaged in her wildest fantasy. Pushing against Gaynor's hand, she then thrust back on Clifford's stalk, moaning out her delight, lost to all but the surrender of her senses. Out of her mind, screaming as she felt Clifford jerk and flood her back passage with his spurts of hot come, only when he and Gaynor drew away did she slump forward on the bed.

Gasping for breath, lying face down to regain a sem-blance of composure, it was with some annoyance she listened to herself being discussed. She heard Gaynor remark what a horny little minx her husband had discov-ered; her ears burnt as Clifford agreed, saying Linda was a natural, a girl born to give and receive sexual pleasure. She'll please many before she's much older, he added, and Gaynor laughed, saying she'd certainly shown her true colours with them.

It made Linda sit up angrily. 'And you two didn't enjoy what you did to me?' she said icily. 'The wife fingered my cunt and sucked my nipples, while she brought herself off. That while her husband was, well, buggering me. Up my bottom. Did you know that, Gaynor? That Clifford fucked

18

my bum? Talk about revealing yourselves in your true colours.'

'There, there, my dear,' Gaynor said sympathetically, taking Linda in her arms and pressing a kiss to her damp forehead. 'Was it your very first time up the bum? Clifford is a notorious arse-bandit. I'm surprised he hasn't had your dear little bottom before.'

'I fully intended getting around to it,' Clifford explained. 'Purely as part of her complete sexual education, of course. The moment seemed propitious, so I buggered her. Took it splendidly too.'

'What an old fraud my husband is,' Gaynor said, hugging Linda to her, breast to breast. 'I'm sure he couldn't wait to get up your tight wee tush. You didn't seem to object. Believe me, it can be *very* arousing for a woman at times. Completely naughty and unusual as it is, how *relieving* for us on occasion to be taken so. To allow the ultimate humiliation, become so abandoned we want to be used and abused. And we get to like it too much. Yes, even strong and intelligent females like ourselves.'

'Couldn't have put it better myself, my love,' Clifford agreed. 'What do you say to that, Linda?'

'I think it's time I left,' she said reluctantly, disengaging from Gaynor's embrace, the kisses pressed to her mouth and the cupped hand fondling her breasts. She smiled at Gaynor to show she appreciated the attention. 'I have to be home before dawn, much as I would like to stay. Will you be here next time I call?' she asked.

'For a few days,' Gaynor replied sweetly, 'before I take this reprobate of a husband of mine off to Ibiza to finish the book that your visits have been delaying. Until then, I shall expect you. We both shall.'

Linda eased herself off the bed. She felt a pleasant throb in her bottom, sticky with the leakage that seeped from her anus. Now she was a complete woman, she decided proudly, her virginity taken in both orifices.

'Would tomorrow afternoon be too soon?' she said wickedly, looking down upon the two naked figures. 'It's Saturday. I'm sure my parents wouldn't mind paying for some extra lessons before you leave. I'm learning so much!'

Chapter Three

MATURE MENTOR

Aunt Joyce was conspicuous by her absence when Martin went down to breakfast. He had shaved, showered, brushed his hair and put on a clean shirt and jeans to impress, his mind still filled with the wonder of the previous night. To be joined in his bed by such a hot and hungry woman, taken in her urgency as he had been, was the very stuff of dreams. He toyed with the breakfast his mother had put before him, at last enquiring (as if barely interested) where Joyce was. Olivia Compton adjusted her spectacles, glancing up from her *Financial Times* and a study of her investments.

'Off to the beach,' she said, resuming her perusal of the stock market returns. 'It's such a nice morning she said she'd make the most of her last few days here. A good day for you to mow the lawns, Martin. I shall be over in Southampton for most of it, seeing my accountant and shopping. Joyce will get your lunch and I'll expect to see the grass cut when I get back.'

'I'll do it later,' Martin complained. The sun was streaming in the window of the kitchen and he had other, more important, things in mind. Joyce, he knew savagely, had fled the scene rather than face him. He would seek her out and his mother's timely absence gave him the space to cajole, coerce and otherwise work his wiles to make Joyce amenable

21

again. He hastened the short distance to the promenade, scanning the early arrivals on the sandy beach, few in number as yet. The heat haze rose in shimmers and the sea sparkled, making him wish he had brought his bathing trunks as he saw Joyce standing shoulder-deep in the water. To his delight she started to emerge, walking directly towards him to her towel and clothes on the sand, unaware she was being observed.

Martin enjoyed the spectacle of her full figure in her clinging wet one-piece bathing costume. Years before, he and his best friend, Norman, brother of the delectable Linda, had first admired her mature body on the beach. Naturally, they took an avid interest in matters sexual and Joyce's figure moulded in the sodden swimsuit intrigued them. How the wet material clung to her full breasts, revealing each shapely globe perfectly to young inquisitive eyes. Her broad buttocks and the bulging mound at the join of strapping thighs were plainly outlined. The soaked costume clung skin-tight to every curve of her ample body. Even the split of her quim was evident, the wet fabric at her prominent crotch drawn in by suction.

The boys had furtively ogled her, agreeing she was splendidly abundant in all parts of the female form that attracted their adolescent curiosity. Watching Joyce approach now, Martin recalled how he had seen all. He called to her from the cast-iron parapet railing of the promenade. She looked up startled, flushing an angry red. Aware he was looking down at the big orbs of her breasts and the deep cleavage between, she snatched up her towel.

'Go away, Martin,' she said firmly. 'I want to get dressed. And I don't want you here. Leave me alone.'

This was not the tremulous Joyce that Martin had expected. He leapt over the rail to land beside her. 'But I want to be with you,' Martin began as Joyce silenced him, putting her fingers over his lips. *Why can't it be like last night?* his expression said. *It was great by me. You started it. What makes you think I wouldn't want more of the same?*

She understood his look fully. 'What happened,' she said calmly, 'was unforgivable. Entirely my fault. I don't blame you but I'm old enough to be your mother. It must have been the sherry I drank with your mother though that's no excuse. What would *she* think if she knew? It will never happen again and I trust you'll never breathe a word of it. I want you to forget it ever happened, Martin.'

'Well, I can't,' he said bluntly, 'because I thought it the best thing that's ever happened to me. I thought we could do it again. I could tell you really liked it too. Be a sport, Joyce.'

'Sport!' she shouted, furious at his attitude. With a sudden swing of her arm she caught him a smarting smack on his cheek, sending Martin staggering. 'Get away from me. Go!' she blazed, making people on the beach nearby turn in surprise.

Discretion being the better part of valour, Martin slunk away, rubbing his cheek ruefully. He decided he had blown it, gone about the operation entirely with the wrong approach. You must take the lesson to heart and learn about women, he instructed himself. He'd received his first slap in the face for not employing more guile. He would work off his deep frustration mowing the lawns as his mother had instructed. At least he'd got a fuck out of Joyce's lapse, he consoled himself.

Waiting on the step of his front door as he walked up the drive was Mandy Field: sweet seventeen, plump and cuddlesome in her cotton-print dress. Beside her on the gravel path lay her bike with a rolled-up towel containing her bikini in the handlebar basket.

'Where's your Becky, Martin?' she enquired. 'I thought we'd go for a swim as it's so hot. I've already called on Linda but she's still in bed, lazy thing.'

'Becky's gone to Southampton for the day with my mother,' Martin said, thinking of Linda Simon still in her bed and how he'd like to be there with her. Nevertheless he ogled the jiggle of Mandy's big tits while the girl arose from the step and straightened her dress. She still had some puppy fat and was cock-stiffeningly curvaceous, with plump thighs and a broad bottom. After the sight of Joyce in her costume, Martin was as randy as a bucket of frogs. 'Come in,' he invited. 'Have some of my mother's home-made lemonade. I'll put ice in it too. You look hot.'

'Not the kind of hot you'd like,' Mandy giggled, following him through the door as he opened it. In the coolness of the panelled hall he immediately made a grab for her, pinning her comfortable frame to the wall, her breasts hard against his chest. 'Dirty beast,' the girl laughed unabashed. 'I can feel your big thing pushing into me. What would Linda say if she knew what you were doing? You're stuck on her, aren't you? What if I tell her?'

'Tell her what you like, she's a stuck-up bitch,' Martin assured her. He pressed his mouth to Mandy's, getting a response, his tongue probing. For a few moments he fondled her breasts through her dress, enjoying the fleshy pliancy. 'Let me see them, Mandy,' he ordered, pleased to find he was so authoritative. 'Bring 'em out.' He fumbled at the buttons down the front of her dress. 'I'll bet they're two beauties. Have they ever been sucked?'

'What a thing to say,' the girl giggled, but at the same time her fingers took over from his to unbutton herself. His hand delved in while she leaned back against the wall, allowing him to pull both her breasts up over her bra, the ample mounds thrusting out above the lacy cups. 'There, now you've seen them,' she teased. 'Shall I put them back?'

His answer was to cup them, bury his face in the warm

24

damp cleavage and seek out a nipple with his mouth. With delight he heard Mandy give a low moan and felt her hand searching at his crotch for his rampantly straining prick. He unzipped for her, bringing it out, directing it to her hand, then sought under her dress. The skirt was bundled up quickly and he felt her smooth belly, going down inside the waistband of her briefs to meet a soft growth of hair and a fat prominence with inrolling lips. Her grip on his stalk was tight, her movements jerky and inexpert, almost painful. He was not about to complain. His curled finger entered her cunt and she jerked herself on it agitatedly.

'Let me fuck you, Mandy,' he begged. 'Let me put it in. I know you want to fuck. It's good, isn't it?'

But even in her throes she muttered no, she didn't trust him or herself. 'Keep doing what you're doing,' she urged and, with a loud gasp, she came off on his hand, her bottom bumping against the wall. She rubbed at his shaft strenuously in her excitement and he came too, in a series of spurts, his spasms matching hers until she stopped and pushed him away.

'I hope you're satisfied now,' she complained, holding up fingers covered in his gooey emission. 'What horrible stuff. Just imagine if I'd let you put that inside me. You're a dirty beast, Martin Compton. No one has ever gone that far with me before. I'll never trust you again.'

'You're all the same,' Martin said. 'You love it and want it, then claim you didn't. Come through to the kitchen and you can wash your hands.' He grinned at her while watching her replace her breasts in her bra and button up her dress. 'It wasn't bad, was it, Mandy? I think you deserve that drink now. Made you come, didn't I?'

'I suppose you did,' she admitted with a shy smile, 'but don't look so smug – you came too. It's a funny feeling, isn't it? Makes your tummy go all trembly and shivery. I suppose

25

it's even better with the real thing. You know, when people *do* it.'

'Absolutely,' Martin assured her. 'Next time I'll have a supply of condoms handy. It's better to be safe than sorry. You and I could go steady if you like, Mandy. Would you like that?' He gave her a hug, thinking the willing girl would provide a good regular supply until he tired of her. 'What do you say?'

'I'd like that,' she said, returning a kiss. 'It's not just because you want to – do it to me – is it?' A sudden thought struck her as he was about to protest. 'This won't go down well with Linda. She always says she can have you anytime she likes. I mean as her boyfriend. She's so sure of herself. Of course she's so pretty, not plump like me.'

'All the more of you to enjoy,' Martin said. 'As for Linda, she can get stuffed, not that she'd allow anybody to do that.'

He watched Mandy pedal away and danced a little jig in the doorway at the thought of going the whole way with her next time. There was a sexy body on her too, even if plump, and he was going to enjoy fucking that tight little quim.

So the day had not been such a complete disappointment. In his cheerful mood he pulled off his shirt to tackle the grass cutting, a chore always good for a fiver from his mother. He heard the front door close and footsteps in the hall. Glancing out from the kitchen, he saw Joyce about to go upstairs. For a long moment their eyes met, then she hurried on, her large breasts bobbing in her haste.

The enticing sight was not lost upon Martin who, despite his recent orgasm with Mandy, felt a responsive twitch and stirring in his jeans. He recalled the sight of Joyce's big tits bouncing as she'd shed her dressing gown last night. Going into the hallway, he admired the swaying cheeks of her ample behind disappearing upstairs. He stood there some-what forlornly, wistfully thinking what might have been when he heard her call his name. Going up, he knocked at the bedroom door and was invited to enter. Joyce had an open suitcase on the locker at the foot of her bed, packing her clothes.

'Aunt Joyce,' Martin said sincerely, remembering his vow to handle situations more subtly. 'You surely don't have to leave. Mother would wonder why. I'm sorry I acted like I did on the beach. You know I'd never mention what we did to a soul.'

'I believe you, Martin,' Joyce smiled. 'You're quite a young man, aren't you, I'm very fond of you. Too fond, I think. I'm sorry I smacked you, sorry I started all this. Tell your mother I had a telephone call and that I'm needed at the shop.'

'Stay,' Martin pleaded. 'Don't upset yourself about what happened. I'm seventeen and not such an innocent,' he assured her. Risking a further rebuff, he slipped an arm about her waist and kissed her cheek. 'It was perfectly understandable, we all feel that way at times. I know I do. I blame my mother for giving you sherry; you're probably not used to drink. I'm glad I was there for you – when you felt like that.'

'Were you, dear boy?' Joyce said, smiling. 'Then perhaps I shouldn't feel I'm such a terrible woman.'

'A lovely woman,' Martin told her, squeezing her waist as suggestively as he dared, cunning in his sincerity. He sensed a weakening in her resistance and her body relaxing. 'I've always thought you very beautiful,' he said, laying it on. 'Couldn't we? Please—'

He did not wait for her answer, holding her tighter, catching her unaware as his seeking mouth clamped to hers. For a long moment the kiss held, her lips responding, opening, allowing his tongue to probe. Then he lowered her across the bed and was on her, pressing against her breasts

27

and thighs, pushing into her crotch. In his moment of triumph she tore her mouth apart from his, thrusting at his chest to get him off her body.

'You randy little sod,' Joyce said with some amusement. 'You can see why I've got to go. I'm not safe with you around.'

Martin took that as a compliment. Both sat up, breathing heavily, regarding each other as if awaiting the next move. 'You've not the goody-goody Aunt Joyce we all thought you were,' he challenged her. 'That's just an act when you stay here. I like the new Aunt Joyce much better.'

'Well, keep your distance,' she laughed, adjusting her hair. 'Who would have thought it, the little boy I used to hold on my knee wanting into my knickers? It's not on.'

'Speak for yourself,' Martin said boldly. He rose to stand before her. The bulge in his jeans thrust directly before her face. 'You get in my bed and just about rape me, then expect me not to want a repeat?' On an impulse he unzipped and pulled out his prick and balls. The bolt upright stalk was rigid, the plum-head swollen and glistening red. Joyce stared at it and gulped, her eyes fixed on its length and thick girth. 'Come on,' he urged her. 'Do something about this.'

'No, not with you, Martin,' she answered kindly. 'Once was an unforgivable lapse on my part. Twice would be deliberate. Don't make me, please! Be kind. I really don't want to.'

She stood up, smoothing down her dress and going to the foot of the bed to continue packing. Disgruntled, Martin slumped down across the bedcover, on his back with legs over the edge, his engorged cock as upright as a flagstaff. He saw Joyce eyeing it surreptitiously, her attempt at packing faltering. Wordlessly he held out his hand to her and pulled her towards him. He placed her fingers around the rigid stalk. For a moment her clasp lingered, then she tore her hand away as though burned by its heat.

'Not with you, Martin,' she repeated, her voice thick with emotion. 'I've always been your Auntie Joyce. I feel like your aunt.'

'You're just my mother's best friend,' Martin said sullenly. 'You're not a real aunt. Do something about this. I know you want to.'

The woman sighed, shaking her head as if the situation was beyond her. She reached out to grasp the prick rearing up so appealingly and looked upon its straining length and girth. 'If you must.' Martin barely heard her throaty whisper, unsure whether she referred to him or his prick. 'Yes, it is a lovely big one, so thick and hard. I shall feel eternally damned for this but I *do* want it—' She sank before him, on her knees between his legs, holding his stem upright, gently stroking it before her spellbound eyes. Then, with a hollow groan of submission, she covered it with her mouth, sucking greedily while making little mewing sounds of intense pleasure.

'Aunt, oh aunt,' Martin groaned in his excitement, clutching at Joyce's thick tresses and spontaneously lifting his hips to fuck her face. The avid and increasing suctioning on his stalk at once drew molten fire from his balls, surging up the pipeline to spew a glut of creamy come into her throat. Still she sucked, swallowing and smacking her lips until his spurts became dribbles and his prick softened and shrank.

Lying back, delightfully sated, he savoured his limpness in her mouth. She continued to lap and lick his tool like a mother cat cleaning her young. When she released it her head fell forward on the edge of the bed between his knees and remained there.

Martin smoothed her hair with a loving, grateful hand. 'That was out of this world,' he told her sincerely. 'My first cocksuck. I've read about it, thought about it – it was marvellous! You were marvellous, Joyce. Have you ever done that before?'

'You'll make me blush,' she said, her head still lowered. 'Yes, I've done it before. We have no secrets between us now, have we? I'm too fond of it; I can't resist wanting it in my mouth. Yours was especially tempting, so young, hard and upstanding. Shall I go on and finish packing now?' She gave a wry shrug. 'You know what will happen if I stay. We'll both want each other.'

'Then stay,' Martin declared joyfully. 'I insist.' He tilted her chin in his hands, looking at her appealingly. 'Say you will.'

'You're a very naughty boy,' Joyce chided him, 'but leaving now would be like closing the stable door after the horse has bolted. We'll have to be very careful, you know.'

Martin pressed a long kiss to her lips. 'Not for the rest of today,' he reminded her. 'Mother and Becky won't get back from Southampton until late. We can really make hay.'

'I would hardly call it that,' Joyce smiled, amused at his youthful eagerness. 'I shall probably regret all this so you'd better make love to me before I change my mind. Shall we undress?'

Chapter Four

WOMANLY LOVE

Noon came and went before Linda awoke, bright sunlight streaming through the drawn curtains. Her waking thoughts were of the night's stolen hours. She smiled and stretched luxuriously, reliving the erotic threesome with Clifford and his wife. It had been a revelation, getting such powerful climaxes from another woman's sex-play. Lesbian tendencies? Not me, she thought, but it *had* been good in the heat of the action. After all, what about all the arousing things Clifford was doing to her at the time? Her nipples still felt pleasantly swollen and tender, a legacy of Gaynor's gluttonous suckling of her teats. Tender too were both her lower orifices: her quim was puffy and moist; her back passage tinglingly sensitive.

Her mother peeped into the bedroom, coming in to sit on the bed. She frowned and smoothed her daughter's brow. 'I don't know how you sleep so late and yet look so drained,' Marion Simon said solicitously. Linda pulled the duvet tight around her to cover her breasts and raw nipples. 'Are you working too hard at your studies, dear?'

'I'm all right, mother,' Linda told her snappishly. 'I want to have a shower now, so please go.'

'Lunch is ready,' Mrs Simon announced. 'You must eat

31

something before you go out. What are you planning to do this afternoon?' she added, in a change of tone, sounding awkward and hesitant.

Did her mother suspect something? Linda wondered. But how could she? She would not mention her intended visit to the Maine's cottage.

'It's a perfect day for the beach. I'll go swimming with Becky and Mandy. Don't expect me back before evening.', She allowed her mother a smile. 'I must make the most of summer before I start work in September.'

'That's another thing,' said Marion Simon. 'Your father and I think you'd do better going to university instead of this local newspaper job. Anyway, Mandy called for you earlier and said she'd be at the beach. Your father and brother have gone fishing.' She stood up, looking pleased. 'Lunch in ten minutes,' she ordered.

Linda had more on her mind than to worry over her parents' interest in the afternoon's arrangements. Intending to spend as long as possible with Clifford and his wife, she ate quickly. Her mother made her some sandwiches which she packed with her bikini and towel in the basket of her cycle. Then she pedalled off with mounting excitement at the prospect of more sexual pleasure.

At the cottage she parked the bike out of sight in Clifford's garage, noting with a frown his car was not there. When the back door of the cottage opened, Mrs Gaynor Maine stood there, smiling a welcome.

'It was pleasant last night, wasn't it?' she said as she greeted Linda, but it was more of a statement than a question. Linking arms, she led her visitor through to the cosy lounge. 'Do make yourself comfortable, my darling,' she said, leading Linda to the couch. She lovingly smoothed the back of her hand down Linda's cheek. 'I've been eagerly awaiting your return, sweet child.'

'Hardly a child,' Linda maintained. 'Not after last night. Where's Clifford?'

'Patience,' Gaynor advised. 'He'll be back later. He was called to an urgent appointment just before you arrived.' She pursed her lips as if stifling a secret smile. 'I'm sure *we* can manage without a man for a while.'

She sat close beside Linda, cupping her face, studying it. 'You're so hard to resist,' she said, pecking quick kisses on her eyes, nose, cheeks, finally lightly mouth upon mouth as if to test the reaction. 'It was your first time with another woman, I know,' she smiled, 'but it excited you. I suspect that such a naturally sensual creature as you can be equally aroused by male or female. So no false modesty, please. I could teach you so much.'

'Did Clifford go out to leave us alone?' Linda pouted. 'I think I might have been consulted.'

'He really does have a pressing engagement. Forget him meanwhile and look at me. I can feel you trembling. Would you like to see my breasts?'

'I've got breasts of my own, thank you,' Linda retorted. 'Why should I want to see yours?'

'You may find it nice to touch them and fondle them. Or suck upon them even,' Gaynor said pleasantly. Linda's mouth was suddenly dry, her throat constricted, a strange excitement churning in her stomach. She looked at Gaynor and saw a handsome, intelligent woman of about her mother's age, calmly awaiting an answer. Her bobbed hair, fringed across a broad intellectual forehead, was tawny and expertly cut. Her mouth was wide with generous lips. She wore only a floral cotton housecoat, loosely tied at the waist.

Gaynor toyed with the opening of the housecoat at her neck, revealing a tempting glimpse of the upper swell of her large creamy breasts. 'Shall I?' she invited.

'If you insist,' Linda heard herself saying in a low voice.

With widening eyes she watched the robe drawn apart to open to the waist, saw Gaynor lift her shoulders and arch her back. A truly magnificent pair of heavy rounded breasts thrust out before her.

With trembling fingertips, she trailed one hand over a smooth slope, circling the thick nipple. 'They're so huge, so firm and tight,' she murmured. She took them in both palms, hands shaking as she felt their mass and weight.

'Do as you wish with them,' she heard Gaynor tell her.

An impulse to bury her face between the warm mounds, to press kisses all over them, fasten her mouth in turn to each taut nipple, surged through her. Choking as she found the words, Linda said, 'Would you like me to suck them, Gaynor? Is that what you want?'

'I think it's what you want, my dear,' Gaynor said sweetly. 'Come to my arms, little girl.' She cradled Linda into her, holding up a breast and directing the nipple to her mouth. 'There,' she soothed. 'Suck on me to your heart's content. This is nice, isn't it? The *hors d'oeuvre* before the main course. Kiss me, my darling, give me that sweet mouth.'

Raising her lips from a saliva-covered nipple, Linda eagerly pressed her mouth to the other woman's and found the kiss as passionate as any with Gaynor's husband. Their tongues touching, probing, lapping, with a sob of gratitude Linda broke off the kiss to lower her face and seek the sweet nipple on which she been gorging greedily.

'More of that later,' Gaynor said, disengaging herself. 'There are even nicer things we can enjoy.' She rose, leading Linda through to the bedroom. Kissing her as she helped the girl undress, she let her robe slide to the floor, entirely in command of the situation. Body to body they hugged for a long moment, breast to breast, thigh to thigh, before lying side by side on the bed.

'Now,' Gaynor instructed. 'No haste to begin with. For a

while let us just kiss and touch, explore each other's bodies. When it all gets beyond you, my dear, I shall know. I'll have a special treat for you then.'

Linda went willingly to her arms again, kissing mouth and breasts, her hand venturing between Gaynor's thighs to find her warm wet cunt to fondle. It all seemed so perfectly natural to want to do so, her arousal growing as Gaynor expertly did the same to her. Then she was pushed flat on her back, her legs parted and Gaynor's head was lowered to her crotch.

'Yes, please yes, y-e-s-s,' she groaned as an avid mouth clamped over her outer lips, a searching tongue entering to swirl around her clitoris.

'Don't come!' came a muffled command from Gaynor as Linda grasped her head and bucked in pleasure. 'Do as I say, girl, hold back for later! You must learn to retain the feeling – I won't disappoint you.'

Delaying a climax was no new experience for Linda but, with a mouth and tongue applied with an expertise not even Clifford could match, it was with relief she saw Gaynor's head lift. Her body had fought to prevent the final surge, stiffened as each time it seemed she would scream out and come.

'Good girl,' Gaynor praised her, her big breasts bobbing. 'I know that took great willpower. Now I shall reward you for waiting.'

Lying across the bed, still fighting off shudders and spasms and resisting the temptation to finger herself to a longed-for orgasm, Linda wondered what Gaynor had in mind. She watched her cross to the dressing table, her ample buttocks swaying, and take out an object which she held behind her as she turned.

'What is it you most desire right now, with a repressed climax boiling in your sweet cunt, Linda dear?' she asked teasingly, still with whatever she was hiding held behind her back. 'The truth now, I won't mind. Admit it.'

'I should like to be fucked,' Linda confessed, her mind and body aching for complete satisfaction. 'Fucked by a big prick until I come and come. Why isn't Clifford here?' Her voice was almost a sob as she complained, 'Is that what you wanted to make me say? I need a prick, a good hard one up my cunt.'

'Then you shall have one,' Gaynor announced. Crossing to the bed she held out an V-shaped contraption with inch-wide elastic straps dangling from it. Focusing her eyes upon it, Linda saw it was two replicas of the male penis joined at the base from where the straps hung. 'Clifford's otherwise engaged this afternoon, but I've never had any complaints about this. It doesn't suffer from premature ejaculation and can't possibly stay anything but beautifully rigid. I've already oiled it for your visit, Linda.'

'Have you fucked other women with it before?' Linda asked, sitting up. She watched closely as Gaynor bent at the knees to ease one half of it inside her, stepping into the looped elastic straps and adjusting them. In place, the dummy prick remaining outside her crotch thrust up like the real thing, with a thick stalk and bulbous knob. Worn by a well-built woman with large breasts and strapping thighs it looked lewd in the extreme. 'Yes, I've fucked other women with this,' Gaynor said. 'I haven't kept count but a dozen at least. And the identity of one who returned for more might surprise you.'

'Who?' Linda began only to be silenced as Gaynor sought her mouth and lowered her on her back.

'It's not important right now,' Gaynor said, her hands squeezing Linda's breasts, pinching and plucking at her nipples. 'You're here, and it's just you and I, my sweet. I promise to drive you out of your senses. Kiss me with open mouth and tongue, you little bitch. Now reach for it, take it in your hand. Doesn't it feel good? Like the real thing? You'll soon be begging for it, I promise.'

With the warm, pliant flesh of Gaynor's nudity pressed to her, her kisses on her mouth, breasts and nipples, and her finger titillating an already throbbing cunt, Linda cried out for relief.

'Fuck me! Go on, fuck me!' she urged desperately. 'Shove it in me hard. Now!' With the girth of the double dildo projecting from Gaynor in her hand, she rolled her bottom and sought to be penetrated. Knees raised, legs clasped around her partner's waist, Linda thrust forward. A loud heartfelt groan and it was in her to the hilt and filling her, Gaynor's soft belly and pubic bush pressing on her own.

'There,' Gaynor announced triumphantly, smiling down at a face contorted by abandon. Beginning a slow movement of her hips, she was hauled closer as Linda jerked frantically to get full measure. 'You *are* desperate, girl. Don't worry – I can fuck you with this all day.'

'Then do so!' Linda shouted, hoarse and wild-eyed as she writhed beyond control as her climax came. It rippled from her cunt like an electric surge, the shock waves undulating her belly and tingling her breasts. She bounced her bottom to meet Gaynor's increasing thrusts and was lost to all but a desire to maintain a lustful, continuing orgasm. Above her, Gaynor was out of control too, mouthing lewd words and fucking strenuously. At last, exhausted by their efforts, both lay still and panting to regain their breath. Gaynor remained on top of Linda with the dildo fully embedded.

Their bodies were sweat-soaked, their breasts clammy and sticking to each other. 'Shall we shower?' Gaynor suggested, kissing Linda. 'Personally I quite like feeling hot and sticky between bouts but perhaps you'd like to freshen up. Am I too heavy for you?'

'Stay where you are, I like it too,' Linda said. 'Don't pull away, I want it to stay up me.' She gave a wicked chuckle. 'I'm going to need it again before long. We didn't need Clifford after all, did we? You made me come and come.'

'I've truly never met anyone who loves sex like you do,' said Gaynor thoughtfully. 'I suppose you consider yourself completely uninhibited. But are you, Linda?'

'I let your husband fuck and bugger me,' the girl replied, wondering at the serious tone Gaynor employed. 'And you've had me too. And how! Isn't that uninhibited enough for you? I don't think anything could shock or surprise me.'

'Shall we test that?' Gaynor asked.

'Fire away,' Linda said lightly. 'You're going to tell me that Clifford is out screwing some other female. I don't mind in the least.'

'That might depend on who it is,' said Gaynor. 'How about your mother?'

She awaited the reaction, watching Linda closely. Surprise, disbelief and wonder all were shown in Linda's eyes until she burst into a short laugh. 'Are you saying that while we're here, Clifford is fucking my mum?' she said in obvious amusement. 'So that's why she wanted to know where I'd be this afternoon. Good for her, she deserves a good fuck, I'm sure. How long has this been going on?'

'Since she met Clifford to discuss your studies,' Gaynor said. 'She's a lovely woman, an older edition of you, my dear. Of course, my husband tries it on with all attractive females. It seems she lets him, quite often too. She comes here in the afternoons. I'm so glad you don't mind.'

'Mind? I find it hilarious. My dad's not up to satisfying her. So we're all at it! Everybody's fucking.' Linda thought deeply for a moment. 'You say she's a lovely woman – have you met her?'

'Yesterday afternoon for the first time,' Gaynor admitted

with a sly smile. 'She came to visit Clifford and found me here with him—'

'—And you try it on with attractive females just like Clifford,' Linda said delightedly. 'I can't believe this! It's too good to be true. You're making me randy with your talk; push a little into me again. Fuck me and tell me how you seduced her.'

'You're a hopeless case,' Gaynor laughed, pushing with her hips, withdrawing the dildo out of Linda and making her rear up to retain its depth. 'Actually your mother was embarrassed to find me here. You know Clifford, he actually introduced her to me as his lover. She was in a daze when he led her off to this bedroom.'

'That I can believe,' Linda giggled. 'I'll just bet she was. But it didn't stop her letting Clifford fuck her, did it?' She settled into a regular motion, rotating her bottom on the bed and lifting it to enjoy full penetration. 'Oh, I shall come again soon,' she announced. 'And you no doubt joined in, Gaynor. Did you fuck her with this big thing that's up me?'

'It was quite a session,' Gaynor agreed. 'I think she was more than surprised when I joined in. She returned my kisses quite passionately, enjoyed me fondling her and held me when I sucked her nipples. Your breasts are so like hers,' she said, looking down on Linda's. 'When Clifford had fucked her and I approached with the double-dildo strapped on, she turned her face away as if embarrassed by her desire. All the same, she held up her arms and widened her legs to receive me. Like mother, like daughter,' she added mischievously. 'She couldn't get enough of it. Marion, isn't it? Well, it must have impressed her, for she came again last evening. She said she was passing, so she called in.'

'A likely story,' Linda grunted, working herself off with ever-quickening thrusts. 'So the pair of you filthy beasts had her again—'

39

'I hesitate to tell you how,' Gaynor said smugly, the dildo inside her shunting away, increasing her lewdness. '*She* mounted me, it was what she wanted. Of course, with Clifford watching, his big stiff prick in his hand, he had to put it somewhere. I saw him bending over us, heard your mother groan and guessed where.'

'He went up her bottom while she was impaled on you!' Linda almost screamed out as her climax came upon her and she bucked furiously into Gaynor. 'We must do that, we must do that!'

'We certainly will,' the women heard Clifford's voice booming out from the doorway. 'As soon as you two wanton creatures have completed the disgraceful lesbian coupling you are enjoying so much.'

He came up to the bed and sat down to watch the final throes of the pair. 'How delightful, two bodies steaming after hectic sex. My favourite sight in all the world, for more stimulating than any scenic grandeur. The Pyramids, the Taj Mahal, the Grand Canyon – I'd sooner see *your* grand canyons, my lovelies.'

'Clifford, you are full of shit,' his wife said, laughing. The length of the dildo she wore, now withdrawn from Linda, ran with juice. 'I trust you spent a worthwhile afternoon?'

'Fucking my mother,' Linda said cheekily. 'Aren't you ashamed, having a married woman *and* her daughter?'

'It's always been a favourite thing of mine,' Clifford said, standing to take off his clothes. 'There's a *piquancy* about a mother and daughter both being fucked by the same man. I've even had them together, at the same time. But much as yours is so keen on being put to the cock, Linda, I don't think she's quite ready for that. It's a nice thought though, and it might have happened in time. I'm rather sorry we have to leave for Ibiza so soon.'

'That would be gross,' Linda considered. 'I can't imagine

it, not my mother.' She suppressed a giggle. 'It would be strange.'

'Stranger things have happened, and they will with you,' Gaynor told her. 'It's in your nature. Look at Clifford. Standing there raring to go. Are you ready to mount me and let *him* have you at the same time, like you said you wanted to?'

'Why not?' Linda said easily. 'Like mother, like daughter, you said it yourself. It seems I've inherited her nature, as well as her looks. She's quite gone up in my estimation!'

Chapter Five

MOTHER'S BOY

Autumn came with Martin long bereft of Joyce's company. It had been so good while it lasted. Every randy youth should have an obliging older woman who allowed him to fully experience the great joy of sex. That being his belief, how could he fault his friend Norman for indulging in a similar liaison when the chance came along? A surprising affair, too, taking place under his very nose! Martin had been too engrossed enjoying frequent carnal bouts with the ample-bodied Joyce to notice. Once she had conceded to satisfying her desires with Martin, she'd become as eager as he to make the most of her stay in the Compton household.

Martin had had little thought for anything else but Joyce's silent arrival in his bedroom each night. There was no false modesty or hesitation on her part now. She eagerly slipped off her dressing gown as she got into bed beside him in all her comfortable nakedness.

Martin's mother had often wondered why such a handsome and well-formed woman had never married. A partner in a Wimbledon flower shop, each summer she stayed a few weeks in the Compton's large house by the sea. Martin's parents had separated years before and though not strictly a boarding house, the many spare rooms were used for paying guests, relatives or long-term friends. And lovers, too, that summer.

Fondling and kissing, Joyce soon became more urgent as she'd tell him in plain language to fuck her. She surprised and delighted him with the imaginative things she wanted him to do. Back, front, sideways, woman superior or doggy-fashion, Martin proved a willing accomplice on her nocturnal visits, striving to give satisfaction.

Once his big cock was well up her there was no denying her delight in a good shafting. Afternoons when they were alone in the house proved an opportunity for her to give vent to loud groans and cries while being fucked – noises which were necessarily toned down in their nightly couplings. Martin loved to hear her vocal accompaniments: the pleading and begging, the commands and the lewdest utterances. He knew of no better way of spending time than on his bed with this full-bodied woman. Sunshine streaming through the window, perspiring bodies heaving together, it was all that he ever dreamed of and more. And after sex, Joyce would stretch and relax by his side. He revelled in the sight of his mature lover displaying all her ample charms, the variety of intimate female parts laid bare for his close inspection. One day, unable to resist such a model, he fetched his pencils and sketch book and, sitting on a chair beside the bed, he drew her from life.

She lay in the posture of a woman after satisfying sex, arms raised, cushioning her head while her hair spread out over the pillows. With breasts swollen from her arousal, nipples tautly projecting, legs parted and relaxed, offering full sight of her hairy mound and sex, she allowed Martin to work busily without altering her position. When he finally turned the page of his sketch book to her, offering it out proudly, she sat up to take it. She laid it across her knees, looking down over her heavy breasts at the drawing, reaching for her spectacles and placing them on her nose. For a full minute she was silent while he awaited her response.

'My God,' she said at last, 'it's me, all of me. My breasts, thighs—' She gave a giggle. 'And my *you know what*! It's, it's a work of art, Martin. It's so real I find it embarrassing. Am I so Rubenesque?'

'You're beautiful,' Martin said, pleased with her comments. 'If you turn the pages you'll see others, done from memory.' He watched as she lifted each cartridge paper sheet on its spiral binding, each drawing studied with an amazed shake of her head.

'You like my breasts, I can tell,' she teased him. 'You've drawn them over and over on this page from every angle. And my back and bottom too. You *are* very expert. Such talent shouldn't be wasted, young man. Look how you've drawn my face here, with my hair down, it's like a photograph. Such a memory for detail.'

'It's imprinted on my mind from what I've seen of you,' Martin told her saucily, but in absolute truth. Always before, lying back basking in the afterglow of a protracted fucking, she had allowed him to explore her. When pleasantly languid from several climaxes, she would let him lift, squeeze and play with her breasts as if they were toys. His minute scrutiny of her sex showed it still pouting, the swollen outer lips parted to reveal the inner pink with its glistening folds of soft flesh. Rolling over at his request, he had admired her rear perspective: full rounded cheeks which, when drawn apart, disclosed a tightly puckered anus and the splendid bulge of a mound big as a split peach, festooned with curling hair around the cleft. Once on impulse he had put his mouth to it, used his tongue to taste the moistness, probed and felt her body stiffen, heard a soft moan of pleasure.

'You really are a wicked thing,' she'd said in a strained voice, her buttocks trembling. 'How did you know to do that? You'll make me come, so you will.' Continuing until her shudders ceased and she lay gasping for breath, he'd congratulated himself for obeying the impulse, her prostrate form evidence of his new skill.

With her departure he realised what a lack there was in his life. He now considered regular sex as necessary to his well-being. The summer season ended, depressing enough in a small seaside town, leaving him without relief except by the one obvious method available. Linda Simon was still keeping him at a distance and Mandy, ignored while Martin had Joyce to satisfy his lust on, had found herself a steady boyfriend. He even saw less of Norman as the weeks proceeded; it was as if he were being avoided. Once he and Norman had been inseparable, playing soccer for the local junior team together, attending the cinema, discussing what sexual delights girls could provide. Now he hardly saw his closest friend. Fed up with feeling an outcast and determined to find out why, he called at Norman's house one evening to discover the reason.

He was let in by Mrs Simon, from whom it was evident Linda had inherited her good looks. Never seen without make-up, chic in her dress, an expensive perfume assailed Martin's nostrils. 'Linda's out with her boss at the newspaper, covering some story on the local lifeboat,' she said, giving him her customary smile.

She thinks I'm stuck on her daughter and it amuses her, Martin thought, as ever admiring the swell of her breasts bulging her blouse. That painted mouth could give one a glorious suck-off too.

'Poor Martin,' she added sympathetically. 'You never give up, do you? I think it's a shame the way that daughter of mine treats you. She doesn't deserve to have such a nice young man interested in her.'

Interested in having her tits out and getting into her

knickers, Martin could have said, instead of nodding his head sadly as if in agreement. He always played along with Marion Simon's wishes, aware it did not hurt to have her on his side, pitying him and consoling.

'Actually I've called to see Norman,' he said, as if making up an excuse for Linda's absence. 'It's school stuff. The exams are coming up and I said I'd help him. He's a year behind me so his papers will be like I had last term.'

'How thoughtful,' Marion Simon praised him, a long tapered hand covered with rings reached out to touch his cheek. 'That's more than his sister offered to do. She can really be a selfish little bitch. Norman is in his bedroom studying hard, I know. Go up, Martin dear. When you've finished I'll make supper for you both.'

'Thank you, Mrs Simon,' he said, making a move towards the stairs when her hand clasped his shoulder and stopped him. Once again he was treated to an almost seductive smile.

'I think you can call me Marion, don't you?' she said. 'You're seventeen and a very handsome young man.' She watched his reaction, adding, 'Off to art school soon, I hear.'

'The Southern College of Art,' Martin said.

'Yes, well, you must come and see us before you go. And don't be so noble with that girl of mine. I've noticed you let her walk all over you at times. Show her what you're made of,' she advised. 'She'll respect you all the more for it.'

You don't think I've tried that, and everything else to give her one? he thought, going up to Norman's bedroom. He found him studying the pictures in a popular nudist publication. 'That's for me as soon as I get a bird willing to go along,' Norman stated, holding up a colour page illustrated with several nude and shapely young women posing beside an outdoor swimming pool. 'I've decided to become a dedicated naturist for my health's sake. You get to see all the bare boobs and bums on show. Do you know there's a couple

47

of nudist camps and a beach where people can go bollock naked right here on the Island? The only snag is they don't allow single chaps. You've got to bring a female partner along.'

'Tough,' Martin agreed shortly, intending to get straight to the point of his visit. 'Look, Norman, have you been avoiding me lately for some reason? Have you got a bit on the side? I told you all about screwing Aunt Joyce, didn't I? Come clean and tell me who you're shagging.'

'I should be so lucky,' Norman laughed evasively. 'It don't grow on trees, does it?' Martin studied his friend's face to see a sign of catching him out. 'Who do you think I'm fucking then?' Norman asked defensively. 'I'd be the first to tell you if I was getting the leg over. I'd be delighted to.'

'I thought maybe you were,' Martin said moodily, 'you and I not being around like before. You've even quit the football team and we could use you on Saturday against Wellow. You'd tell me if you were hanging out of somebody, wouldn't you? There's no secrets between us.'

'More to the point, have you hung out of my sister yet?' Norman switched the subject neatly. 'Time you did, Marty, for I reckon she's a horny slut on the quiet. I can prove it. Come with me and I'll show you something that will bug your eyeballs. Quietly now, we're going to investigate Linda's room.'

Norman led the way in, Martin looking about the tidy feminine bedroom and thinking of her undressing there each night. He imagined slipping into the bed with her to sample her lush young charms. 'Over here,' Norman was indicating, the drawer of her dressing table pulled open. 'See what you make of this.' He held up a lacy black bra and tiny matching briefs. 'Like to take these off her, wouldn't you?'

'I've tried,' Martin admitted, holding the briefs to his nose and sniffing appreciatively. 'I've tried my hand a thousand times but she keeps her legs shut tight. She's a prick-teaser and enjoys it; all the more for being so bloody good-looking. She just will not fuck.'

'She's a stuck-up bitch and I wouldn't fuck her with your dick,' Norman laughed. 'Linda treats everyone like she's royalty. She's always resented me, her step-brother. Didn't know that, did you? My old man was divorced and married to my step-mother when I was four. We came here to live and Linda was five at the time. She made it obvious she didn't want a new brother.'

'I didn't know that,' Martin said. 'Kept it quiet, didn't they?'

'They don't spread it around that both were divorced when they met,' Norman said, 'and don't you mention it. As for goody-goody Linda, what do you think of this?' He rummaged carefully below folded layers of scanty underwear and pulled out a long black object. He held it out for Martin to see. 'How would you like a dong like that? It's bigger than yours Marty.'

'Jesus, a whopping great dummy prick!' Martin exclaimed, his face wreathed in a huge grin. 'Would you believe it!'

'Dildo I believe is the correct description,' Norman laughed. 'Think of that length going up snotty little Linda. Imagine her giving herself a going-over with this brute.'

'I am,' Martin said wistfully. 'That I'd love to see.'

He watched Norman carefully replace the dummy prick. Back in his friend's room they heard Marion call to them that supper was ready. When it was time to leave she saw Martin to the door, standing on the step with him. 'Goodnight, young man,' she said sweetly, bending her face to his. For a moment he thought she was about to kiss him on the mouth, but at the last moment she twisted her face to peck him on the cheek provocatively. 'Do come and say your farewell before you leave for college, won't you? Maybe Linda will be kind to you for a change. I'm sure your luck will improve some day.'

I should be as lucky as that big dummy dong she gets off on, he thought, going on his way considerably tickled to be in on such a revelation. Discovering others' sexual secrets was both arousing and intriguing, something he would always seek to know. Linda had definitely soared in his estimation. There couldn't be much wrong with a girl horny and wanton enough to fuck herself with a substitute prick. His kind of female, in fact. The world was full of such wonders, he surmised, and it boded well for his future. They were all out there waiting for him and he would make sure he'd find them.

On Saturday he cycled in a downpour to the local football ground to find it under inches of water. The goal nets were not in place and marking the pitch was impossible. In the little hut that served as a dressing room he found Sam Hicks, the trainer, sitting with other despondent members of the local side. 'Game's off,' he was told. 'Cancelled till next week. Too late for you, Marty, we hear you're off to art college.'

'I didn't fancy playing on that pitch today,' Martin said. He stood in the door of the hut until the rain abated somewhat, then rode off towards his home through deserted streets. Drenched, he wheeled his bicycle down the path at the side of his house, parking it in the garden shed before entering by the back door. All seemed quiet in the large house as he stood in the kitchen drying his hair with a hand towel hung behind the door. His mother and sister must be out, he concluded, helping himself to a slice of cherry cake and going on through to the passageway off the main entrance hall. What he heard there drew him up short, mystified by the sounds, making him cautious as he went silently to the door leading into the Compton's lounge.

He found the heavy door ajar just the inch or so necessary to peer in to clearly see the fireplace and the large over-stuffed couch, one of a pair either side. On it, showing the reason for the muffled grunting and moans he had heard in the passageway, was a lifting and thrusting bare backside, its owner busily engaged in strenuously fucking whomsoever was on the receiving end. In front of the couch and fireplace lay an untidy jumble of clothes, as if thrown off in haste – the haste of desperation to get at it. Riveted by the sight, Martin stared and recognised Norman's longish head of hair. He got an instant straining erection as he watched the action. 'The horny sod,' he chuckled to himself. 'That's why he's been too busy to see me or play football. He's shagging my sister!'

A moment later he was surprised even more, drawing back from his viewpoint as the partners switched positions. Rolling over among the cushions to change to the woman-superior posture and hardly ceasing in their ardent coupling, Martin recognised his mother. Broad, womanly buttocks bounced as Olivia Compton bore down on Norman's upraised prick, inches of it being shunted in and out of the cling of her cunt lips. Martin heard her grunt at each determined thrust as she engulfed Norman's stem, heard the sliding of it in and out. With her agitated bobbing, her breasts swung sideways, out under each arm in turn, until with a great shudder she impaled herself to the hilt. As his mother squirmed her ample bottom on Norman's cock, Martin heard her cry out, 'Faster, harder! Fuck, fuck me, Norman, thrust it right up!'

Obeying manfully, Norman grasped the globes of her buttocks, striving against the weight on him to lift her. Relentless in their pursuit of pleasure, both gasped loudly and shuddered out of control.

'He made her come!' Martin told himself in wonder at the sight. 'My mother!' As they lay quivering in their pleasure, he was certain this was not their first time. It had been too wholehearted, too uninhibited – too practised. Mrs Compton eased herself up off of Norman, his flaccid dick falling out of the mouth of her cunt, the condom he wore glistening with her juices. In a trance, Martin nudged against the door and with horror heard it creak open slightly. It was enough to warn the loving pair on the couch that they had been observed.

Olivia Compton sprang up like a scalded cat, leaping to the carpet, leaving Norman spreadeagled among the cushions. For a long moment she and her son stood frozen, long enough for him to note the rounded fullness of heavy breasts, the mature curves of hip and thigh, the thickly forested mound between her legs. Transfixed, he saw her swoop down to snatch at her clothes, uptilted tits falling forward to become long tubes of flesh. She brushed past him in haste, garments clutched to her bosom, darting into the passageway and up the stairs. He followed to shout his apologies after her, that he hadn't meant to spy, but she fled before him.

Chapter Six

WORKING GIRL

'Looks good,' Hugh Bembridge said, leaning over Linda's shoulder and scanning the screen of her word processor. 'We'll use it word for word. I like what I see.' She turned to smile gratefully up at him, noting he looked fixedly down the neck of her dress at the cleavage of her young breasts.

'Am I showing too much, Mr Bembridge?' she asked coyly, the words chosen to test his reaction. 'This neckline *is* rather revealing. If you think it's not quite appropriate for wearing at work . . .'

'Not a bit,' he assured her, patting her shoulder and leaving his hand there. 'Pretty girls with assets like yours should be dressing for effect. It won't do any harm when you interview people either. Guys especially always open up to nice-looking female reporters. Remember that, Linda. And cut out the Mr Bembridge bit, love. Call me Hugh. We're all bosom buddies here.' He attempted a snide joke. 'More so in your case, I'd say.'

Linda lowered her eyes, her tongue in her cheek, gauging the ambition of her new employer. It was to fuck her, no doubt, and she idly wondered what advantages would be offered in return. Bembridge was in his thirties, twice her age and not unattractive if somewhat overweight. A former Fleet Street journalist, now owner and editor of the weekly *Island*

Investigator, even at her interview Linda had seen through him. Her looks and figure had undoubtedly got her the job, despite experienced applicants. He could teach her a lot, at least about writing for public consumption. About sex, after Clifford she had little to learn.

'Get your coat, honey,' Bembridge said, breaking into her reverie. His affected transatlantic accent was a hangover of his days as New York correspondent for a national news-paper. 'You've done well for your first few days and it's late. How do you get home? Bus, bike, or boyfriend in his car?'

'Bus,' Linda replied. 'There's no boyfriend, Mr Bem-bridge. I mean Hugh.'

'It's no trouble to drive you,' he smiled. 'It would be my pleasure. Do you drive?'

'Yes, I've passed my test. I've used my father's car. I'd have it tonight but he's using it.'

'We'll have to see about a company car,' he promised. 'The paper's still struggling but circulation is rising. Finish your probationary period to *my* satisfaction, Linda and I'll see what I can come up with. Your own wheels. How does that grab you?'

As she got up from her desk he gave her bottom a friendly pat, lingering just a moment too long as if savouring the feel and testing her reaction. Waiting beside his car while he locked up the office, she pondered how far he'd attempt to go with her on the ride home. Since Clifford's departure she had been without sex, apart from self-pleasuring, and after Clifford masturbation seemed a poor substitute. She had even considered seducing Martin Compton in his last week before leaving for art college. Now it seemed likely she had another prospect, Hugh Bembridge, married but with the look of one who played away from home. The stirrings of arousal pulsated her sex like a heartbeat, oiling her vagina as she considered the possible outcome of accepting his lift.

Thoughts that it would help her career gave her a thrill too. It was almost prostitution.

On the drive Hugh pulled off the cliff road into a square of picnic area overlooking the sea. Crowded in the summer, now it was deserted but for another car. He parked far away from it. The full moon appearing behind a fleeting cloud silvered the expanse of sea. 'Very picturesque,' Linda said almost mischievously. 'Did you bring me here to admire the moonlight?' His knee pressed to hers and he slid an arm across the back of her seat, his fingers smoothing her neck.

'Come off it,' he laughed crudely, a different Hugh Bembridge. In the moonlight she saw his eyes gleam lustfully, his mouth almost watering. 'What do you think's going on in that other car? Can you see anybody sitting up admiring the view?'

'I wouldn't know,' Linda said spiritedly. 'What do you think?'

'That they're at it. Fucking. They're probably both married, too, up here for an illicit jump. Some guy with a bit on the side.'

'*You're* married,' Linda taunted him. 'Do you consider me a bit on the side? What makes you think I'm that kind of girl?' She disengaged his hand from seeking her breast. 'You don't waste much time, do you? I think you're crude.'

'Some like it crude,' he laughed, pushing her hand away to grope again at her breasts. 'And I think you're trying it on, coming the hard-to-get bit. You knew Clifford Maine, didn't you?'

Linda felt her face redden. 'What's that got to do with it?' she snapped. His fingers were busily unbuttoning the front of her dress, sliding in to cup each breast in turn outside her bra while she sat up stiffly. 'What if I did know Clifford Maine? He was my writing tutor.'

'He certainly knew you,' Bembridge stated laconically. 'In

55

the biblical sense too, didn't he? Said you were the horniest little piece he'd ever tutored. He wrote your reference, advised me to employ you. We had quite a chat.'

'The bastard,' Linda swore. 'Both of you are bastards.' She felt his large hand inside her bra, squeezing the plump flesh, plucking at her tightening nipple. Despite the unsolicited arousal she felt churning her innards, she forced herself to protest. 'I suppose if I don't let you, I lose my job. That's blackmail.'

'It wouldn't go that far,' Bembridge asserted. 'You're a good little writer. But coming across wouldn't exactly hinder your chances. You want it, anyway, I can feel you trembling.' He took her hand and she allowed him to draw it down to the warmth and steely hardness projecting from his fly. 'There,' he said. 'Try that right up you, girl. What about a backseat job?'

Linda could not suppress a giggle at his forthrightness. 'God, you're a crude bastard,' she said. 'And out of luck too. You can't fuck me – I'm not on the pill.'

'Then get on it if you intend to work for me,' he advised, his hand leaving her breast to cup her chin. 'So what about that pretty little mouth? That won't get pregnant, will it? Or a ride at your gorgeous tits, maybe? There are good alternatives. Are you getting in the back seat?'

'Under duress,' she told him, but with mounting excitement at the prospect. 'You're a filthy beast.'

'A bit of rough,' he agreed, 'and I've found that's often what the ladies like. So-called nice ones too, the nicer the better. So get in the back and take off your clothes, or shall I smack your bum?'

'You wouldn't dare,' Linda replied hotly, discovering it was strangely exhilarating to be spoken to like this. 'Or perhaps you would,' she added, sounding petulant but finding the idea exciting. In the rear of the car she obediently undressed while Hugh Bembridge did the same. She noted in the silvery light that his penis still reared admirably.

'There,' she announced, finally nude, proud to show off her lovely body as she stretched out with breasts uptilted and her legs across his bare thighs. 'That is all of me. What you see is all I've got.'

She heard his sharp intake of breath with pleasure and was sure that in time she could wrap him around her little finger. 'And what a lot you've got, girl,' he told her admiringly, his hands sliding up her thighs slowly, then suddenly parting her legs. 'That's a well-fucked cunt, I bet,' he uttered coarsely, 'but all the better for that. I haven't got time to waste on seducing virgins. Give me ready-made whores every time.' His hand went to her sex, a curled finger roughly invading her cleft, causing her to arch her back and yelp a protest. 'One like you, well broken in. You've juiced up a flood. What have you got in there, Linda, a running tap?'

'You really know how to compliment a girl,' Linda said sarcastically, teeth gritted as his finger probed, her arse rotating helplessly. His hand sought her large clitoris, rubbing the quivering projection between his fingertips. Groaning with pleasure, Linda could not survive the expert rubbing.

'Oh God!' she squealed, squirming her hips and spending gloriously, out of control. She sat up dazed from the magnitude of her climax, seeing Hugh Bembridge watching her mockingly, holding up two glistening fingers. 'Let me go now,' she asked humbly. You've done what you wanted.'

'We haven't even started,' he informed her casually. She felt a growing fear of him, and resented the arrogance of his manipulation. With her looks she had always considered that men would do *her* bidding. This man was over-powering, demanding obedience as his right. She was not the obedient type.

'I'm dressing,' she announced, summoning her will, reaching for her clothes. He grasped her wrist, twisting it so that she was turned to face him. 'Let go of me,' she said as calmly as she could. 'You take too much for granted.'

The short laugh he gave showed he would not be reasonable. 'Not used to being treated like a slut, are you, Linda? But that's what you are, so why not accept it? Do you think you're too good for the likes of me? You came off like a firework just now, so don't kid me you don't love it. A word in your shell-like if you want to work with me. Coming across for the right man will take you to the top. It's the way of the world, girl, so enjoy the trip. Do we understand each other?'

'I've never been spoken to like this,' she complained.

'Then it's time you were,' he said. 'I've no doubt there'll be plenty of men willing to worship at your feet in time. This one won't, so you know what you're in for if you stay.' He held up the two fingers that had pleasured her. 'Lick them, Linda. Lick my fingers clean—'

The fingers stayed unwaveringly before her lips while she considered what to do. She could push them away and refuse angrily, but a stronger urge direct from her still palpitating cunt made her want to comply. Taking the palm of his hand she muttered, 'I was right, you are a beast,' before sucking each finger one at a time in her mouth.

'You're learning,' Hugh Bembridge said as she did so. 'That wasn't too bad, was it? You wanted to, didn't you?'

'What if I'd refused?' Linda asked.

'I'd have smacked that nice little bum of yours good and hard, like I shall do if you annoy me or your work's not up to standard,' he promised. 'That's rule one. Now let's get down to the nitty-gritty. Just lie back and enjoy it, girl.'

He roved his mouth over her face, kissing, licking like a cat lapping milk, going down to her breasts and sucking each nipple in turn. The treatment made Linda sigh. She directed his head lower, raising her knees and guiding him to her source. She felt his stubble, welcomed his thick tongue, groaned and worked her pelvis in jerky motions against his face. Brought to the brink once more, the fire in her cunt at white heat, she moaned in frustration as he pulled away. His mouth wet with her juices, he moved forward over her; a staunchly erect prick nudging her inner thigh. The knob rubbed and teased at her pouting sex lips, making no attempt at further penetration. Awaiting her response, he maintained the outside contact, tempting but proceeding no further.

It came as he'd expected. With a low moan of submission, Linda hoisted her bottom wantonly and engulfed his whole length. 'You pig,' she swore, working her hips, 'I told you not to but – oh, fuck me – yes, fuck! Shove it in, shove it up! Oh, God, do it, do it!'

Above her, Bembridge looked down goatishly on her twisted features, supreme in his triumph, matching her stroke for stroke, knowing this volatile girl with her over-sexed nature was his for the taking. As she came in a long series of heaves and thrusts, he disengaged at the crucial moment, jetting hot spunk over her heaving stomach and sprinkling her breasts.

'Better out than in, that lot,' he told her cheerfully as she lay recovering slowly along the car seat. 'See that you go on the pill in future, I'm not mad on leaping off in mid-thrust.' He looked down at her spread-apart breasts silvered with his come, her gaping cunt still retaining the round shape of his girth, almost visibly throbbing. 'Dry yourself with this,' he said, offering a handkerchief from his jacket draped over the front seat, 'then you can dress and I'll get you home. I presume we understand each other a little better now. You are aware of our working arrangements?'

'Yes,' Linda said meekly, dabbing at her breasts.

'Very good,' he said, 'we'll make a journalist out of you yet. And don't be late in the morning, that's a punishable offence.'

Chapter Seven

FOND FAREWELLS

Leaving his house the evening before enrolling for art school, Martin weighed up his chances of going out with a final fuck on his home ground. The best venue for hopefully getting off with an obliging local girl had to be the Winter Gardens hall. That night the dance floor would shimmer beneath the mirrored globes reflecting dappled coloured lights over walls and floor and couples. Local group Mort Titian and The Shrouds would belt out the beat, and the atmosphere would reek of sweat and cheap perfume and nubile female bodies, a powerful aphrodisiac to a randy youth.

It was almost a week since he had discovered that Norman was his mother's lover. It had been an awkward few days. Her eyes either avoided him or looked accusingly at him when they were together. As if he cared! He wished he could tell her he was happy for her. He had tried to that night as she fled past him clutching her discarded clothes. Dashing to the bottom of the stairs, unable not to note the jiggle and bounce of her amply rounded buttocks and the growth of hair peeping from the divide of her cheeks, he had tried to reassure her. Then, turning back into the room where the romp had occurred, an irate Norman faced him, stark naked but for a wrinkled condom on his deflated dick. Only when he saw Martin's face wreathed in a huge grin did he relax,

61

and accept that his friend was not outraged by what he'd seen but was hugely tickled.

'Everybody's at it,' Martin grinned delightedly. 'Great, isn't it? Aunt Joyce and now even my mum. Restores one's faith in human nature, doesn't it?'

'Rotten sod,' Norman said goodnaturedly. 'We thought you'd be playing football. So now you know, your ma and I have been at it. Do you mind?'

'Do I look like I do?' Martin laughed. 'I'll never blame anyone for wanting nookie. Never,' he emphasised. 'Kept it quiet, didn't you? How long has this been going on?'

A month or two, he was surprised to learn. Whenever Martin or his sister was out of the house. 'I never would have thought she was like that myself,' Norman agreed, gathering up his clothes. 'I came here for you one day when she was hanging out washing. It was blowing a gale and the wind whipped her dress hard against her. It really flattened it against her and showed the cheeks of her arse and the split like she was bare. When she turned to me her big tits were like that too, the wind pressing the dress between her crotch and against her thighs. She saw me eyeing her up and this sudden feeling come over us both. I was trembling, so was she.' He paused, as if assuring Martin that this was gospel. 'We walked back into the kitchen and she asked me how old I was. Her voice was all trembly too, and we stood close enough almost to touch. We were breathing heavily too, you know how it is. Then we were kissing, really going at it – frenching and gum-sucking. It was frantic, Marty, like it was a dream. Next thing I know I had her dress up and knickers down and was shagging her up against the sink. I made her come off.'

'You caught her on blob,' Martin said sagely. 'I'm sure she hasn't been getting any since my old man left. What did she say afterwards? That it was all wrong, it must never happen again and stuff like that? Joyce did too. Evidently my ma didn't let that stop you fucking her.'

'She's all for it,' Norman said proudly. 'Can't get enough of my cock now. At first she tried to fend me off when I called but I hung around until she gave in. That's why you never saw me lately, I'd wait till you and your sister were out. She used to complain, but then she'd let me kiss her and grope her boobs. She told me I was a wicked boy, looking at her with eyes like a puppy begging, but soon the heavy snogging got to her and we fucked again. After that she let me every time I was here. It's great and she thinks so too.'

'I can tell that from what I saw,' Martin agreed, 'and from the two used French letters I see in the fireplace as well as the one on your dong. You must go at it like rabbits! How many times do you reckon you've got across her?'

'Dozens,' Norman grinned. 'Sometimes she'd see me waiting across the road. When you went out, I went in, and she'd call me upstairs from over the bannisters, waiting with her clothes off, bollock naked for me. We'd give the bed a fair old pounding. I've sucked her tits, licked her fanny, and she's sucked me. We've done the lot.'

'No more than what I did with Joyce when she was here,' Martin had to say defensively. He heard his mother calling down to him and his eyes met Norman's.

'I'm going,' his friend announced. 'I don't want to be here for this. I just hope you haven't spoiled it for me.'

Martin mounted the stairs and entered his mother's bedroom to find her fully dressed, her hair brushed and looking serious with her spectacles on her nose. She had always been a strong-willed woman, now he wondered what approach or excuse she would adopt. 'I've been very foolish,' she began. 'I allowed something to happen today that never should have. I'm a lonely woman, you know, and what you saw will never happen again. It was the first and only time.'

She told the lie with complete aplomb. 'What you do is none of my business, mother,' Martin said, stifling his grin. 'If you are so lonely, then I don't blame you.'

As he entered the dance hall he felt he couldn't blame anyone for giving in to temptation. He was feeling horny as never before after his recent lack of success. He saw curvy Mandy Field clinging possessively to her new boyfriend as they danced, ruefully conceding that he had missed out with her. Every girl seemed either to be partnered or not the kind to come across on short acquaintance, so after several futile dances he went to the bar to order a lager. On the stool beside him sat an attractive blonde woman with heavily made-up eyes and lips, drinking vodka. Middle-thirties, Martin guessed, liking the look of her, liking painted women. His scrutiny did not go unnoticed, his own appearance being given the once-over.

'Good crowd in tonight,' he said for want of a better opener. She was not the usual sort who frequented the Winter Gardens. She was apparently unescorted, older and wearing an expensive silk dress. The rings she wore looked the real thing too, one of them a thick gold wedding band and a rock of a diamond engagement ring with it. Her rich perfume reeked headily in his nostrils. 'Good crowd,' he repeated.

'You'll have to do better if that's your chat-up line, young man,' the woman giggled, obviously well oiled with drink. 'What comes next? "Do you come here often?" '

'It was actually,' Martin grinned, warming to her sense of humour. 'Or even, "What's a nice woman like you doing in a dump like this?" I'm just a local yokel, an Island caulkhead. You tell me what I ought to say.' He gave her his best winning smile, aware she was regarding him with a secret and amused look.

'You could start with, "Can I buy you a drink?" ' she said,

stifling a hiccup. 'Or better still and more to the point – "I suppose a jump is out of the question?" '

If Martin was taken aback, he fought not to show it. Hadn't he promised himself to be all things to all women? This one, he figured, was well off, drinking to forget, probably after one hell of a blazing row with an errant hubby. This was her way of getting her own back. 'Is it?' he asked meaningfully. 'A jump being out of the question?'

'Have you a flat or a car we could use?' she said, seeming to sober up somewhat. 'My bastard of a husband has mine; he says he's working but no doubt he's out screwing some young slut. It's *my* money he's throwing away to stay in business and keep him sleeping around while it goes bust. Why shouldn't I do the same?' She stared defiantly around. 'Order a taxi, whoever you are, I'll take you home. My days for a quickie under the pier or up against a wall are past.'

Tempting as the offer was, Martin did not relish an irate husband returning. 'I know a good place,' he said, leading her off by the hand, down steps at the rear of the hall to a door that led under the stage. So far she had followed dutifully but now she hesitated. 'Warm, dry and safe,' he assured her, ushering her into a long space about five foot high and putting on a light to reveal the area filled with curtains, clothes, furniture and stage scenery. 'Not very quiet though,' he had to admit as The Shrouds thumped out rock music overhead, 'but there's a bed in here somewhere.'

'You know your way around,' she giggled, clutching his hand as they stumbled forward. 'Do you come here often?' For the first time he kissed her, enjoying the feel of her full tits against his chest, his erection firming flush on her mound.

'I painted the scenery for the dramatic society,' he told her, leading her to a bed cluttered with costumes and curtains. As he stood before her she sat up and unzipped his jeans. 'I'm glad I did now.' With his stalk fiercely erect he leaned back slightly as the woman bent to kiss its bulbous knob almost reverently. Her tongue lapped and licked its way up the stem. 'You've done that before,' he said. 'Suck it. Eat it!'

'Yes, yes,' she muttered dozily, as if the effect of her drinking was telling on her finally. 'You tell me to suck it, eat it. I like to hear that. Talk dirty to me.' She took him deep in her throat, sucking and slurping away greedily. 'Fuck my face,' she mumbled with a full mouth, but her suctioning eased, slowed, and suddenly she fell back across the bed sound asleep. About to grasp her head and work his hips, Martin's prick bobbed up free from her lips, glistened with her saliva. With a feeling that he had been cruelly robbed, he sat beside the woman and listened to her deep breathing. When she came to drunkenly with his repeated shaking, she allowed herself to be led outside to the taxi rank. He almost had to lift her into the back seat, glad that a taxi was waiting.

He heard her mumble her address to the driver, made sure she had her handbag clutched to her hand, and watched as the car drove off. He didn't even know her name, he recalled. At least he'd be able to say it had been an adventure, a near-run thing. On the next street was the Simon residence and, hoping for better luck, he decided to call to say his farewell. The night was but young. Perhaps the haughty Linda, feeling kindlier with his departure imminent, might for once relax her defences. Reaching the door, he heard raised angry voices, Linda appearing to slam it behind her as they met on the steps.

'My mother,' she swore heatedly, 'is an interfering bitch. All the time wanting to know where I'm going.' She glared as if he too disapproved. 'I'm going to work, that's what. I've told her repeatedly a journalist hasn't got set hours. Why are you here at this time of night? Norman's out.'

And I can guess where he is, rogering my mother, Martin

could have said. 'I'm off to the mainland tomorrow, art college, remember?' he reminded her, thinking what a delectable piece she was. He pressed closer to her until she was backed against the door, her gorgeous breasts barely an inch from his chest. 'I came to say goodbye. I thought we could go for a drink, or to the dance. Or something . . .'

'I know your something,' Linda said sarcastically. 'Anyway, my boss is picking me up. He should be here. Do you have to stand so close? Piss off, Martin, go and play with yourself.'

'I'd rather play with you,' he said, holding her, seeking her mouth as she twisted her face around to foil him. The pliancy of her soft young body against his made his erection return sturdily. It fitted comfortably into the fork of her thighs and he moved his hips slowly, sensuously, to rub it against her dress and the sexual part beyond. He felt her stiffen up, then relax her body, suspected a slight movement to push her crotch to meet his tentative thrusts. His hand rose to cup a breast and squeeze and fondle, feeling a tight nipple in his palm. Then they were mouth to mouth, his tongue probing and her hips working to his increasing thrusts. Suddenly she pushed hard at his chest, holding him off, shaking now with anger.

'You dirty little swine!' she berated him, her voice almost a screech. 'Who do you think you are? Grow up! I'm not one of your easy things. If I ever want you to do that, I'll be the one to say.'

The door opened before Martin could tell her to fuck herself with her dildo. Mrs Simon stood in the doorway, looking at them both. 'What *is* all this noise about?' she demanded. 'I could hear the commotion inside.'

'Ask Martin,' Linda said snidely. A large car had drawn up before the house and a horn sounded. 'That's for me, my work chariot,' she said. 'Expect me when you see me, mother. As for you, Martin, better luck next time. I'm sure you'll do well at your college.'

They watched the car depart, Mrs Simon shaking her head. 'I don't like that man she works for or his sleazy little newspaper. Linda has changed completely lately. We've just had an upsetting row about her attitude. Of course her father wasn't here as usual when I needed his backing. Night fishing now, as if all day long wasn't enough. Did you come to say goodbye before going off tomorrow?'

'That was the idea,' Martin said. 'We fell out.'

'You poor boy,' Marion Simon sympathised. 'She's argumentative, rude to me and not a nice girl at present, I think. You're better off being keen on someone else, Martin.' She ushered him into the house, sitting across from him in an armchair, crossing long shapely legs and showing a length of sheer stockinged thigh. 'Just what was going on out there?' she asked good-humouredly. 'Did your passion get the better of you? It sounded like it, you naughty boy.'

'It got to a kiss and cuddle,' Martin admitted, 'then she went berserk. I didn't mean to push it. You know, expect to . . .'

'Go the whole way?' Marion Simon finished for him, laughing. 'I should hope not, at least not in our doorway. You haven't had much luck with my daughter, have you, Martin?'

'Her or any other girl,' he admitted, half in jest, wondering about the direction of her questioning and where it was leading. Across from him he noted the enticing jiggle of Mrs Simon's large tits as she laughed at his reply. Once again he was reminded how much she was an attractive older version of Linda.

'But you've had your moments,' she insisted smilingly. 'You're not exactly a virgin, are you? Not a handsome boy like you. I'm sure my daughter hasn't been the only fish in the sea.'

'Then I must be using the wrong bait,' he said, an inner presentiment telling him to appear regretful and to appeal to her sympathy. He felt the stirring in his stomach that preceded arousal and sensed the charged atmosphere in the room. 'I should be so lucky,' he added dolefully. He noted the change in his voice, thick with emotion. 'Maybe going to college will improve my love life.'

Marion Simon tut-tutted, shaking her head beguilingly at his admission. 'You are a poor soul,' she smiled, 'but I'm certain your luck will change.' Her voice, too, sounded different to him, almost a husky whisper. Rising, she crossed to Martin, kissed two of her fingers and pressed them to his lips. Then she walked off with a sway of her hips, glancing back once to give him an amused pout of painted lips. From his seat, looking out into the hallway, he saw her mount the stairs, each step working the firm cheeks of her buttocks under a skintight skirt.

Martin sat, wondering at her sudden departure, unsure of her motive. She had probably gone upstairs for no other reason than to use the bathroom and left him with a promising hard-on from her teasing. She's having me on, he concluded, certain she would return to offer no more than coffee. Ten minutes passed, fifteen, and he grew restless, deciding his last foray in town had proved more frustrating than profitable. Mounting the stairs to inform his hostess he was leaving, he tapped on the main bedroom door and found it open. Inside, Marion Simon was laid out in wait. She posed for his arrival completely nude, big breasts lolling, legs parted, one languidly stretched out while the other was raised and bent at the knee. The posture maintained was lewd in the extreme, intentionally inviting. It revealed to full advantage the thick triangle of pubic hair curling down to surround her plump *mons* and the cleft lips of her cunt.

'It's not Linda, but perhaps her mother will do?' she enquired coquettishly. 'You do deserve a going-away present, Martin, so for this once I'll allow you your way. Do you like what you see?'

He walked slowly around the foot and side of the bed, feasting his eyes. 'I didn't dare hope,' he admitted. 'I like, I like! I've pictured seeing you like this since I was a kid, when you were on the beach in your bikini.'

'A rather overflowing bikini,' she laughed. 'So you did take notice? What a naughty boy. And now you see me. I've a confession about you too. Our two families were having a picnic at Whitecliff Bay last year. When I handed you a sandwich your towel fell from around your waist. I was *most* impressed by what I saw.'

Martin remembered, recalling the flush of pride he felt when Marion Simon's eyes had widened at the sight of his endowment. 'Do you think I should be the only one undressed?' she added sweetly. 'Don't just stand there, young man. Let me see you. Has it grown at all since last year? Am I awful to hope that it has?'

'It's grown,' Martin assured her. 'Seeing you stretched out like that made it even bigger.' He tore off his clothes, eager to let her see the rigid stalk he was so proud of, that would soon be fucking this splendid woman. As he stooped to peel off his underpants, the final garment, he saw with alarm a bright red ring of lipstick circling the girth, a memento of the drunken woman under the stage of the Winter Garden. He covered it quickly with his hand, standing before Mrs Simon with long inches of thick prick projecting from his fist. She scrambled to her knees, muttering her admiration, crawling forward to him. Thankfully, she replaced his hand with her own curled fingers, covering the offending ring, and with a low moan, as if unable to resist, devoured him. It was more

70

than Martin could endure. His knees buckled, and his hips jerked, as he shot long spurts into her throat, the suctioning continuing until he was limp and drained.

'I've got lipstick all over the poor thing,' Marion Simon giggled as she released the flaccid dick from her mouth and inspected it. 'Did I really swallow all that? Come on the bed with me, Martin dear. Do you want to feel my breasts and suck them? Do whatever you wish, so long as we can make *him* go big and stiff again. You know what I want you to do, don't you?'

'Say it,' Martin told her, getting on the bed beside her, their lips and tongues meeting, his hand seeking a plump breast. 'Say it, the word that means what you want. I like to hear a woman speak it.'

'Fuck?' Marion Simon asked amusedly. 'You want to hear me say fuck? I don't know if I want you to be friends with my daughter, a forward boy like you. All right, if it will help. I want you to fuck me, fuck my cunt, make me come and come with your lovely big prick. Suck my nipples, darling, suck my big tits.'

'Yes, you have lovely big tits,' Martin agreed, fastening his lips to the breast she held up to nurse him. He suckled each hard nipple, feeling the stiffening of his prick as Marion massaged it sensuously. 'Is it bigger than your husband's?' he mumbled against her breast, while below his finger entered her cunt, sliding in an oiled crevice to titillate a tautened clitoris. 'Bigger and better,' she moaned hoarsely. 'Lick me out, please, darling. Lick out my cunt. You do that, don't you?'

Delighted with her obvious excitement, Martin obediently slipped between her thighs, parting them and delving in with open mouth. He sucked her labia and penetrated her with his tongue, swirling it around and poking at her swollen nub, exulting in the sudden wild churning of her bottom and her gasps. With her climax evident by the increasing convulsions of her body, he knelt between her legs, his ramrod entering and piercing her to the hilt without guidance of hand. Below him Marion bucked furiously, moaning out her extreme pleasure, cradling him tightly in her thighs with her legs circling his back.

'Fuck! Go on, fuck! Fuck me!' she repeatedly ordered, and 'Keep it in, shove it up harder!' even as the spasms of a wracking orgasm overtook her. At the same time Martin came in her, thrusting manfully to his last spurt.

Kissing, touching and fondling each other, in their sated condition they both fell asleep. Waking with a start to find his partner slumbering beside him, he covered her with the duvet and dressed quietly. Well past the midnight hour, deciding it was prudent to leave while all was quiet, out on the landing he came face to face with Norman.

'Just in myself from your place,' his friend grinned. 'This makes us even, Marty. You were right, everybody is at it, your old lady and mine as well. It's great, isn't it?'

'And we've only just begun,' Martin promised.

Chapter Eight

ON THE JOB

'Ms Mannering will probably see you next, dear,' the effeminate young man smirked. Behind a huge desk in the outer office of the executive director of Merlin TV, he beamed an ingratiating smile at Linda, enjoying her agitation. Kept well over an hour for her interview, seeing others shown into the executive director's office ahead of her, she ignored his amused look and stared ahead, briefcase on lap and knees together. The job she was hoping to get made the waiting necessary, even if she was inwardly furious at being ignored.

Linda had interested herself in studying the decor of the office: awards won by the company on the walls, photographs of stars and personalities who had appeared in programmes, posters of productions of 'The Magic of Merlin Television' sold worldwide. Now, curbing impatience, Linda decided the treatment was deliberate, designed to show her insignificance. The message was that she was lucky even to be considered as an employee of such a prestigious concern.

'I'm Giles French, personal secretary to our lady boss, the beloved Hope Mannering,' the smug man said, breaking the oppressive silence. 'H.M. for short, get it? Her Majesty. More of an old dyke than a queen really, but that's what we call her, H.M. Not to her face, of course.'

'Should you be talking about her like this?' Linda frowned.

'Certainly not,' Giles agreed. 'She's undoubtedly got this office bugged. H.M. knows everything worth knowing about everybody, including me. She'll love you, dearie. You're dishy. Tell me, are those big tits for real? Or just padded out for effect?'

'Whatever they are, would you be interested?' Linda replied coldly. 'I hardly think so.'

'You're so right,' Giles agreed affably. 'Obvious, isn't it? Having cleared that up, what are *you*, luvvy?'

'That's of no interest to you either, I imagine.'

'No,' Giles conceded. 'But to someone else not miles away, yes. Play along and the job's yours. Not a great salary but a bright future for an ambitious researcher. The chance of writing, producing or directing programmes if you're good enough and survive long enough with Merlin Television. That means surviving H.M., of course—'

Whatever Linda intended to answer was stifled by an audible whimpering issuing from the office of Hope Mannering. It was followed by a swish and loud crack, an anguished cry mixed with the sound of leather striking bare flesh. Linda directed enquiring eyes at Giles, noting him grinning sadistically. The cries, yelps and shouted pleas continued with the thrashing noises.

'That's little Louise getting her botty reddened,' explained Giles happily. 'Corrective treatment for a junior researcher who got her facts wrong for a Merlin documentary. H.M. caught it before being televised, of course. She misses nothing but it's still a punishable offence in her book. How she loves wielding that strap—'

'On her employees?' Linda began.

'I know what you're thinking,' smiled Giles. 'It's harassment. They could report it, be awarded compensation by some industrial tribunal or whatever. But they don't. H.M. is an excellent employer. She initiates training, promotes from

74

junior staff who are loyal. Louise won't complain. No one ever does, get it?'

The door to the inner sanctum opened and a girl appeared, red-eyed and stifling her sobs. 'Miss Simon?' she enquired tearfully. 'You are to go in now. Ms Mannering will see you.' Rubbing her bottom through her skirt she fled the room, Giles' taunting look following her.

Linda entered the office reminding herself the post would be a big step forward in her intended career. She found a tall angular woman in her mid thirties seated at her desk glancing over a folder, large horn-rimmed spectacles on the end of an aristocratic nose.

'Not an extensive record of employment, Miss Simon,' she began curtly, without any words of token politeness. 'Twenty now, I see, with local newspaper experience followed by local radio work south of London. I've obtained tapes of your radio work, by the way. So now you hope to move up in the world? We do need an intelligent being in our research department. Suppose I take you on?'

'I'd work hard to be efficient and do whatever was asked of me,' Linda said with hope rising. 'Anything.'

'Anything?' Hope Mannering smiled subtly, rising and walking around her desk to lean against it facing Linda. 'Just what do you mean? Now, think before you answer. Anything at all?' Linda stepped back a fraction, overpowered by the scent of the woman, noting the beautifully coiffured hair and expressive face, the expensive suit and jewellery. The woman's smile broadened at Linda's indecision. 'Come, girl, you've got a tongue, haven't you? I sincerely *hope* so. I'm not going to eat you, or am I? Speak up.'

'I would like to work here,' Linda said boldly. 'Whatever I'm expected to do. Is that what you want to hear?' To be propositioned so early in her interview surprised her, but the woman was attractive to her and she wanted the job.

'Then we should get on, if you're as flexible as you claim,' Hope Mannering decided. 'I'll offer you a month's trial period to uncover what hidden talents you may have; and see what you're prepared to do on the job.' Her eyes searched Linda's face. 'Don't let it go to waste, Simon, there are hordes of young women out there eager and willing to work here under me. Remember that.'

'Yes, ma'am,' Linda said humbly, controlling the elation she felt on hearing of the trial period. To be accepted after that as a Merlin employee meant more than being good at her work, she knew, but also pleasing this powerful and attractive woman before her. Undoubtedly sexual favours would be required.

'You're such a pretty thing,' Hope said, brushing the back of long fingers over Linda's cheek. 'Quite lovely, in fact.'

Here comes her opening move, Linda decided, her heart pounding and body trembling at the touch. Excitement churned in her mind and sex, she was so easily turned on. Though she was ready to fall into the other woman's arms, she nevertheless judged that apparent reluctance would be the more appreciated by her seductress. The corruption of innocence would add spice to the encounter.

'You're trembling, girl,' Hope said smiling kindly at her. 'Do I have such an effect on you? What do you feel?'

'I don't know, Ms Mannering,' Linda replied, her voice suitably quavery. 'I feel – so strange – so weak. Like there are lots of butterflies in my stomach. I've never known such a feeling.'

'Is it a nice feeling?' Hope asked sympathetically. 'Do I disturb you so much? I'm not such an ogre. I think perhaps you should lie down. Come, I've a bedroom *en suite* to my office for when I work late.'

'If you say so,' Linda said meekly. She felt a light kiss pressed to her mouth and blinked through real tears at the pleased face before her. She saw with amusement that Hope paused to speak into the inter-com on her desk. 'Hold all calls and no visitors, Giles,' she ordered. 'I shall be engaged with Miss Simon for her interview.'

Thus Linda was led into an adjoining room with the waiting bed. She was hardly a lamb to the slaughter, she told herself, recalling other times and other interviews when her youth and beauty had worked for her.

Sex for advancement seemed par for the course in her case. She did not mind at all provided it helped her career as a broadcaster and writer. Hugh Bembridge had taught her the rudiments of newspaper journalism well, fucking her throughout her year's employment with him. She had used him as much as he had used her, leaving to join a local radio station when the newspaper began to fail, thanks to Hugh's philandering and squandering of the profits as well as his wife's money. For her last months there Linda had run the weekly by herself – she was anything but a lazy girl and enjoyed the experience. When she left the paper had been sold and Hugh had departed for pastures new.

Radio had been a useful experience too. At first a general 'gofer' who did everything from make the interminable cups of coffee to filing news reports, her good looks did not go unnoticed. Neither did her application to her work, and her suggestions and occasionally her written items were broadcast. But her big break-through came when, after a late-night session in a pub with the station manager and a disc jockey, they had adjourned to discuss new programmes at the DJ's bachelor pad. As ever, she had gone a willing victim.

This was her first experience of two men at a time and the hectic threesome had given her a taste for double satisfaction. The drinking had continued and the business talk tapered off. Both men began to flatter her, agreeing she was worthy of writing scripts and interviewing on the air. From

lack of chairs in the small flat, Linda had sat on the bed and
in time the two men had joined her, sitting on either side. An
arm had sidled about her waist, a kiss pressed to her cheek.
Both then kissed her mouth in turn and two different hands
had cupped a breast each. It had been agreed that clothes
were a hindrance and they had all stripped off.

Linda remembered with pride and pleasure the effect on
the men of her glorious naked body. Her breasts were
fondled and praised, their mouths on her nipples arousing
her, making her demand someone take her. One at a time
she was fucked across the bed and licked out, then fucked
again and again. The last bout was near dawn on her hands
and knees with a cock working in her cunt and another in her
mouth. This was an enjoyable method of getting better
assignments at work, she thought as, after showering and
dressing, she left the two exhausted men slumped on the
rumpled bed. Now the wheel of sex had turned again and she
was being led off by Hope Mannering to take her chance at
TV success.

'Let me take off your jacket and loosen your blouse,'
Hope said as she sat Linda on the bed. Her hands worked
expertly, removing the coat and unbuttoning the neck of the
blouse to reveal the swell of Linda's breasts in a lacy bra.
'Kick off your shoes too,' she ordered, 'make yourself
comfortable. What a pretty blouse, it would be a shame to
crease it. We'll just slip you out of that, too, and your skirt.
You feel so warm. Isn't that better now? Lie back, girl.' She
held a cool hand to Linda's brow. 'You really are lovely,' she
said.

'Do you think so?' Linda asked coyly. 'You've been so
kind, and I feel such a nuisance. I don't know what's come
over me. I'm so worked up and excited – I can't explain . . .'
Above her Hope was staring avidly at her body, clad just in
bra, briefs, suspender belt and sheer stockings. 'Please don't

look at me like that,' she begged, deciding that was appropriate to her Little Miss Innocent act. 'You make me . . . make me—'

'Feel strangely aroused? Do you want me to do nice things to you?' Hope suggested. Again she stroked Linda's cheek and bent to press a soft kiss on her mouth. 'It's nothing to be ashamed of. It's quite normal in fact for you to feel this way. I'm pleased for you. Would you like me to kiss you properly?'

'I want you to – but would it be right?' Linda said plaintively. 'I mean, two women. I've never before—'

'Of course it would be right if you feel that way,' Hope insisted. 'You silly goose, you must learn to give in to your desires. Guilt about sex is such a wasted emotion. Between women, it can be so fulfilling.'

'But would *you* want to?' Linda said, as if she wasn't well aware of the other's interest. 'You wouldn't do this just to please me?'

'With such a lovely creature like you it would be a pleasure,' said Hope. 'Enough talk. You want me to hold you, kiss you, make love to you. Say it then. Say you want me to make love to you.'

'I do want you to – make love to me,' Linda pleaded. Hope lowered her face to Linda's, her lips unhurriedly kissing her eyes, cheeks, mouth and the soft flesh of her breasts swelling out of her bra. 'Do you like them?' Linda asked shyly. 'I think they are too big. I want you to see them. Kiss them . . .'

'Of course you do, they're so beautiful,' Hope soothed her. 'I want to see them too.' As Linda sat up, her bra was unhooked and cast aside and her bared breasts thrust out in all their fullness, the pink nipples uptilted. 'God, I could eat them, they're so perfect.' Hope cried. 'Such fabulous tits on such a slip of a girl.' She noted Linda's look of surprise.

'That's what they are – tits,' she affirmed. 'Tits and cunts and arseholes are what we have, and mouths and hands and other things to pleasure them. I find the use of supposedly crude terms in love-making can be so erotic. Do I shock you? You have much to learn.'

'Then teach me,' Linda said. 'I think I would like that.'

'Good girl. First, we don't rush things. We won't be disturbed. Let us both go naked and unashamed, lie together awhile and slowly discover what pleases us most.'

As Hope took off her clothes, Linda watched. The older woman slipped out of panties and suspendered stockings to reveal pear-shaped breasts and a shaven cunt. On the bed, the pair kissed passionately, tongues entwining, hands fondling. Linda had her nipples ardently sucked and her cunt fingered, moaning her appreciation as her ardour increased.

'I wonder if you're as innocent as you make out,' Hope suddenly announced, sitting up over her bedmate, regarding her suspiciously. 'If you hadn't appeared so naive, I'd say you were a horny little slut. Have you been leading me on?'

'No, no!' Linda protested, 'I got carried away by what you were doing. Honestly! It was you – the things you did to me – you made me feel so *excited*. I didn't know I could—'

'Become so aroused by another woman?' Hope said doubtfully. 'You'd better not ever lie to me, young woman. I will not be fooled. I demand truth and loyalty.' Taking Linda's shoulder she rolled her over face down.

'It *is* the truth, please believe me.' Linda begged. 'I couldn't help myself – or *want* you to stop.' This last was true at least and she hoped it would reassure Hope and make her continue the sex-play. She felt a soft hand smooth its way over her raised bottom, then give it more than just a playful smack. Linda decided it was prudent to let out an anguished howl. With an effort she blinked tears into her eyes and turned her face to Hope, distraught at being accused.

'All right, I'll accept I made you over-excited,' Hope conceded, looking at Linda's brimming eyes with self-satisfaction. Her hands parted Linda's bottom cheeks. 'You didn't want me to stop, you say?' She pressed ardent kisses over both cheeks. 'How peachlike. So sweet. Part them for me, girl. Open your legs.'

'What is it you're going to do?' Linda said, pretending she had no idea. 'Shouldn't I be turned to face you?'

She received several sharp stinging slaps to her bottom, making her cry out. 'Damn you, just do as I tell you,' Hope snapped impatiently. 'Now I do believe I've got a novice on my hands. Tell me, do you like this?' she asked, two fingers curling into Linda's rear-directed cunt. Hope twirled them, stroked, plucked at the engorged clitoris, felt the girl's buttocks rotate, heard her low moans.

'Oh yes, I like it,' Linda admitted. 'It's lovely. It makes me feel like I did before – so queer and funny, all trembly inside—' She awaited Hope's next move and a tongue replaced the two fingers, surprisingly long and probing. Linda gave a squeal and pushed back against the face pressed to her bottom cleft. She jerked and convulsed, coming to a sudden climax that left her sprawled out on the bed limp and sated.

She sat up in time to see Hope sitting beside the bed watching her revival with amused interest. 'That was – was – your *tongue*,' Linda said as if in wonder. 'I didn't know. I mean I would never have thought—'

'And you liked it,' Hope said smiling at her *protégé*. She leaned back in her chair, hands gripping the wooden arms, legs parted to reveal her clean-shaven lippy quim. 'Now I should like you to do the same for me. Come here, girl.'

Linda knelt in front of the woman and was taken in her arms. She was kissed fondly, a hand cupping each breast in turn. 'Lick me now,' she was told, being eased down until her face was at the same level as Hope's parted thighs. The darker outer lips protruded from the paler shaven mound, now parted by Hope's fingertips to reveal the inner folds of a wet furrow and a prominent clitoris. The scent of her sex was strong as Linda moved her head forward, mouth and tongue poised.

'Go on, you'll get a taste for it,' Hope urged. Sucking and lapping as if new at the act, Linda felt her head grasped and Hope's thighs working against her face. Soon the muttered *aghs* and gasps from above told of Hope's approaching climax as Linda probed with her tongue, now sucking hard at the thumb-like clitoris. As she came, Hope lifted in the chair, groaned out loudly in extreme pleasure, then flopped back as Linda drew away her mouth.

'Now leave me,' Hope ordered suddenly. 'Shower and dress and go. You start your trial period tomorrow. I need hardly add that what has taken place between us is not for discussion.'

'I would never breathe a word,' Linda promised. 'It was so nice, what we did,' she dared to add, 'I hope you will want me again. I've heard of women making love, of course, but I never thought it could be so wonderful. I want to thank you.'

'We shall see,' Hope said in her official voice. 'Don't expect any favours because of what occurred during your interview. Should we come into contact during your work, you will neither regard me nor address me as other than your superior. Reception will direct you to our research department when you report at nine sharp in the morning. I shall expect good accounts of your work. Do I make myself clear?'

'Yes, Ms Mannering,' Linda said deferentially. 'Whatever you say.' She began gathering up her clothes, her pert bottom turned to her boss, resisting the urge to give it a wiggle in her elation, certain that with her wiles special favours would be assured.

'I've no doubt that with your stunning looks,' Hope Mannering said as if in afterthought, still lolling completely naked in her chair, 'certain members of my male staff will make advances to you. All they will want is to sleep with you. Ignore them. You are here to work.'

And save myself for you, Linda thought slyly, wondering how long it would be before they would share a bed. 'I hope in time that I might write scripts for you,' she said. 'There's no chance I'd allow any involvement with a *man* to interfere with my work.'

'Ambitious little witch, aren't you?' Hope said, allowing herself a brief smile. 'I think there's more to you than meets the eye, young woman. One other thing—'

'Yes?' Linda enquired. She placed her clothes on the bed and stood obediently erect awaiting the order, knowing her breasts and cunt were enticingly on offer.

'I don't like pubic hair,' Hope informed her. 'Remove it. Such pretty little lips should be given air, made more kissable. It is something I shall insist upon – for any future meetings . . .'

Once showered, dressed and with her make-up replaced, Linda went triumphantly through to the outer office where Giles sat smirking behind his desk. 'You were a time in there,' he grinned suggestively. 'I presume you got the job from the look on your pretty puss. Or is that glow from some other cause? Did you let H.M. seduce you? I knew she wouldn't be able to resist a sweety like you, it's her one weakness. Not that I blame you for letting her. You even look like you enjoyed it.'

'Maybe it was I who seduced her,' Linda could not resist saying. She leaned over the desk to tickle him under the chin. 'Now that I work here, just you watch out that I don't seduce you. I'm sure I could if I set my mind on it.'

'And I'm sure you couldn't,' Giles said, suddenly serious.

'Nor would I advise you to try, with me or anyone else, male or female, while H.M. considers you her personal property. Because that's what you are, Miss Simon, if she's just had you like I'm sure she has. You've just sold your body and soul to her for as long as she wants. One indiscretion on your part, anything that displeases her, and you'll be out on your ear, deary. You're cock-a-hoop now, but you've put yourself in hock to a possessive A-one tyrant. Don't ever cross her if you want to continue working here. She's a dominating dyke, who can be an implacable enemy. Take this as a friendly warning.'

'No one owns me,' Linda retorted boldly. 'I shall do my work well and be my own person. And I don't frighten easily.'

'Wait and see,' Giles shrugged. 'The call will come and then you'll realise. You'll find what a dark side there is to her world. Just don't enter it.'

Chapter Nine

BED AND BAWD

Martin had to disengage himself from the clinging girl to rise from her bed. Reaching for his underpants, discarded hurriedly the previous night with the rest of his clothes, he braced himself against her sobbing. Facing him in the dressing table mirror he saw Bronwen sitting up on her knees. Each sniffling intake of breath set her neat little tits bobbing. Forced to relent he turned, sitting beside her to smooth strands of dark hair from her wet cheeks. She grabbed his hand, kissing it possessively, drawing it down to cover her left breast. This is not going to be easy, he considered. Didn't she know she'd been just an available ride?

'Bron,' he said, trying to curb his impatience, 'this was bound to happen. It's been great, but it's over. You knew that from the start. We've just been good company for each other.'

'You call it *company* – wanting sex morning, noon and night?' she complained bitterly. 'You just used me, you filthy beast!'

He considered that rich, coming from a girl who had guided his hand to her bare tits and was now groping at his limp dick. 'We're a couple of lonely students,' Martin reminded her, allowing her stroking hand to continue as his prick responded. 'You were as keen to go at it as I was.' It seemed the only way was to be brutally frank. 'Christ, you couldn't get enough – even now you're after to me to fuck you again.' At her anguished howl – while still manipulating him to full erection – he put in his cruellist jibe. 'Anyway, Bron, what about the boyfriend you're engaged to back in Wales? Training to be a minister of the Baptist Church, isn't he?'

'You knew that too,' the girl sulked. 'It never stopped you doing all those dirty things to me. Like you want to now, don't you?'

'It's hard not to,' Martin agreed, 'with you wanking away at me. But there isn't the time, honestly. I've a train to catch – a really important meeting later this morning.' He appealed for reason. 'It's a job opportunity I can't miss,' he said, finding himself being pushed flat across the bed. Any further protest was silenced as she leaned forward to drape her breasts over his face. Twisting her shoulders, she swung them like bells, brushing pointy nipples across his lips, pausing to tempt him to capture one. He felt his stiff shaft gripped roughly and yelled in pain as she straddled his thighs and sought to force it up her cunt. His howl as she impaled herself to the hilt made her all the more aggressive and she rammed her pubic bone hard to his, hair to hair. 'My poor prick!' Martin screeched. 'You bloody near broke it off, you bitch!'

'Bastard!' Bronwen returned promptly, heatedly, bouncing her arse and grinding it into his crotch. 'See how you like it!' Martin could hardly fail to do so, pinioned below her weight with his prick being urgently shunted up and down the tight-fitting channel of her cunt. Hot blood pumped up his rigid shaft as she rode him, wild in her angry lust, determined to get the response she desired. Caught helplessly in the heat of such wanton behaviour, Martin heaved his pelvis up to meet each downward thrust, his hands slipping around to grasp the rounded cheeks of her bottom. Her gyrations increased as he hauled her harder in to him, giving a croak of triumph as she jerked out of control and climaxed, the shock waves of pleasure pulsating in her cunt and belly.

'You will come, you will!' she screamed. 'I'll make you come inside me.' In her continuing spasms her mad onslaught buffeted him mercilessly, her arse a blur with her pounding. 'Fuck, fuck!' she yelled with each thrust. 'Fuck it up me, give me a baby – a baby, you beast! Go on, on—' Martin in his frenzy could only surrender to the inevitable, his spunk rushing from his aching balls and surging from his prick. Shuddering and moaning, his thighs jerked uncontrollably as he shot gushers of come deep into the recess of her cunt.

She collapsed beside him, breathing deeply, perspiring from her efforts. 'I knew I'd make you,' she said, a note of pure malice in her voice as Martin stirred beside her and made to rise. 'And what if you've got me pregnant? You didn't take precautions, and I'm not on the pill. What would you do about that, Martin?'

'Plead rape,' he said, gathering up his clothes. 'You can't come that with me. Go and fuck your boyfriend like you did me. Let him make an honest woman out of you. Goodbye and good luck!'

But as he made to depart, she reached for him and grasped his hand. As he looked down at her slim naked body with the pointy tits he had enjoyed and the tight little quim he had fucked so regularly, a kinder tone came to his voice. 'I don't believe you came off the pill, Bronwen, and I don't know why you said it. We've had good times, but that's all there was in it. I'm sure your fiancée is a lucky man. Let's part friends, shall we?'

He escaped with relief to shower and shave, returning to

his rented room to dress and go downstairs with his suitcase. As he crept past Bronwen's room he heard muffled sobs from inside. Possessive girls, strictly brought up in close Welsh communities, were to be avoided in the future, he decided. Nevertheless, prim and engaged as she was, Bron had been a great fuck and had made his stay in digs more bearable during his last months at college. He looked into the kitchen to say his farewell to his landlady, finding her at the table drinking tea and reading the morning paper. Teresa Quinn was comfortably built, fortyish and rarely seen before midday in anything but a dressing gown and slippers. She regarded Martin's appearance with sly amusement.

'I thought you two would bring my ceiling down saying goodbye,' she said. 'How did Bronwen take it?' She gave a short laugh. 'I mean, your leaving here, not what you put into her. That girl got too fond of you, I know. Too fond of what you were doing to her as well. You *are* a good-looking devil, Martin.' She glanced at her wall clock. 'Have you time for bacon and eggs? You've got to keep your strength up the way you go at it. I've made you sandwiches for the train.'

'That will do and I'll get coffee on the journey,' Martin said. He accepted the sandwiches and took his case to the front door, followed by Teresa. 'Thanks for everything,' he said, offering his hand. 'Maybe you'd look in and console Bronwen after I've gone. It's not all my doing, you know. She's even engaged to some guy she knew at school, her childhood sweetheart, poor sod. Now that she's qualified as a music teacher she should marry him, and play the organ at his church.'

'Like she's been playing with your organ,' Teresa laughed. 'I don't blame either of you. Stolen fruits are the sweetest. I'm not letting you get away with just a handshake, either. Don't I get a kiss?'

With his back up against the door he was confronted by

Teresa's mischievous scrutiny of his face. Her arms went around his neck and she kissed him fiercely and lewdly, rolling soft wet full lips over his as a long warm tongue probed his mouth.

'That's a goodbye kiss?' Martin laughed nervously, shaken to the core, her belly and crotch moving slowly and sensuously against his. Despite his recent strenuous sex with Bronwen, he felt the throb and stiffening rush of blood engorge his prick. Again her mouth clamped hard to his, ardent in her passion, the pliant mound between strong thighs continuing an insistent rub-rub against his hardness.

'You couldn't see the forest for the trees while you've been here, could you, young man?' Teresa informed him teasingly, her waist now encircled by his arms in the heat of their embrace, palms cupping the large moons of her buttocks. Glancing down he saw that, in drawing apart and leaning back slightly from him, her dressing gown had fallen open to the waist. Standing crotch to crotch, cunt to cock, he was regaled with the sight of her bare breasts. Creamy white, slightly pendulous with their size and weight, they were a real woman's tits. He compared them with Bronwen's small neat bosom and, as if reading his mind, Teresa thrust her breasts out by arching her back. 'You've been too busy screwing that chit of a cry-baby to know what was available under your nose,' Teresa reprimanded him mockingly. 'It was all there for you. I'd have taken my turn, I'm not greedy. You could have had us both. Wouldn't you have loved that? Two fucks under the same roof.'

'Now you tell me,' Martin complained, allowing her hand to reach down between them, draw down his zip and infiltrate inside. 'I'm not usually so bloody slow. I'd have jumped at the chance. But Bronwen wouldn't leave me alone, she wanted it all the time.'

'And you're complaining?' Teresa taunted him, pinioning

him to the door with his rigid length in her hand. 'I can't blame Bronwen wanting lots of this.' She gave a low lewd whistle. '*That* is what I call a cock! You weren't at the back of the queue when they dished them out, were you?'

Martin preened himself, peering down at as fine a pair of big tits as he'd seen. With his prick being expertly stroked between her forefinger and thumb, he shrugged as if modest about his endowment. 'I've been told it's a reasonable size,' he said, trying to sound as cool as Teresa. 'There's been no complaints. You'd have been welcome to try it. But with your old man around the house there wasn't much chance, was there?' He had one large creamy tit in his hand, circling his palm over the firm orb. 'I did think about it,' he admitted ruefully.

'He's not here now,' he was informed meaningfully. Suitcase left at the door, he found himself drawn by the cock back into the kitchen. There Teresa pushed aside her breakfast dishes and lowered her back onto the table top, opening her dressing gown wide to reveal herself full frontal. Her breasts thrust up, cupped in her hands, fingers plucking each thick nipple. With thighs separated and knees drawn up, her cunt was offered to his gaze, a lush growth of curling hair surrounding a full-lipped cleft. 'Fuck me now,' she said simply. 'Use that huge dong to excite me. Let me see how good you are, young man.'

It was a challenge Martin could not resist. A glance at the wall clock as he hastily kicked off both trousers and underpants told him his train would be pulling out of Southampton station without him. But the sight of the brazenly displayed cunt tilted for his use assured him he had his priorities right – never look a gift cunt in the mouth when offered. Make this good, he told himself, placing his palms on her upper thighs and parting them wider. First he dipped his head and kissed around the soft flesh at the fork of her legs, moving on to slowly draw his extended tongue along the length of her outer labia, flicking them, lapping, sucking. 'Oh, yes, do that,' he heard Teresa sigh dreamily. 'Lick me out, love. Tongue-fuck me first.'

Martin applied himself, his nose and chin soaked by her copious juices, urged on as his tongue probed by the lifting and churning of her pelvic area, the arousing pungent odour of her sex. *I've got her going good*, he congratulated himself as her torso writhed and she pulled his face hard against her crotch. Neither did she pause as she saw, over Martin's bobbing head, Bronwen standing at the kitchen door. Rooted to the spot, the girl looked on wide-eyed, completely mesmerised by the sight before her. 'I want to come with your prick up me,' Teresa uttered hoarsely, her agitation increased by being watched. 'Show me what you'll be putting into me, let me see it!'

Keen to oblige, Martin stood up with his erection rearing mightily. Leaning forward, the horny woman nursed it between the cleave of her tits and bent to suck momentarily on the swollen helmet before lying back spreadeagled for the desired penetration. Bending over her, Martin entered to the balls at first thrust, drawing a gasp from her throat as its length and girth lodged home.

'Fuck it up! Oh, make me come,' she begged, curling her legs around his back, lifting to his thrusts. Her bottom raised from the table's edge, Martin clasped both cheeks to pull her hard against his pounding cock, one finger insinuating into the crinkled crevice of her anus, driving her wild, increasing her lust.

Teresa came with rapid undulations, working her arse like a piston, crying out in her relief and pleasure. There was nothing to compare with bringing a woman to such wanton heights, Martin thought as he spurted his tribute of hot jism deep into her as she trembled in her final throes. Still belly to belly, their sweat bonding them, he grinned in her upturned face. 'You can say you've just been well and truly fucked,' he said with the arrogance of youth. 'Does your old man screw you as well as that, Mrs Quinn?'

'More to the point, does Bronwen screw as good as me?' Teresa said levelly. 'We should ask her, seeing as how she's been standing there watching us at it.' Startled, Martin was about to turn his head when Teresa stopped him by placing a hand on his cheek. 'Don't get agitated, she didn't attempt to stop us,' she said, obviously amused. 'In fact watching us rather excited her. Didn't it, Bronwen?'

'You're a pair of dirty beasts,' the girl said irately, coming to the table. Her face was flushed and her Welsh accent pronounced. 'Now I know what kind he is, then I'm glad to be rid of him. I don't know why I ever thought I might love him. He doesn't compare with my fiancé, Kenneth. If there's any justice, then Martin should be bloody well hung.'

'But we both know he is, don't we, dear?' Teresa said pointedly, easing herself out from under Martin. 'As for what we've been doing, it is only what you and he have been at like sex maniacs for weeks under my roof. I've listened to you night after night. Can you blame me for wanting my share? I don't condemn you for sleeping with him. I'm married, you are engaged. We'd both be better saying no more about it and better off with this young man out of the house.'

On the train later, Martin cherished the memory of his parting but now he had to think of his future. He found the office of Bembridge Publications, splashing out on a taxi. A ground floor flat of two rooms, the publishing firm was not as he had imagined. He waited in the outer office which was crowded with filing cabinets and a desk behind which a woman was engaged on the telephone. When she replaced the receiver and looked at him with a smile, he thought he had never seen such a pleasantly attractive face. Serene, kindly, composed, her features were set in well-cut fringed and bobbed brown hair. It was difficult to determine her exact age – middle-thirties, he conjectured, and nice with it; extremely nice. She was a cut above this shabby establishment, he decided.

'Martin Compton,' he introduced himself, returning her smile. 'I've an appointment with Mr Bembridge and I'm over an hour late. The train was delayed, I'm afraid. Will he still see me?'

'When he arrives,' the pleasant woman assured him. 'Even if you'd arrived on time, Mr Compton, H.B. wouldn't have been here. He's just telephoned to say it will be at least three o'clock before he looks in. He asked me to apologise to you.'

'It works both ways,' Martin said, relieved. 'Had Mr Bembridge been in, it wouldn't have looked good for me, turning up late. I take it you didn't inform him that I wasn't here either. I mean when you were talking to him on the phone just now, Miss—'

'Mrs,' she corrected him. 'Mrs Jessop. Hortense to you, young man, now that you're going to work here.' She stood up from behind the large old desk. Hidden as most of her had been by the desk and a grubby-looking word-processor, he was impressed by her smart appearance and figure. A white chiffon scarf was knotted fashionably about a graceful neck, and her purple silk blouse was stretched tight at the buttons by a high and ample bosom. She smoothed down her tweed skirt over shapely thighs and offered her hand. Its touch was soft and cool. He was reluctant to let it go.

'I had no reason to tell him you weren't here,' she said, smiling. 'He wasn't here himself. Because he's decided to add your talents to his staff, no doubt he felt no urgency to be here. Naughty of him, but that's our Mr Hugh Bembridge. Why don't you leave your suitcase here and go for lunch? You can pop back later.'

'You mean I'm employed?' Martin asked delightedly. 'I understood this was to be an interview and that I was one of dozens of applicants.'

'That sounds like the boss,' she said with a further smile. 'He knows your work and is very impressed. There are no others after work of any kind here. This is his way of getting you to work for him for peanuts. You'll be so grateful that you'll accept anything. Don't let him fool you, stick up for a decent salary. London rates. I presume you have a place to stay?'

'Not yet,' Martin said. 'I'll have a scout around for a bed and breakfast while I'm out for lunch.' As she nodded agreement he noted the enticing jiggle of her appreciable breasts, getting his usual urge to fuck any female he found attractive. In her case all the more so because of her 'niceness' and obvious respectability. No doubt also she went home to her husband and a cosy semi-detached as spotless as her person, where she would knit after the evening meal, and read or watch television. And at bedtime? Again, no doubt she would wear a sensible nightdress and sleep back to back with her hubby. On Saturday nights, perhaps, he would lift her nighty and roll on top of her. What a waste, thought Martin, mentally undressing her, imagining the well-developed body naked to his eyes. Out in the sunlit streets he considered his chances of ever seducing such a prize, deciding it was not on with such a wholesome, contented wife who was unaware that she exuded sex from every pore.

He had a cheap pub lunch and half of lager in a corner seat of a large and almost empty tavern. He took his time, watching a big expensively suited man at the bar drinking a succession of double whiskies while chatting up a blonde barmaid. No shortage of cash there, he thought. The tall guy had the look of a man-about-town, handsome in a rakish manner, broad-shouldered and full of himself as the barmaid simpered. Then the morning's sexual excesses took their toll. Seated comfortably, Martin's eyes closed as he nodded off. He dreamed that he and a pregnant Bronwen were married, waking up with relief to find the blonde barmaid gathering his empty glass and the tall man gone.

His watch told him it was past three o'clock. Sluicing his face in the Gents' and making himself presentable, he used the pay phone in the bar to call his mother. He begged a loan, knowing her tightness with financial matters, £50 repayable when on his feet, telling her to send it care of Bembridge Publications, his new employer. He refrained from asking her if Norman still called round, knowing from Norman's letters that the affair was still ongoing and that his mother was being serviced regularly. Replacing the phone, he walked back to the paint-peeling front door of Bembridge Publications. His knock was merely to indicate he'd arrived and he went in to find the outer office unattended with the good-looking Mrs Hortense Jessop absent from her desk. A moment later he heard a moaning noise from the inner office, the noise repeated and tailing off into a long, heartfelt whimper.

At once he recognised the sound of a woman in the throes of being fucked. He knew that moan, had revelled in producing it from women himself. His blood pounded, he was aroused and eager to see the cause. Cautiously he made his way around the desk, increasingly intrigued as the cries and groans continued. Mingled with the noises of a woman in bliss, Martin clearly heard the grunt and gasp of a rampant male. *Someone is in there getting well and truly screwed*, he said to himself in delight, enjoying the wailing sounds from a female in extremis. He peered in, risking pushing the door open a further inch or so. He saw the thrusting flanks and muscled buttocks of the large man he had noticed at the bar of the public house.

The man had discarded his jacket, tucked up his shirt, and dropped trousers and underpants to his shoes. Bare from armpits to ankles, he pistoned away into the woman bent over before him, her bottom up-tilted and upper body draped across a desk. It was with surprise and shock that Martin realised she was Hortense Jessop. How wrong he had been about her! Now she was gyrating in lust, the full white globes of her bottom trembling as her lover worked like a stallion to service her. Martin could see the rapid shunting of the thick organ embedded in her cunt, could hear the sliding and slapping of belly to buttock as they fucked madly. The man's balls bounced and the lips of her grotto gripped the huge root's girth, stretched to a perfect circle.

'Go on, fuck it into me,' she urged him. 'Give it to me, I've never wanted it so much.'

I should have known, Martin told himself amused by her abandon, *even the best of them fuck*. Hortense certainly did, her squeaks and whines and working of her arse showing a true wantonness and carnal nature. She would be well worth his attentions, he thought as he admired the way she gave herself over to pleasure.

'Yes, now, now!' he heard her shout. 'The back way – finish there – I like it in my bottom. Go on, Hugh, do as I say. You like it too.'

His prick withdrew, red and glistening, thick and wet. He guided the bulbous knob to the crinkled orifice an inch or so above the hole he had been poking. Hortense Jessop whimpered as her rear passage was forced and took in inch after inch of the big cock, despite its girth.

'Give me all of it,' she gasped. 'I want all of it. Go on, go on! God, it's splitting me – give me more!'

Hugh gave all he could, becoming heated and relentless with all of his thick stem up her bottom. Martin watched them with envy, their cries growing lewder as they shuddered in their lust. Wondering how long such a coupling could continue, he saw Hortense's backside jerk furiously in protracted spasms as she came. The man grasping the flesh of her hips buckled at the knees and groaned, his quickening motions revealing the spurting of his come deep into her receptive back passage. When he at last withdrew, spunk trickled from her still-gaping anus. Hortense lay flat out, sighing with relief.

It was time, Martin decided, to depart and keep their secret. Highly elated and greatly aroused at what he'd witnessed, he pictured himself pleasuring Hortense in a similar situation. He walked around for a reasonable time so the pair could recover, then went back to the office. Even as he entered he heard the clicking of the keyboard and saw Hortense busily working away, her hair in place and looking composed, if a little flushed in the face.

'I'm afraid you've missed Mr Bembridge again, Martin,' she said affably. 'He's come and gone. However, he said you are to start tomorrow. I open the office at nine. It will be a bit cramped but I've ordered a desk for you. As for your salary, work that out when you see him. Did you find a place to stay?'

'Not yet,' Martin admitted, wondering how the woman could appear so normal and businesslike after what she'd been doing. 'I'd better get out and find something. The few places I've tried weren't cheap. I'll perhaps have more luck trying farther afield.'

'You've just left college, haven't you?' she said kindly. 'You won't have much money to spare until you begin to earn. I understand the position. I'll talk to Mr Bembridge about an advance.'

'I'm expecting money from home, thanks all the same,' Martin said, touched by her concern. She was obviously a good fuck and a good woman as well. 'I'd better get out and find a

97

bed for tonight.' He saw her study him thoughtfully, write something down on a slip of paper and hold it up to him.

'Here's an address just a mile away,' she said, smiling. 'It's where I live with my husband and there's several spare rooms. I'll be here working for an hour or two yet but you say I sent you.'

'I couldn't impose,' Martin said, suitably grateful and hopeful she would not take him at his word. She silenced him by pushing the paper with her address into his hand.

'Don't be silly,' she ordered. 'Jessop will be glad of your company for a few days at least and it will allow you to find a suitable flat. Shall I call a taxi for you? It's not a terribly long walk.'

'I'll walk,' Martin said, picking up his suitcase. 'You've been more than kind to me. I'm sure I'll enjoy working here with you very much. It's a pity I missed Mr Bembridge again.' Tongue in cheek, he asked, 'What's he like? Is he a demanding boss?'

'I'm satisfied working for him,' Hortense said. 'He has big ideas at times, hoping to build a magazine publishing empire. You're a part of his plan. But he can be a bully. Don't let him get on top of you. Stand up for yourself.'

From what I've seen, Martin chuckled to himself as he walked down the road, *I certainly won't let horny Hugh Bembridge on top of me or anywhere else.* As for standing up for himself, he'd hopefully stand up for Hortense given the chance. Stand rigid and give her some of what he had to offer. It was a nice thought to have at the start of a career. Once again, he felt, he had landed on his feet. He approached the address she had given him. It was a detached two-storey house, set off the road in a tree-lined avenue. He went up a gravelled driveway and rang the bell, wondering what kind of husband Jessop was to have a wife who fucked so wholeheartedly away from home.

Chapter Ten

TALK OF THE DEVIL

The apartment was luxurious and spacious, as befitted Hope Mannering's lifestyle. Crowded into the lounge were a host of famous faces from the television and pop scene, drinks in hand. There were evening-suited men and women in *haute couture* dresses rubbing shoulders with a younger element in jeans and loose shirts. In a simple off-the-shoulder black gown that revealed the sweep of her superb breasts to full advantage, Linda felt quite at home. The silky cling of her dress was moulded to her hips and buttocks, and she noted the covetous eyes of both male and female guests upon her.

It was only her startling beauty they admired, she knew, but one day she vowed she would take her place among them, famous in her own right. She would be introduced as Linda Simon, best-selling writer, and revered not just for her dark good looks. And whatever she had to do to further her ambition she would do. Two months had passed since beginning her job at Merlin Television, good experience in the media world which she intended in time to use as background for a block-buster novel. She applied herself to the work and as a lowly researcher did more than just gather facts, presenting them in script form. Some of her suggestions and actual words had been used on screen. Her efforts had been noted and even encouraged by Gerald Lyle, a senior producer whom she knew was dying to bed her. Though Linda had no objection, she still had Hope Mannering, who considered Linda as her private property, to take into account.

For over a week after their encounter during Linda's interview, Hope had remained unseen to her new employee. Then, working in the research office late one evening, Linda looked up to see her lady boss regarding her like a predatory male. Kisses had been exchanged and Linda had been taken to the apartment where she now stood. On a huge silk-sheeted bed they had indulged in every permutation of female lust and sex until dawn. Trusted to keep their liaison secret, Linda had been called to Hope's inner office on several occasions since. As if in reward, the invitation to this evening's celebrity gathering was received by Linda as a further step up the ladder. She was informed that this was not so by Hope's male secretary, Giles French, who now approached her through the throng, flamboyant as ever in a green velvet suit and huge floppy bow tie. Champagne glass in hand, he gave her a knowing smirk.

'You didn't heed my warning, did you, dear?' he said. 'Don't think you are here for your intellect and your standing as a valued member of Merlin's staff. It's for those splendid big tits you're showing almost to the nipples. You don't know what you've let yourself in for. You'll be playing rough with a big bad crowd. A bit of lesbo hanky-panky with the lecherous H.M. is just for starters. Inviting you here shows she's got you in mind for stuff you'd never imagine. The very depths.'

'Drop dead,' Linda told him, smiling as she spoke under the gaze of nearby guests but with venom in her voice. 'You'll give me a bad name, talking to a perverted queer. I can take care of myself.'

'Luvvy,' Giles smiled, 'every single person here is perverted, if not queer unfortunately. You should be so lucky. This shindig has not even begun. Later the chosen will gather in conclave. Leave now.'

Giles placed his empty glass on the tray of a serving girl in a French maid's outfit who was passing and helped himself to another. 'You recognise little Louise, of course,' he laughed, delaying the girl by holding her arm. 'Look what H.M. has got her tarted up as. She'll do anything to keep her filing job in the research department, won't you, Louise?' The girl pulled away from him, blushing deeply, hurrying off with her tray. 'You recall she got her bottom smacked for some misdemeanour on your first visit to our office,' Linda was reminded. 'Now that girl is completely in the power of H.M. Wait and see later tonight if you're intending to stay. You'll end up the same way, jumping through a hoop.'

'I don't think so,' Linda said. 'Louise is hopeless at her job, but I'm good at mine.'

'So we've heard,' Giles sneered. 'Ambitious little whore, aren't you? Writing scripts and getting in with Gerald Lyle, hopeful that our star producer will want you on his team. Has he fucked you yet?' He regarded Linda in mock sadness. 'Forget it, girl. He could fuck you rigid but nobody gets promoted without H.M. agreeing. She's well aware of what you're up to. Stick with her and forget Lyle if you hope to make it. She doesn't forgive easily. In fact, never.'

He excused himself as Gerald Lyle joined them. 'He's a dangerous creep,' said the young producer. 'Everything he hears gets back to the boss. You look especially lovely tonight, Linda, the best thing at this bloody awful party of poseurs and pimps. It's breaking up now except for Hope Mannering's clique, who remain to indulge in the unspeakable. Devil worship, satanic rites, witchcraft and black magic nonsense, all in fun, they claim. Can I offer you a lift somewhere? My place, for instance?' he added hopefully. 'I do want a serious talk with you.'

'I'll see that Linda gets home safely, thank you,' Hope Mannering said firmly, joining them suddenly. 'It's time you were leaving, I believe, Gerald. Aren't you on location at first light tomorrow?'

She led Linda off by the arm. 'Just what is your relationship with that man?' she demanded. 'Has he made certain promises to you regarding your future? He just wants your body, young woman. Our Mr Lyle is notorious for bedding susceptible girls. I want you to meet some special people now that the party crowd is thinning. You'll find them more important to you in your career.'

'Mr Lyle and I have no relationship,' Linda reassured her. 'Whatever I've done is in the course of my work.'

She was taken to a group of about a dozen who stood drinking at an ornate glass-topped bar in a corner of the lounge. Hope had an arm about Linda's waist, an intimacy acknowledged by her guests with knowing grins, exclamations of approval and even a wolfish whistle. Their ages ranged from smart but portly fiftyish men with their stylish women to a long-haired youth destined for pop stardom. At his elbow stood his minder, a huge black male once a contender for a heavyweight boxing crown. He held out a card to Linda, on which was printed a telephone number and the words 'Wayne will expect your call'. It was taken by Hope, who smiled graciously but dropped it into an ashtray on the bar. This too was noticed as a possessive gesture.

'Greedy, greedy,' admonished a tall distinguished man, but taking care to make it sound like a joke. 'Are you intending to keep that ravishing girl to yourself, Hope? You may well be outvoted.'

'The connoisseur as ever, Mr Ambassador,' Hope acknowledged. 'I suggest we see how the night's convention develops. Shall we now go up and prepare ourselves? *He* will be awaiting us expectantly.'

This time Linda was led up a curved stairway to a small entrance hall where the men and women separated. The room she was directed into with the other five women had long white robes hanging from a wall rack. Beside her, Louise was already shedding her French maid's dress and all around the other women were doing the same. 'Get out of your clothes, Linda,' the girl whispered to her. 'Then pick a white robe and put it on. You will have to now that you're here. If you don't they make it worse for you and perform special rituals to initiate you. It's better to cooperate. I always do.'

'No doubt you do,' Linda said, never having had a high opinion of the submissive girl. But she could not help admiring Louise's shapely tits and the slim neat body revealed as she stood naked. Around the room women were stripping off showing a variety of breasts and buttocks. 'All this is just a rigmarole for a good old-fashioned orgy, I think,' Linda said, getting out of her gown. 'Who was the "He" that our boss spoke of in such reverent terms? The master of ceremonies?'

'Just The Master,' Louise said devoutly. 'He who must be obeyed. I'm deadly serious.'

About to laugh aloud, Linda obediently stood silent as Hope approached, clad in a flowing black gown. 'Get your robes on,' she ordered impatiently. 'We are ready to present ourselves. Do you find this amusing, Linda? I can assure you that it's not. You are privileged to be considered one of our secret sect. I demand that you act accordingly. You'll find it most enlightening.'

I'm here because of my body, Linda could have told her. *Fresh tits and a cunt to be used, but I'll use you as much in my turn*. The robe she put on was of purest silk, clinging

103

sensuously to her flesh. Following the others obediently, she
entered a long room illuminated by dozens of thick black
candles in ornate stands, the air heavy with the smell of
incense. As her bare feet trod a thickly piled carpet, she felt a
hand slip into the slit of her robe and fondle her bottom. A
twist of her head showed it to be the tall distinguished man
Hope had called Mr Ambassador.

He smiled, inclined his head politely, making her move
forward with a finger in the cleft of her cheeks, its tip
stroking the lips of her cunt and entering to titillate her
clitoris. Feeling his hand between her cushiony buttocks, she
stifled a low moan of pleasure as his upright thumb pressed
to her anal orifice and intruded its full length. Thus intimately captured, she leant back against his chest, giving little
jerks in response. He guided her to join the other robed
people standing in a half-circle. Before them a stage was
curtained off with heavy black velvet drapes on which was
emblazoned a pentagram, the five-pointed star used as a
symbol in black magic circles. Despite her mounting arousal
as the man behind her made free with his hand, Linda took in
the scene with interest. The hushed disciples standing obediently, the dramatic atmosphere, all was excellent research
material. One day it would be included in her best-selling
writing. Come what may, whatever rituals or challenges she
would undergo – all sexual she had no doubt – Linda would
comply to gain the insight.

The curtain before her parted and the assembled gathering
knelt. Slow off the mark, she was brought down on her knees
by the man who gripped her by the cunt and arsehole. *They
cannot be serious*, she thought impiously as the people
around her began to chant in unison. *All this crazy rigmarole
so they can fuck each other*. However, this fun and games
turned them on, no doubt. On the stage three figures sat in
throne-like chairs, draped in black robes. She recognised

Hope. The central figure was a seated model of a larger-than-life male. It had the head of a goat with a pair of curved horns protruding over the ears. On the other side sat a tall imperious man, black-garbed, with a mask covering his face.

No doubt this was the mysterious Master, Linda surmised, still finding it all highly amusing. Hope lolled back in her chair, opening the skirt of her robe and parting her legs to reveal her shaven cunt to her audience. The Master then did the same, showing a large flaccid prick curved over heavy balls, his pubic area shaved clean. One by one the devotees mounted the steps to the stage. Each man in turn went on his knees and kissed and licked Hope's out-thrust pussy before returning to his place. Many of the women did the same before crawling to The Master and taking his cock in their mouths for a short ritual sucking.

'You must show your obedience,' Linda heard the Ambassador say as he released his hold on both her highly agitated orifices. As he bent close over her, she could feel a straining erection against her thigh. 'I'd sooner you fuck me,' she whispered. 'I'm sure this crowd would like to witness that. Fuck me now, you've made me want it. I know you want to.'

'Go on the stage like the other women and suck The Master's penis,' he advised seriously. *So even you, an educated and sophisticated man, are taken in by this bullshit,* Linda thought. He read her mind. 'I strongly advise you to comply, young woman. You have fellated men before, I presume? Tonight you will have many of them in your mouth.' He allowed her a brief smile before urging her forward. 'As for your stated desire to be fucked, you will have more than enough to satisfy you before we depart.'

Linda mounted the steps, noting that Hope was gripping the arms of her chair as Louise avidly licked and tongued her boss's quim to an impending orgasm. Behind the naked kneeling girl, Giles French stood flicking a many-thonged whip across her pert upraised bottom cheeks, striping them rosy pink. Last in line of the women, Linda knelt before The Master, finding him staunchly erect and glistening wet from other mouths. 'Welcome, daughter,' she heard him intone in a sepulchral voice. 'Thrice welcome as a convert to The Covenant. To hear is to obey, to enact our Rites of Natural Lust is obligatory. You understand, Novitiate Linda Simon?'

Sure, sure, she nodded hiding her increasing amusement. *Daughter indeed. No doubt he got a kick out of that incestuous inference.* All the same, the stander rearing before her was a good one, thick and rigidly long. She clasped the big balls and used her right hand to grip his stalk, drawing the bulbous knob to her mouth. Still with a persistent throb of excitement in her lower regions from her recent handling, she could not resist the temptation to enjoy a good prick in her mouth. Unsure that she could just go ahead without his permission, she said humbly, 'May I, Master?'

'Well said, Linda,' she heard Hope say. Glancing sideways she saw her sitting up in her chair, flushed of face in the after-glow of orgasm. Louise was still on all fours between her spread legs, greedily mouthing and licking clean the shaven pubis. 'Will you anoint her, Master, and finish in her mouth?' Hope added. 'She shows proper obedience, worthy of that privilege. Or do you consider her deserving of your ultimate accolade, to fuck the latest daughter of your worshipping family? See how she kneels in homage before you, gripping your mighty sceptre with hope in her eyes.'

'She has not qualified for that honour yet, surely?' Giles French said, cunning in his intention. 'Let her ride the goat as is ordained for initiation.' He ignored glares from both Hope and Linda; the former because she fancied seeing her protégé being fucked, the latter because she was eager to be had.

'We shall first observe how well she suckles,' The Master

decided gravely, drawing Linda's face forward. 'Eat of my flesh and console yourself on The Master's penis, daughter. Show how worthy you are, then I shall decide.'

To stop herself giggling, Linda took his prick into her mouth. Sucking in the whole length, bobbing her head, turned on by the feel of a hot throbbing stalk between her tongue and palate, she determined to have him come by her efforts. She felt the tremble in his legs, the stiffening of his body to keep a semblance of composure. *This horny bastard has got it made*, she told herself, *making out he's doing me a favour in going down on him when he's as keen as any man. He may fool the other idiots here, but I'm not taken in.* The big cock in her mouth pulsed and leapt, as if ready to surge hot come down her throat. Lost in the pleasure given and received, Linda's buttocks twitched. She fought an urge to finger herself and wished that someone, man or woman, would come behind her kneeling form and oblige. Better still that someone came and fucked her. To her intense aggravation and frustration, she felt the prick withdrawn from her mouth.

'I have decided,' The Master said, despite his best efforts unable to disguise a voice thick with emotion. 'I shall anoint her. Prepare her. Do it quickly.'

Linda found herself pulled back from him, held by Hope and Louise. Giles French heaved her head forcibly back, stretching her neck and gaping her mouth. Directing his prick at the target, The Master gasped and gave a helpless shudder, jetting glob after glob of thick come over her tongue and down the back of her throat. Allowing a moment for her to gulp and swallow her mouthful of his glutinous emission, he fed the diminishing cock back into her mouth.

'Cleanse it!' Linda heard Hope order sharply. 'Clean every inch thoroughly.' In her aroused state the girl welcomed the opportunity. She eagerly lapped its length, ran her tongue lasciviously around the knob and gobbled noisily on inches of still-pulsating stalk. Her cunt and bottom twitching in her heightened state, through her well-stuffed mouth she managed to utter 'Please! Somebody fuck me – anybody – fuck me!'

Glancing around, still with The Master's prick snug between her tongue and palate, she begged for relief with her eyes. 'She is on heat,' Linda heard intoned above her as The Master withdrew his prick. 'Let her receive the satisfaction she craves. She shall ride the goat. It is my will. Place her—'

Linda found herself lifted to her feet, noting that before the stage the faithful were pressing forward for a closer view. 'Let Linda ride the goat, it has been willed,' they cried as they threw off their robes and groped each other. Giles French drew the covering off the seated model. It was complete in detail, a well-sculpted figure of a male with outstretched arms and perfect in all but its large head and the realistically shaggy goat's face. It had glowing red glass eyes and curved horns. Held by Hope and Louise, brought face to face with it, Linda saw the seated figure had its legs parted and bent at the knees. Hooved feet were affixed to the platform on which it was placed.

Hanging between the spread thighs, the big balls were as round as oranges in proportion to the oversized model. She saw this was in sharp contrast to a mere inch or so of stubby penis, no more than a fat plum-shaped knob, projecting above the scrotum. *If I'm expected to squat over that*, Linda considered, *I'll hardly feel it*. She felt acute disappointment, thinking that this degenerate bunch would at least have provided the thing with a dummy phallus appropriate to its size.

'Place her so that her convulsions may be seen by all the faithful,' The Master ordered. 'Let her face be in full view

108

and observed.' The hands holding Linda turned her, lowering her onto the lap of the beast as Giles French drew off her robe to reveal her naked. There were gasps, intakes of breath and exclamations at her beauty. 'You've really got some tits, girl,' Giles said crudely to her face. 'Horny little cow, aren't you? You're in for a treat, believe me.' Spoken in a low whisper only heard by Linda, she thrust out her tongue at him, snarling back that he get fucked.

'No,' he laughed softly. '*You* are about to be fucked. Are you sitting comfortably?' He gave her a slight push so that she fell back to the massive chest, finding it as comfortable as an armchair. Padded leather, she presumed. She parted her legs to drape outside those of the model's. Shifting her bottom she felt the fat knob nudge her cunt lips. A squirm and a push down forced its passage barely inside her. *I'm expected to give an Academy Award performance on* this! she thought cynically; *I'd rather they'd given me something worthy to fuck myself on. I wouldn't have disappointed them. Damn them, I shall use my fingers too.*

She touched herself, rubbing her clitoris while the thickness of the knob inside her began to make its stubby presence felt. Her arousal mounted as she looked out at the upturned faces before the stage.

'Let the ride commence,' she heard The Master order, followed by the sound of a click. Suddenly the model's arms came forward to encircle her below her breasts and from inside the figure she became aware of a faint whirring noise. At once the goat began a gentle see-sawing motion, thrusting up against her spread arse cheeks, shunting the plum knob in and out of her cunt. It seemed to have grown.

'It's a machine, a machine is fucking me,' Linda groaned, her tits bobbing as she ground and gyrated her bottom to get in as much as it allowed on its forward motions. With head thrown back and mouth agape, she cried out in her pleasure, demanding more as if the object of her delight was flesh and blood.

'She wants more. Increase the length and speed!' came shouts from the audience. Linda felt the figure's hips accelerate in its thrusting and realised the false prick was enlarging inside her juicily moistened sex tunnel. Opening like a telescope, inch after inch began to fill her. Out of her mind with lust, she met each upward lunge with a matching downward thrust, gabbling incoherently as climax after climax wracked her body. She was drunk on successive orgasmic surges that had her slumped forward, unaware of where she was. At last she was helped off the stage and laid out on cushions while Hope held a champagne glass to her lips.

'Relax awhile, my dear,' Hope soothed her, kissing her sweat-soaked brow. 'Others want you, but you have done more than enough for one meeting to prove your worthiness. Let them anticipate the joy of having you at later gatherings. You did well.'

Linda returned the kiss. 'It wasn't difficult,' she admitted, acting coy. 'I just came and came again riding the goat. I've never known anything like it.'

'You'll discover delights beyond all comprehension now you are truly one of us,' Hope smiled. 'Always permit what is demanded and erotic pleasures denied others will be yours. And you will demand them, too, of others here, male and female. Our rule is for all to give themselves whatever the request. Now you can enjoy a little entertainment I've arranged. It's quite wicked even for me, really. You know Louise, of course.' Hope pursed her lips as if to reveal something extremely underhand. 'The silly girl still has inhibitions and a deal of reluctance in her nature. We're going to make her change for the better tonight. Teach her to accept and learn to enjoy.'

'I thought you had her well trained,' Linda said. 'I mean she accepts you spanking her for misdemeanours and I saw her licking you out quite thoroughly tonight.'

'All that with me, yes,' Hope agreed. 'The silly goose is afraid I'll dispense with her services. But I want to see how the shy creature will react with a macho male. She's engaged to a boy in our mailing department, a real wimp, and I know she's as moony about him as he is with her. It will be fun to see her well fucked, won't it? That's what we're about to witness.'

Linda could imagine Louise waiting in the wings, trembling and fearful of what awaited her. All around the room the naked throng lay expectantly, the men fondling buttocks and breasts, the women idly stroking pricks, but refraining from doing more as they waited for the reluctant Louise to provide the entertainment.

A cry of approval went up as the huge former boxer, the minder of the pop star, walked to the centre of the room and took up his position. Legs apart and hands on hips he presented a magnificent spectacle of brute male perfection. Broad of chest and narrow of waist, legs like the trunks of trees, his frighteningly massive penis hung flaccidly over heavy balls.

'Hung,' Linda heard herself saying. 'My God, but he is hung. Even slack it's a monstrous thing.'

'All for Louise,' Hope said lewdly. 'First she will have to get it up for him, of course. She'll be made to do it. What a pity her pathetic boyfriend isn't here to witness her initiation. That would be the icing on the cake.' She poured more champagne into Linda's glass. 'Lucky little Louise, wouldn't you say?'

Anything but is how she feels right now, Linda decided, seeing Louise being led into the room stark naked and looking around with eyes like a frightened doe. Beside her,

Giles French playfully flicked his whip across her pert bottom, urging her onward. Coming face to face with the huge black athlete, she drew back in alarm, giving out a little whimper that was patently a stifled cry of alarm. It turned into a yelp as Giles swished his flail across her cheeks.

'The bitch needs a lesson, a lesson in submission,' Hope called out from beside Linda. 'Proceed, gentlemen. The Master has willed it.'

You liar, Linda thought, *this is for your own salacious pleasure*. Before her, Louise whimpered again as Giles grabbed her hair and forced her down on her knees at eye level with the great black limp appendage.

Chapter Eleven

FANTASY HALL

Martin's first sight of Hortense Jessop's husband was of a furtive face peering around a slightly opened door. 'Who are you?' he asked nervously. 'Are you a cop?'

'Mr Jessop, I presume?' Martin said, passing in the note Hortense had written. 'I'm Martin Compton and your wife offered to let me stay a few days – until I get fixed up.' A chain was released from the door. It opened to reveal a slight, bald-headed man of middle age wearing a woman's frilly apron.

Both men regarded each other. Martin considered it little wonder the good-looking Hortense fucked so wantonly with her boss, having such an apparent wimp of a husband. Jessop spoke his thoughts grumpily. 'She shouldn't invite any Tom, Dick or Harry she fancies to stay here. Doesn't she get enough?'

'I wouldn't know about that,' Martin said, intrigued. It sounded like Hortense handed it out to deserving causes. 'I only met Mrs Jessop today. I'll be working for Bembridge Publications and had nowhere to stay.' He was ushered into a spotless hall, shown into a large and well-furnished lounge. 'What made you think I was The Bill?' he asked.

'You looked like a policeman to me,' Jessop said gloomily. 'Big young chap like you. One or two of 'em know about us and call to enjoy the amenities, you know. Got to keep 'em sweet.' Seeing Martin's puzzled look, he explained, 'It's the parties. We do have occasional evenings when special guests come here. They're harmless entertainments, but there's others might not think so.'

'I'm all for harmless entertainments,' Martin offered, to show he was no threat. Did arranged orgies take place in this outwardly respectable house? 'Whatever you do is your own business,' he added. Once again, he hoped, luck had steered him to the unusual, something decidedly sexual in promise. He followed Jessop up carpeted stairs, along a landing with the doors of bedrooms on either side. His room was at the end, furnished with a single bed, wardrobe and dressing table.

'It will do me splendidly,' he said to his host. 'It's quite a house, eh? So many rooms.'

'I do the housework,' Jessop said proudly. 'Hortense makes me, but I like it. There are three bathrooms up here if you want to clean up. Dinner will be served at seven.'

After Martin had unpacked he decided to investigate and went into several of the bedrooms. They were feminine in the extreme with king-sized double beds and lacy drapes, mirrors on the walls and ceilings. He opened a wardrobe door to find a leather suit hanging inside along with a variety of silken cords and whips and canes. *How kinky can you get*, he thought delightedly. This was the paraphernalia of a way-out sex establishment catering for diverse tastes. In a drawer of a dressing table were realistic dildo and vibratory devices: singles and doubles, with strap-on belts, and masks, handcuffs, creams and porn magazines.

It was an Aladdin's cave, he decided, furnished with the goodies one never expected to stumble upon. He turned on a television set in the corner of one room and on the screen appeared a naked black girl. She was giggling as she evaded the clutches of a plumpish white man in late middle-age. With pert tits swinging, she at last collapsed into an arm-chair, hooking the back of one knee over the padded arm to reveal an out-thrust cunt with a bush of wiry hair surrounding the inrolling lips. At once her face became fiercely arrogant and she pointed a finger at the floor before her. Her other hand gripped a short leather strap and, Martin noted, the scene was being enacted in the very room in which he stood. The plump man fell to his knees before the girl, getting a fair crack across his fleshy buttocks. With her free hand, using two fingers like an inverted 'V', the girl divided the lips of her sex as the man went in head first.

'Home movies, made on the premises,' Martin said aloud. 'What a place! I could be right at home here.' He sat on the bed to watch, a growing erection in his trousers. The man licked and lapped the girl, tonguing deeply, getting a good whack on his reddening arse each time he paused for breath.

'So you like eating black pussy, do you, you filthy wretch?' the girl demanded. 'Tell me!' She was assured anxiously that he *loved* eating black pussy. 'And what would your wife and House of Lords colleagues think of you doing this to me, your poor slob?' she added harshly. Again he lifted his head momentarily to admit they would be scandalised, the disgrace would be too much to bear. 'Yet you come back for more,' the girl laughed derisively, laying on the belt. 'Keep going, make me come! You pathetic creep.'

Fearing discovery, Martin reluctantly switched off the video, and went to run a bath. He shaved, dressed in a fresh shirt and walked downstairs to find Jessop in the kitchen basting a large piece of pork with golden crackling.

'Roast, baked potatoes, parsnips and peas,' Jessop informed him proudly. 'My own special gravy too, of course. Go through to the lounge and I'll serve you a drink, Mr Compton.'

'Martin to you,' the young man replied. 'You'll spoil me.'
Feeling ravenously hungry, Martin decided Jessop wasn't a
bad old sort at all, despite appearing a downtrodden character. However, it was no doubt his thing, and whatever turns
you on as they say. In the lounge Jessop went to a sideboard
crammed with bottles. He poured two sherries and sat
opposite Martin on the edge of his chair.

'Had a look around up there, did you?' he said slyly. 'I saw
you from the kitchen. Close circuit throughout the house.
Not much goes on that isn't seen – or taped.'

'I was being nosey,' Martin admitted. 'It's some house.'

'Known to our guests as Fantasy Hall or the Fun Palace.
Got to be careful about that. Mrs Jessop obviously trusts
you.' He spoke in a lowered tone. 'How well do you know
her? Did you fuck her?'

'I only met her today,' Martin protested, noting that
Jessop's face registered disappointment. 'I mean, not that I
wouldn't like to, given the chance and if you don't mind.
You've got a very attractive wife, and a kind one too.' Hope
sprang in his breast. 'Would you like me to fuck her? Are
you into watching?'

'Whether I am or not, she's more than enough for one
man,' Jessop said, ruefully. 'Have you come across the word
nymphomaniac truly applied to a woman's nature?'

'Not often enough,' Martin said cheerfully.

'She's one,' Jessop said, set to launch into revelations
regarding Hortense's sexual activities. 'Not that she was like
that when we were married. She's changed. I didn't make her
like it, unless you count not giving her enough. But then she
never complained. It was that trip that done it. Never the
same woman after that.'

'Do you want to tell me about it?' Martin encouraged him,
sure by the way Jessop leaned forward and his eyes glowed
with excitement at the prospect. Beads of sweat gathered on

116

his pink bald pate. A sex-talker, Martin classified him. Getting his kicks relating his wife's promiscuous infidelities more than from his own sexual triumphs, if any. It must be that her sexual triumphs were his own at secondhand. 'What about the fatal trip?' Martin asked quietly.

'She went with other adults to a week's conference on book-keeping and accountancy. It's her profession,' Jessop began, sounding aggrieved and almost wringing his hands. 'A chartered bus drove them to a hotel. At dinner that evening the driver, a brute of a man, sat beside Hortense and got familiar. He made it plain that he fancied her. She told him she was a married woman. Later, when she was in her bedroom and in bed, she heard a knock at the door. It was *him*, with a bottle of wine and two glasses he must have got from the bar. He insisted on entering her room and, frightened, she allowed him in for one glass.

Persistency obviously pays, Martin thought, admiring the bus driver's determination. 'Hortense was extremely uneasy about him being there,' Jessop continued. 'She was not that sort then, she was a very quiet and private woman, in fact. He sat on the bed beside her and wouldn't go until she'd had several glasses of wine. She begged him to leave. Then the swine put his arm around her waist and kissed her neck. Rather than make a fuss she allowed it under protest. I mean, it would have awoken the whole hotel.'

'The rotten bastard,' Martin swore, filled with admiration for the bus driver's intended act of seduction. 'I'll bet your wife was all nerves, just anxious that he left her alone.'

'He began kissing her mouth, using his tongue,' Jessop said miserably. 'Had her laid back on the bed, and though she struggled the beast got her nightdress off, leaving her naked.'

'A fine figure of a woman too,' Martin consoled him,

recalling Hortense's big breasts bulging her blouse and the rounded tightness of her buttocks. 'What happened next?'

'He used his mouth on her, and performed what's called cunnilingus. Despite her protests, she became aroused and had an orgasm. Do you know I'd never given her one in our marriage? She weakened and he took off his clothes and got in bed beside her. He fondled her breasts, played with her sex, and then had full intercourse while she was still protesting. Again he brought her to a climax. After that, falling asleep fitfully, she awoke to find him aroused and so she was taken again – twice more before morning. The surprising thing is he made her come each time, several times, she admitted. She also told me he had insisted she suck his penis, something we had never done.'

'She'd hate that,' Martin commiserated, stifling his grin. 'But it's strange to think she came off so strongly. I mean you can't have a come without enjoying it, can you?'

'That's what puzzled me,' Jessop agreed sadly. 'She told me all about it on her return home. Rather than be shown up, she kept quiet about it at the hotel. He went to my wife's room every night, sleeping with her and using her for sex. It changed her completely. Only after that did she start to complain about *our* sex life. I was content the way it was. Now you can see what we've come to.'

'Tough,' Martin agreed, certain that it admirably suited both. He had no doubt Hortense had enjoyed her fling and been sexually awakened. 'You've stayed together. You didn't throw her out.'

'We were business partners at the time, as well as man and wife,' Jessop said glumly. 'Besides, she did admit all on her return.' He paused, looking at Martin as if for understanding. 'It had the strangest effect on me, arousing me like never before. For once, I badly wanted her. Discovering sex like that turned her into a completely different woman. She does what she likes now, goes with whoever she wants. I just have to live with it.'

'Gives you a hard time,' Martin sympathised to encourage him in his telling, priming him cunningly. 'It must be hell for you.' Anything but, he knew, noting the excitement Jessop got from baring his soul, the tremble of his hand holding a glass. Set to launch into further revelations regarding his wife's seamy lifestyle, Jessop was cut short as Hortense walked into the room. The two men got to their feet, Martin in a gesture of politeness but Jessop leaping up as if caught out slacking. The woman smiled bleakly as if expecting little else from him, drawing a finger along the sideboard and inspecting it for non-existent dust.

'I've cleaned in here and dinner will be ready in time, dear,' he assured her hurriedly, all but cringing. Martin felt like applauding. 'I was merely making your young guest feel at home.' He left for the kitchen, scurrying away and leaving his glass of sherry on the coffee table.

'Jessop!' Hortense called to him sharply. 'Glass!' Mumbling his apologies, he turned and picked it up, continuing his exit. Watching the act, Martin thought it a perfect example of mistress and slave, obedient lackey and dominant woman. Both played their roles without prompting, as if it were normal procedure, neither appearing self-conscious or embarrassed by the presence of an interested observer.

Looking across at Hortense's serene face, remembering her kindness to him, Martin thought her the last to dominate anyone, even the wimpish and docile Jessop. She relaxed in her armchair, kicked off her shoes and gave him a welcoming smile. Again he admired the contours of her large breasts, the splendidly alluring curves of her mature figure, the shapely calves and ankles. When she'd been fucked over her boss's desk she'd been very much the submissive party, as he had witnessed. Now she could evidently switch roles effectively on arriving home. It was the best of both worlds, Martin concluded, as ever highly intrigued by the sexual practices of others.

She saw his look, read his thoughts, her smile changing to one of amusement. 'Come now,' she said lightly, 'I'm sure you must have got my husband figured out for what he is. Didn't he unburden himself about our marriage to you? I don't think he would miss the chance – it excites him sexually. He's harmless, really. It's his way.'

'I'd say it suits you both,' Martin said. 'And why not?' He saw her nod agreement, ignoring her husband as he returned to the lounge with a glass on a tray. Hortense took it without thanking him and he retreated once more, leaving them alone. 'My evening gin and tonic,' she announced after a trial sip. 'Jessop knows exactly how I like it. He'd better,' she added mischievously.

'Service with a smile, or else,' Martin grinned, feeling a liberty to say it. 'And he loves it obviously. He did tell me something of your way of life. Other men? That turns him on too.'

'Jessop wouldn't have it any other way,' she admitted casually. 'He enjoys my having lovers, enjoys the humiliation and being so subservient. Don't lift a finger while you're here, let him look after you. We mustn't spoil him. Does all this amaze you?'

'Sounds like the ideal situation all round,' Martin began, about to add something on his own behalf as to his past sexual history when the front door bell interrupted. Jessop appeared, hurrying through to answer the call. Returning, he went to his wife to report. 'Mr Cameron has called,' he announced, and was followed in by a tall elegant man who glared in annoyance at seeing Martin.

'Who's he?' the newcomer asked abruptly, used no doubt to speaking his mind regardless. 'You know I don't like strangers here when I call. Get rid of him.'

'Colin,' Hortense said apologetically, 'I didn't know you'd be calling. You always phone to say if you are.'

'I happened to be passing,' the man said shortly. 'Who is he? What's he doing here? You know our arrangement.'

'He's a nephew of mine,' Hortense stated. 'He's staying here for a few days. I didn't think you'd mind.'

Martin wondered at this new turn of events and why she had lied. Who was this arrogant type who acted so confident and overbearing in the Jessop's home? He felt a touch on his shoulder. Jessop was nervously indicating that he leave with him. In the kitchen Jessop closed the door firmly, shaking with excitement.

'What gives?' Martin asked. 'Who is he to come here ordering everybody around? He doesn't own the place, does he?'

'He does. He owns us,' Jessop said, his voice hoarse with emotion. 'There's nothing we can do about it. Want to see what he's here for?' He opened a door, ushering Martin into a spacious pantry, its many shelves lined with tins and jars. Mounting an aluminium stepladder, he slid aside a cardboard carton on the top shelf and climbed back down for Martin to go up.

Gripping the shelf for balance, he saw a round spyhole set in glass on the wall before him. Through it he looked down into the lounge where Hortense now stood facing the lordly Colin Cameron. The enlarged clarity of the view, as if standing near enough to touch, made Martin draw back startled. He looked back down to the expectant Jessop.

'Christ, I'm almost in there with 'em,' he whispered. 'Won't they suss they're being watched?'

'It's safe,' Jessop assured him eagerly. 'They can't see or hear us. That spyhole is a lens; it magnifies like a zoom camera. Made so a camera can be attached to it. This house is full of such gimmicks. The other side is part of a wall light decoration, so well concealed you'd never suspect. Go on,' he urged excitedly. 'See what they're up to. You do want to, don't you?'

You want me to, Martin chuckled inwardly, and I'm happy to oblige. Fixing his eye back to the lens, he saw Cameron unbuckling his belt and pushing down both trousers and underpants to his knees, revealing as he lifted his shirt a large prick curving over balls thick with hair. 'For fuck's sake do something about this, Hortense,' Martin clearly heard a gruff voice command. 'I was at a business conference and all I could think of was how good you are at sucking me off. So I broke off the meeting and had my chauffeur drive here. Rub it up and start sucking, woman.'

'Tell me what's happening?' Jessop piped up from below. 'Give a proper commentary, please. It *is* my wife in there.'

'He's got his pants down and he's ordering her to suck him off, the dirty rotten lecherous lucky bastard,' Martin reported cheerfully. 'She's taking off her blouse, her bra. What tits! She's on her knees.'

'No half-measures with Hortense,' Jessop said proudly. 'What are they doing now? Don't just ogle, tell me, tell me!'

'It's what *she* is doing,' Martin said wistfully. 'Your wife. This is giving me a permanent hard. She's kissing and licking over his knob and shaft; now she's nursing it between her big boobs. Moving her shoulders so that it's fucking her in the tight cleavage, giving the swine a titty-ride—'

'Is he erect? Has she made it get up?' Jessop demanded.

'He'd be dead if it wasn't,' Martin said. 'As a matter of fact he's got her by the ears, moving his hips, fucking her tits. Jesus, I should be in his place. Oh, oh, his knees are buckling. No man could stand much of *that*.' He fell silent, engrossed in the sexual activity enacted, full of admiration for the skill and dedication Hortense applied to her task.

Now she had the engorged cock in one hand, cupping his balls with the other, regarding it with a smile, then lowering her head to take inches of it in her mouth. She bobbed from the neck vigorously, her cheeks hollowing with her suctioning. While she sucked avidly, she lapped the underside of his stalk before taking the full length between her lips again.

Martin saw Cameron shudder, gasp out a throaty groan and begin to jerk his pelvis wildly. It made Hortense suck all the more furiously until, as if reluctant to release it, the prick was withdrawn from her mouth limp and glistening.

'You haven't told me what's happening,' Jessop complained. 'What is she doing now?' Digesting a mouthful of hot jism, Martin could have told him. He climbed down from the stepladder, visibly shaken himself.

'Fucka-me-mucho,' he said weakly, the front of his trousers bulging out. 'What a cocksucker – what a gobble she gives! I don't know what hold that arrogant bastard has over you two, but I'd like some of it.'

'It's a long story,' Jessop said helplessly. 'We're in his debt. He owns this house we live in and comes and goes as he likes. We have to put on entertainments for guests useful for his business interests. He helped us out when Hortense and I were bankrupt and homeless, knowing what he had in mind for us. I told you, he owns us.'

'He wasted no time in whipping out his chopper for your wife to chew,' Martin said thoughtfully, envious of his arrangement with the Jessops. Hortense evidently found it no distasteful chore, either, despite having no choice in the matter. 'When is the next entertainment, as you call it, taking place? I wouldn't mind being here for that, if possible. To help out in any way,' he added hopefully. 'I'd do anything asked.'

'I don't know,' Jessop said. 'The guests are all well-known people. Nobility, business tycoons, show biz, we get them

123

all. They're chary of strange faces, they've got their reputations to consider. I'll talk to Hortense. You could help with serving the guests with drink and food. I'm always run off my feet doing that when they are here. You'd have to wait on them wearing nothing but a short apron. Are you willing to appear like that before others?'

'Only if the apron is a nice frilly one,' Martin laughed. 'See-through if you wish. What have I got to hide? Jessop, old friend, count me in!'

Chapter Twelve

SHOW TIME

Looking around the candlelit room, Linda thought that the elaborately staged setting was nothing more than a means of heightening the eroticism of the occasion. It was a charade, played out to release inhibitions. This was simply a group-sex orgy carried out under the guise of some crackpot black magic circle led by the so-called Master, but no doubt orchestrated by Hope Mannering. As she lay among the cushions being fondled and kissed by her boss, Linda stored it all in her memory – it would be great material for a sensational novel.

So this was how the rich and famous amused themselves, she thought. Doubtless they needed new impetus to arouse their jaded appetites. Her own presence, she realised, was to provide a fresh body for their entertainment. Now, having performed, it was the turn of the reluctant Louise. The girl cowered on her knees before the figure of the black minder, with Giles French standing threateningly over her with his whip. Around the room, reclining spectators muttered their impatience, eager for the seated figure on the stage to order the ordeal to begin.

'Leon is truly a magnificent specimen, if one goes in for that sort of thing,' Hope said, referring to the black giant poised above Louise in the centre of the room. As he waited to enact his role, his oiled muscles gleamed in the candle-light. 'Personally I don't,' Hope added, her tongue tip trailing over one of Linda's taut nipples. 'Never have, although I quite enjoy watching others perform. This should be fun.'

'So you never fuck at these soirées?' Linda asked, surprised. She was fed champagne from Hope's tilted glass. Drops fell between her breasts and she felt the woman's tongue lapping in her cleavage. 'I thought that allowing sex with others was what this was all about.'

'Rank hath its privileges,' Hope said smugly, her hand slipping down over Linda's belly to stroke her sex lips. 'Why should I fuck men when I have delightful creatures like you to amuse myself with? I hate the terms butch and dyke, but on honest reflection I have to admit I qualify. I can't resist pretty young girls. You're a prize, with those gorgeous breasts and sweet little cunt. Even after riding the goat you're still tight.' She heard Linda's low moan and was pleased to note how the girl lifted her hips to the invading finger in her sex. 'You love it, too, don't you? Lascivious baggage that you are.' She pressed a long passionate kiss on Linda's mouth. 'You're mine. Say it!'

A cry of approval from the others prevented Linda from giving her answer. She saw the seated figure on the stage raise a hand and at once Giles French ordered Louise to take hold of the big limp penis dangling before her face. She turned to Giles for mercy and got a sharp swish of the crop for daring to do so.

'Take it in your hand, bitch!' Giles snarled. 'Make it grow for us. Suck! Eat his black cock!'

The girl, on her knees, grasped Leon's drooping stalk in her small hand, inches of it curling over her fingers.

'I can't,' she whimpered. 'I *never* have. It's too big – it will choke me!'

126

'Never mind them,' Hope said fiercely as Linda craned her neck to watch Louise's subjugation. 'She knew what she was in for! She needs a proper lesson in submission. What about you? I asked you to say that you're mine.'

'Of course, if you wish,' Linda said hurriedly. 'What else am I? I make love with you whenever you want. I *am* yours.'

'Then you'd better remain so,' Hope said forcefully. 'Forget about men. I insist upon that. Keep away from Gerald Lyle or anyone else while I'm your lover. No one else can help you advance your career like I can. Have I made myself clear?'

'You didn't mind me riding the goat,' Linda said. 'It was like a man fucking me – it gave me orgasms.'

'That's just a mechanical device,' Hope replied. 'It's not a real prick, and hardly different from a dildo, my dear.'

In front of them Louise was whining as she held Leon's growing erection in her fist, hesitating to put it in her mouth. Two sharp cracks of the crop stung her bottom, made her comply. With wide open lips she encompassed the bulbous purple crown of Leon's prick in her mouth. Sucking tentatively, her moans of despair were plainly heard despite her full mouth.

'She'll soon get to like it,' Hope declared. 'Louise is one of those weak impressionable creatures, easily led, and easily taught. She claims she's still a virgin. She probably is, considering that wimp of a boy friend of hers. I must say she's putting on a good show for us – I'm to be congratulated for arranging it, don't you think?'

'I'd say she was distressed,' Linda dared to say. 'If that's an act it's a very good one. You don't care that you're taking advantage of her?'

Louise was gulping and gasping as Leon, with a handful of her hair in his grasp, fucked her mouth.

'That big brute must be right down her throat,' Hope said

127

with satisfaction. 'She'll know she's sucked cock after this. Just wait until she's being fucked with it. As to taking advantage of her, my dear, Louise and I had a long talk earlier. She agreed it was time she was tutored in cocksucking and fucking. I didn't force her.'

Louise suddenly drew her face away from Leon's crutch, the huge erect prick once free of her lips springing upright, glistening with her saliva. At once Giles whipped her bottom. In the second or two before Leon fed his engorged stalk back into her mouth she cried out, 'God, no! He's going to come in my mouth!' As proof that she had detected this from Leon's increased agitation, hardly was the prick lodged between her tongue and palate before her fear was realised. Holding her head firmly, bucking his hips, he disgorged his load. The spunk was thick and copious, filling her mouth to the brim. Louise was made to swallow it – she was unable to do else – and when he at last withdrew she clutched at his knees for support.

'Now lick it clean for him,' Giles French ordered even as Louise sought to regain her breath. As if fearing punishment for not at once complying, the girl lifted her head, brushing aside the strands of hair that had fallen over her face and recommenced sucking. Leon towered above her, legs firmly planted apart and hands on hips, while she lapped and licked the now subsiding ebony cock. Linda and Hope were joined by another woman, a svelte creature with long pear-shaped breasts. She lay beside Linda, at once reaching over her body to exchange a passionate kiss with Hope.

'She's fabulous, darling,' the woman enthused as their mouths parted. 'Is she an actress or a call-girl you've paid to put on such a show, Hope sweetness, or is she really some little mouse who's fallen into your clutches? I'd like to think she's not acting, but is actually as horrified as she appears, sucking Leon's monster.'

'It's quite genuine, Penelope dear,' Hope assured her friend. 'She's a silly goose of a girl in my employ, quite useless really.'

'She's hardly useless,' Penelope laughed. 'Not when you can use the pathetic creature in such a manner. I wouldn't have thought there were any girls left in London as simple as that. How did you get her to do it? You've seduced her yourself, of course.'

Beneath the two, with Penelope's long breasts dangling right above her face, Linda started to giggle. The effect of more to drink than usual suddenly made her frivolously drunk.

'How do you get her to do it?' repeated Penelope. 'Is it do as I say or you're out?'

Linda gave a loud hiccup and giggled, the image of the two women staring down at her in annoyance blurring in her state of intoxication. She shook her head to steady her eyes but the double vision persisted and the room seemed to circle around her. 'You've both got four tits each,' she said hysterically.

'She's pissed out of her mind,' said Penelope. 'Who is she? Another of your employees, Hope? She's quite a beauty.'

'She's being silly,' Hope apologised, unable not to sound furious. 'I won't have this, Linda. Behave yourself!'

'I thought the idea was to *mis*behave in this perverted crowd,' Linda crowed, laughing so uproariously at her wit that an enraged Hope slapped a hand over her mouth. 'The bloody girl doesn't know what she's saying,' Hope swore. 'She's never been like this before. Damn it, I had high hopes for her. She's turning out to be like any other common little slut.'

Nearby they heard a cry of anguish. Louise was now on her hands and knees with Leon about to kneel behind her. His prick was rampantly erect again and Louise was looking at it over her shoulder with alarm. She gave a moan of humiliation as Leon placed his hand squarely between her spread thighs and cupped the down-hanging bulge nestling in the valley of her buttocks. As his finger delved she groaned at the indignity. 'Please, no, not any more,' she begged. 'Oh God, do you have to do that? Please, please, sir.'

'She wants it, I can hear her squelch,' Giles French observed cynically. 'She's got randy sucking your big prick, Leon. Now fuck her with it. We're all looking forward to that.'

'No!' Louise wailed. 'It's too *big*. Don't, please. No—' Leon withdrew his hand and used it to direct the plum-sized helmet of his erection to her rear-tilted quim, forcing apart the outer lips with an easy forward movement of his hips. Louise squealed that she was sure it would split her in two. For the first time Leon spoke. 'Quiet, little honey,' he said in a surprisingly soft voice for such a huge man. 'Poppa's gonna fuck you good, that's all. You be nice now, you hear?' He spread both palms across her upraised cheeks, lunging inwards.

Her howl of protest was received with cheers of approval from the circle of spectators. Louise looked around wild-eyed, buffeted from the rear and forced forward until she rested on her forearms and knees. With her back dipped, the curved cheeks of her bottom were tilted, aligning her cunt channel to accept the deepest thrusts of Leon's thick stalk. On his knees directly behind her and warming to his task, he increased his pace, fucking her strongly. Two huge hands with fingers spread across her cheeks held her captive, the thumb of his right hand entered beyond the first knuckle in her puckered rear entrance. Despite her cries and protestations, the sliding and shunting of the mighty root penetrating her innards began to have its effect. With a cry of despair she became agitated, working her bottom back urgently to meet Leon's heaves.

'Now he has her!' Hope said maliciously, in the excitement of watching Louise's surrender forgetting her fury at Linda's behaviour. 'See the horny little tart's arse bounce. She's unable to resist the cock in her. Look how Leon is giving it to her, she'll never be the same after this. She'll be cock happy, I shouldn't wonder.'

Leon had risen above Louise, at which angle he was actually changing the direction of his thrusts, poking her in every corner of her cunt. The girl reciprocated by squirming back her rear to get the deepest penetration from each lunge, balling her arse hard against his belly.

'Little Louise has hidden depths,' Hope smirked. 'At least, I hope she has with all *that* inside her. It truly is a monstrous thing.'

'You should try one yourself sometime,' Linda chirped in her tipsy state. She tilted the champagne bottle to her lips, refusing to let Hope take it from her. 'It beats a woman's fingers or tongue, or even one of your dildoes. A real hot stiff throbbing prick,' she giggled, 'There's no substitute for it.' She drank several swallows from the bottle. 'You don't know what you're missing if you've never been properly fucked.'

'You're drunk,' Hope snapped. 'I don't think you realise the consequences of your behaviour.' She was stopped in mid-sentence by a renewed howling from Louise. 'Oh God, no!' she shouted. 'He's making me come – I'm c-o-m-i-n-g! Oh, ooh, *aaaahh—*'

Her convulsions continued as she slumped forward, prone, onto the floor, shuddering as if unable to control her body. On his knees behind her, grinning broadly, Leon still maintained a straining erection. 'Now fuck her arse until her head

131

spins,' Hope called out callously. 'Finish the job and bugger the girl.'

Louise, recovering, heard the words and raised a woebegone face. 'Please, no more,' she begged. 'I couldn't – I'm drained – not right away at least. Please, not there – not there with him—'

Linda, freeing herself from Hope's clutches, found herself crawling past Louise and pausing before Leon, her head on a level with his upstanding prick. 'Use that on me,' she offered tipsily. 'Fuck me with it any way you like. They want a good show so let's give 'em one. I've never had a black one. Let's see how good you are.'

Squatting up on her haunches, she grasped Leon's prick and pulled it with her as she fell back onto the floor. Leon grinned in her face as he was cradled between her thighs, feeling his knob being directed to her cunt.

'Hot for it, babe?' he said. 'The pleasure's all mine.'

The fat monster slid into Linda, the sensation seeming never ending. She groaned out in pleasure, welcoming the black intruder with audible relief. Curling her legs around his waist, she clutched at his tautly muscled arse cheeks to draw him closer in. Frantic to get more up her, desperate to have the big root deeply embedded in her cunt, Linda urged him on. His hands slid under her buttocks to cup and lift as he drove into her. With each heave of his flanks he altered the angle of thrust, his shaft poking every recess of her hungry cunt, jolting her with his power. Ignoring her protests, he withdrew to the hilt then rammed it in again to increase her delirium.

Wild and wanton, Linda bucked against him in her agitation, only her shoulders in contact with the floor. Everyone heard her pleas and breathless demands to be *fucked, fucked harder, faster and deeper!* Spasms of multiple climaxes subsided to leave her inert, sprawled on the carpet alongside

Louise, soggy with Leon's thick come. She heard cheers and applause through the roaring in her ears and, drunk on sex and alcohol, she tried to rise to take the bow she had earned. Then she fell back senseless.

Bright daylight lightened the curtains of a strange room as she sat up in bed, reflecting upon the previous night's happenings. The door opened to reveal Giles French, who entered carrying a tray with a steaming mug of black coffee. He sat beside Linda, shaking his head, and offered the mug which she cupped in her palms and sipped tentatively. She realised her bared breasts were above the duvet and that she was nude. With a steady throb pounding in her forehead she didn't care.

'Go on, say it,' she challenged Giles. 'I made a fine exhibition of myself, didn't I? I had more drink than I could handle. How did I get here?'

'Hope Mannering threw you out after that splendid fuck you had with Leon. He helped me get you in my car,' Giles said. 'Not knowing exactly where you lived, I brought you to my flat. You were quite safe with me, of course. There was hardly a twitch out of you all night.'

'You slept beside me?'

'My dear,' Giles smiled, 'I wasn't going to kip down on my antique *chaise longue* for you. I'm afraid your behaviour last night, appreciated as it was by everyone except H.M., means you are out. Your career with Merlin Television has been abruptly terminated. Hope doesn't allow her chosen to do their own thing. What will you do now?'

'Survive,' Linda said boldly. 'And show that bitch I can make it without being her sleeping partner. Was she really hopping mad?'

'Livid,' Giles agreed cheerfully. 'How we downtrodden loved it. I wish you luck in whatever you do.'

'Luck won't come into it,' Linda said determinedly. 'Let me use your shower and I'll be on my way. Give my regards to those at Merlin.'

'Including the revered lady boss?' Giles asked irreverently. 'Any last message I can pass on to her?'

'Tell her go fuck herself with her biggest dildo,' Linda said, laughing. 'I have better things to do. Starting now!'

Chapter Thirteen

WIFE WATCHING

Hortense sat down to dinner opposite Martin. She chatted amicably as Jessop served the food and poured wine like any fawning waiter, being ignored for his pains while his wife gave their guest her full attention. That same smiling mouth, Martin reflected, had expertly sucked off a prick hardly an hour since. The very house they were in was the venue for sex parties with all the accoutrements handy to fulfil way-out fantasies. Her husband danced attendance on them like a well-trained slave and both were in some kind of thraldom to the overbearing Colin Cameron. Some couple, some joint, Martin concluded happily, studying Hortense and admiring her aplomb.

A fully paid up, actual nymphomaniac, was how her doting spouse had described her to Martin. What he had witnessed so far bore that out and he was eager to be allowed his turn. The print dress she wore was moulded to her shapely figure and left nothing to the imagination. When the meal was completed, they adjourned to the lounge, the obsequious Jessop serving drinks to a background of lilting orchestral music. Hortense talked of business matters and her hope of making Bembridge Publications into a lucrative concern.

'I've accepted a half share in the firm in lieu of salary, so a

lot depends on you, young man,' she said, smiling at Martin.
'It's a half share of nothing so far. Jessop and I act as host
and hostess for rather special parties here and that's our only
means of support right now.'

'So your husband informed me,' Martin said. 'Regarding
that, I'd be happy to help out.'

'How sweet,' Hortense said with a straight face. 'Of more
immediate importance is producing a successful publication.
Our initial attempt to break into the market with *Game Girls*
lost money. Hugh Bembridge's wife's money, at least. It
could have been a good girlie magazine with more effort. But
Hugh is lazy – he's all talk and no action. We'll do the work
and he'll reap the glory if we make it this time. You'll have a
free hand to use your ideas. Hugh's not in the office much.
You'll be your own boss almost.'

'Suits me,' Martin agreed. 'I don't mind an absent boss if I
can put my ideas across.' Thinking back, he recalled Bembridge had been anything but lazy when fucking the woman
sitting across from him. 'I've made a study of girlie mags. I've
got this great idea for one called *Mature*. If we make a
success of the format maybe we could even resurrect *Game
Girls*. It wasn't that bad, I thought.'

'The contributions you submitted as a freelance in college
were the best things in it,' Hortense told him. 'Your car-
toons, and the stories illustrated with your artwork, were
exceptional. You certainly can draw naked females in interesting situations,' she said teasingly. 'Your artwork brought
in our biggest mail. No wonder Hugh offered you a job.
Actually, I insisted to him that he did.'

'Then I owe you thanks,' Martin said, settling back in his
armchair and allowing Jessop to refresh his drink. 'When do
you think we'll get the first issue of *Mature* published?'

'As soon as Hugh Bembridge gets his wife to come across
with the readies,' Hortense laughed. 'She's loaded but

they're not exactly close at the moment. More like at war.'

'Not good,' Martin said, his hopes sinking. 'I need a regular salary to eat and pay rent if I'm to find a place to live.'

'There's no hurry for that, we've the room for you,' Hortense assured him. 'Don't worry, we'll survive even if we do still owe the printers for past failures. They're breathing down Hugh's neck for payment but you wouldn't think so from his lifestyle – the big Mercedes, the handmade suits and his wining and dining.'

While she spoke, Hortense settled back comfortably in the deep armchair opposite Martin, sliding her bottom forward and parting her knees. The dress rode up to reveal bare and shapely thighs. With a start, Martin saw her sex openly displayed, thrust forward by her reclining position. It curved prominently, heavily thatched with soft brownish hair, the cleft separating plump inrolling lips. That's a cunt made for fucking, Martin thought. How it would grip a rampant cock, as he had seen already. Hortense continued talking as if nothing untoward had occurred.

'I'm sure we'll get out a first issue of *Mature*,' she said. 'It's up to you to make it so excellent that there'll be a demand for more. One thing Hugh is good at is borrowing money and dodging creditors. You can live and eat with us here meanwhile. We'll do our best to make your stay – pleasant,' she added with a sly smile and eased herself lower in the chair as if to get comfortable. In doing so she presented Martin with a wider, clearer view of her quim.

'Is something troubling you, young man?' she enquired. 'You seem agitated. Did I make it sound as if Bembridge Publications offered poor recompense for joining us? We'll make it worthwhile. Why such a frown?'

'He's not frowning, he's staring,' her husband said, furtively sidling up behind Martin's chair. 'You know very well

137

he is, my dear,' Jessop went on. 'Fancy flaunting *that* at our young guest. Taunting him with your hairy snatch. You're old enough to be his mother. Why don't you bring out your big tits and let him look at those as well?'

A fair enough suggestion, Martin thought, aroused by the heavy sexual atmosphere pervading the room. He sat back content to let things develop, certain he was a player in a planned ritual.

'Who do you think you are, addressing me in that disgustingly crude fashion?' Hortense demanded of Jessop icily. At once his shoulders seemed to hunch and his manner grow contrite.

'Only your husband,' he dared whimper. 'You desire this boy and are determined to seduce him. I won't allow it. I mean, you are my wife, dear. It's not right.'

'Go to your room, Jessop,' Hortense ordered, rising and adjusting her dress to Martin's disappointment. 'I shall come up and deal with you later for interfering where you're not wanted. Now,' she said, turning to Martin, 'where were we? Did it seem to you I intended to seduce you? Would you have objected?'

'I was considering my chances of seducing *you*,' Martin replied. 'As to where we were, you were in that armchair, showing off—'

'Her greedy cunt,' Jessop put in hoarsely. You're as bad as my wife, Martin. Go on and fuck her then, that's what she wants. See if I care. You're just somebody new to try out.' He stood his ground, trembling. 'Go on, I've seen it before.'

'Are you still here, Jessop?' Hortense said threateningly. 'Off to your room and no sneaking back down. Leave us and I'll come to you later. That's what you want, isn't it? Be a good boy now.'

'It's crazy,' Martin observed as Jessop shuffled from the room mumbling to himself. He stood close to the woman, his chest brushing her breasts. 'With a wife like you he goes off like a lamb, leaving us to it. Mind you, I've no objection.'

'We're doing him a favour,' Hortense smiled, allowing Martin to cup one weighty breast. 'He'll be upstairs watching on closed circuit television, then in time he won't be able to stay away. He'll hover by the door, or even come into the room beside us if he can't contain himself. Would you object to that?'

'Right now I'd fuck you in Wembley Stadium before a capacity crowd,' Martin assured her. He recalled how lewd words had been used while Hugh Bembridge had serviced her and decided to employ the same tactics. 'I've got a hard-on that will screw your cunt rigid. Let's give old Jessop a good show and make his day. I'll make your day for you too.'

'Promises, promises,' Hortense taunted him. 'I hope you're as good as you say, for I take some satisfying, young man. Did I hear you say you considered seducing *me*? That would make a change. Go on then – let's see how you operate.'

You'd better make this good – she's a highly sexed and experienced woman, Martin told himself, accepting her challenge. 'Okay,' he promised, 'one Martin Compton special coming up. But let's not rush things. You're in no hurry, are you?'

'What kind of young man are you?' Hortense said as if complaining. 'I thought you'd be so eager that you'd be all over me by now.'

'That would be very unimaginative,' Martin chided her. 'I'll bet you fucked as soon as you grew tits and hairs on your fanny. And that's how I want you to feel right now,' he added, an idea coming as if inspired. 'You are sweet sixteen, a virgin under my spell. You will do as I say. Everything I say.'

'That brings back memories,' Hortense laughed. 'I once *was* sweet sixteen, an innocent virgin. My lover did make me do everything he told me. He used me as he wished. Really unrepeatable things.'

'But you will repeat them to me,' Martin ordered sternly, at once delighted with her cooperation. He held his right hand before her face, then dramatically snapped his fingers. 'You are now under my power,' he said quietly. 'You will repeat the unrepeatable things your first lover did to you. Every lurid detail. Who was he, the lucky bastard?'

'My mother's financial adviser,' Hortense said on cue in a trance-like voice. 'She dabbled in the Stock Market. He was her broker. Well named, for he swindled her and left the family broke—'

'And broke *you* in as well,' Martin affirmed. 'Never mind that now. Tell me how he did all those naughty things to you when you were sweet sixteen.'

'Must I talk about it?' she pleaded, her head lowered as if ashamed. 'Don't make me, *please*.'

'I insist,' Martin told her forcefully. 'Confession is good for the soul. Consider this a counselling session, to rid you of unnecessary feelings of guilt. What did this man order you to do?'

'Strip naked for him,' Hortense admitted, eyes directed at her feet and speaking in a whisper. 'He'd then make remarks about my body which were quite shameful to hear. I was a big girl, well developed for my age. It was so awfully embarrassing when he talked so crudely about my large breasts or my – my vagina.'

'I can imagine what a lovely young creature you were,' Martin said, envying the man. 'So he ordered you to take off all your clothes. Now do the same for me.'

'I don't want to, you've made me shy,' Hortense complained, trembling. 'Why are you making me relive my past?'

'To get it out in the open so you can accept it,' Martin said, delighted with his act and her response. 'In truth you are aroused, feeling the same wickedly delightful sense of guilt as when your randy old lover had his way with you as a girl. You loved it all the more because you liked to think it was against your will. It wasn't, so why be ashamed? Do as I say now, just as you did for him. Strip naked. Hurry up.'

With a low groan she began to undress, finally standing before Martin as if truly embarrassed to be exposed to his gaze, an arm over her full breasts and a hand covering her sex. 'This is how he used to force me to pose for him,' she began falteringly. 'I hated it.' At his stare she shuddered and moved her hands to her sides, revealing herself full-frontal for his approval.

'You hated the fact that you were thrilled to show off your girlish nude body to the filthy lecher,' Martin informed her. 'It's quite natural for such mixed feelings to be experienced by a young female discovering strong sexual urges. You'd be unwilling to admit a properly brought-up girl should have them. But you did, even if you told yourself he made you do it.'

'He did, he did,' Hortense appealed. 'I was sixteen and a virgin. He was over forty and our family stockbroker. I felt I couldn't refuse him, not Mr Grimes.'

'Where did all this take place?' Martin asked. 'His office?'

'Sometimes,' Hortense admitted, almost wringing her hands. 'Also when my mother was resting in bed and father at work in the afternoons. Mr Grimes came to discuss finance.' She paused, as if reluctant to continue. 'They were having an affair,' she added in the same tremulous voice. 'It was their way of meeting.'

For all her agitated manner, Martin gleefully noted that her face was flushed with excitement and a pinkish glow had spread to her swollen breasts, her nipples stiff and prominent. Obviously the memories were arousing her effectively. 'You mean the stockbroker was upstairs servicing your mother in her bedroom?' Martin queried, his enjoyment increasing. 'Are you making that up?'

'No, honestly,' Hortense protested miserably. 'Why do you insist on hearing these dreadful family secrets?' The woman seemed so anguished that Martin wondered if he had actually succeeded in hypnotising her. If so, he considered it well worth investigating as a further useful weapon in his sexual armoury. Psychiatrists used it to wheedle revelations from patients, he believed, and it appeared to be working for him. 'It makes me more ashamed,' Hortense said unhappily. 'My own mother. Don't make me talk about it.'

'But you must,' Martin insisted. 'Your history gets more involved. How were you certain this Grimes was having you both, mother and daughter? Tell me.'

'He seemed to stay upstairs a long time on each visit,' Hortense said in her shamed voice. 'I'd come home from school and if mother wasn't up after her afternoon lie-down I'd start preparing dinner. Mr Grimes would always start on me when he came down. I dreaded waiting for him.'

'All the time wondering what was keeping him, your breasts and vagina churning with anticipation,' Martin charged her. 'One day, I suppose, your impatience got the better of you. Upstairs your suspicions were confirmed – that he was fucking both of you.'

'It wasn't like that,' Hortense whined. 'I went upstairs to ask what she wanted to eat that evening. Strange noises were coming from the room. I looked in and saw – saw—'

'Yes?' Martin said eagerly, his prick rearing, struggling against a strong urge to put the nude woman on the wide couch and fuck her. 'Your secrets are safe with me.'

'I didn't look directly in,' Hortense responded. 'I saw their reflection in mother's dressing-table mirror. She was sitting up on the bed with Mr Grimes standing close. Her head was turned to his middle and his trousers were down. I realised with a shock that mummy – mummy was sucking his penis. She had it all in her mouth.' She gave an involuntary shiver at the memory. 'Sucking it—'

'You stayed to watch, of course,' Martin said. 'Did she finish him off? Swallow the lot? You certainly discovered what she wanted to eat that evening. Did she finish him off?'

'No. He withdrew it from her mouth and mother lay back on the bed. Mr Grimes got on top of her, between her legs, and they – they—'

'Fucked,' Martin finished for her. 'Your ma was evidently just the entrée, the *hors d'oeuvre* before he came down to work you over. Seeing them at it made you very aroused, I'm sure. The truth now, Hortense – did you play with yourself while watching? Finger your quim, bring yourself off?'

She nodded shamefully. 'You're making me admit such disgraceful things,' came a mumbled protest, 'but I couldn't help myself, truly. The way mother responded to him excited me. I had such a big orgasm that I was still trembling when Mr Grimes came downstairs. He'd seen me in the same mirror spying on them – and what I was doing. I deserved to be punished for that, he said. He was really stern.'

'And rightly so,' Martin said, stifling his grin. 'Continue, girl.'

'He made me strip for him in the lounge as usual. Then he sat down and ordered me across his knee. I cried, saying I was too big a girl to be spanked. It was humiliating. I tried to defy him. "I'll tell father what you are doing to us," I threatened.'

'But threats and sobs didn't save you,' Martin surmised, certain that the randy Grimes knew his victim. 'I think you liked the idea of your bottom being smacked. The thought turned you on.'

'It was horrible,' Hortense protested, 'but what else could I do? I couldn't really tell father his friend Mr Grimes was having both his wife and daughter. He slapped my bottom really hard.'

'But you enjoyed it,' Martin insisted, 'and why not? Submission to a more dominant person can be enjoyable on occasions. So can the sweet pain and pleasure of humiliation. You felt you were being forced into these sexual acts and therefore you didn't feel the guilt you considered you should feel.' It was the kind of guff written by so-called sexologists in text books, and Martin sagely recalled their words as if they were his own. 'It's a common phenomenon, so enjoy, don't fight it.' He sat down before her, patting his knee. 'Across my lap with you, and get your bare bottom spanked. We'll discover how much you hated the treatment, won't we?'

He saw Hortense look at him blankly for a long moment. Then she lowered herself across his knees, placing her smooth plump buttock cheeks directly below his admiring gaze. If she was not actually hypnotised, he had to admit she certainly looked and acted the part. Her docile behaviour was so different from her usual manner that Martin had to believe she was mesmerised. The broad feminine arse squirming on his lap brought him back to the business in hand.

'Be still!' he ordered sharply, his open palm delivering a smart smack that brought instant compliance. Six more of the same followed, leaving the rounded moons pink and warm. Martin happily acknowledged the subtle shift she made to direct her cunt against one of his knees and her tentative wriggles to rub on the hard bone. 'That's got you going, hasn't it?' he said. 'So what did this Grimes do after heating you up?'

'He – he – parted my bottom cheeks wide with his hands,

peering in close and describing what he could see in detail.'

'Which was?' Martin demanded, doing as she'd described, dividing her ample buttock cheeks and spreading them apart. He gazed on her serrated anal ring, tightly puckered, under which a plump and pretty split cunt moistly pouted. 'Tell me what he saw, or do you need another spanking?'

'He described my bottom hole, only he was rude, saying words that made me blush,' Hortense began hesitantly. 'Words about it being a tight virgin arsehole, and his stiff cock would be the first to fuck it. He put his finger in there, making me squirm. I begged him not to. He played with my – cunt – too. Then he accused me of being worked up and said that I was a girl who liked it all. Oh!' she suddenly exclaimed. 'What are you doing?'

'What he did,' Martin said. 'Feeling up your arse and cunt.' With a curled finger and erect thumb he titillated both entrances, noting with satisfaction how Hortense shuddered in pleasure at his touch. 'He was right, you do like it. I bet you wanted him to fuck you then. Say it to me – fuck me!'

'What's going on, what have you done to my wife?' cried a highly agitated Jessop as he advanced from the door. 'I've been watching upstairs, I've heard it all. Are you sure you can get her out of whatever trance you've put her in?' he asked anxiously. 'I've heard these things can go wrong.'

'I put her in, I'll bring her out,' Martin said confidently. 'It seems I've got the gift. So you heard a few things, did you? I guess the randy bus driver who supposedly forced himself on her in that hotel wasn't the first to turn her on. Not by a long chalk. Your wife has been a horny piece from way back.' Desperately trying not to rotate her arse and cunt under the twin probing of a finger and thumb, Hortense moaned and whimpered, unable to prevent the sounds of her excitement. 'Doesn't she just love having dirty things done to her?' Martin enthused to her husband.

'This has been a bare-your-soul exercise, Jessop, old chap. And what a good subject. Stick around and you'll learn a lot more.'

'I do believe you've hypnotised her,' Jessop said admiringly. 'I've never seen the like. Go on, Martin, make her tell us some more. I never knew about her and that Grimes fellow.'

Hortense, draped across Martin's lap, turned her face to him. 'Who is this man?' she sobbed. 'Isn't it enough what you're doing to me? Why have you let him see me like this?'

'I'm your husband,' Jessop explained. 'Don't you know me, dear?'

'Stuff that for now,' Martin said impatiently. 'We're at the crucial bit. She was about to tell me to fuck her and I've a hard that won't wait much longer to wet its nose.' His finger circled the taut nub of her enlarged clit while his thumb remained deep in her twitching, clenching arsehole. 'She's as horny as a bucket of frogs,' he announced proudly to Jessop. 'This would be exactly how she'd be worked up by old Grimes – desperate to be put to the cock.'

'I couldn't help it. He – he – made me want to do it,' Hortense piped up frantically. 'He did the things to me that you are doing now. I should have hated every moment of it but I loved it. There, I've said – I'd tell him that I wanted to be fucked – like I want you to fuck me now.' She twisted her face to look appealingly at Martin. 'Do please fuck me.'

'All in good time,' Martin promised, curbing his own impatience and continuing to manipulate her cunt and arse. 'Is that *all* your Mr Grimes did? Strip you, feel you, spank you and then fuck you?'

'It's enough to be going on with for a sixteen-year-old virgin,' Jessop claimed, his voice croaking with excitement. 'Wouldn't I have loved to have been there.'

'You're here now, which is the next best thing,' Martin told him. 'You can watch me fuck your wife instead.'

'There were other things,' Hortense suddenly spoke up, as if deciding to admit it all. 'H-he made me let him d-do things to my breasts too. You know – apart from sucking them.'

'He tit-fucked you,' Martin nodded. 'Of course. What else?'

'Like mother, he put his thing in my mouth.'

'Who can blame him?' Martin said.

'And *worse*,' Hortense mumbled.

'Then let's hear it,' Jessop encouraged her. 'Tell us!'

'Sometimes he – he – put his big stiff penis in my bottom hole and did it to me there.'

'Enough is enough,' her husband gulped, almost hopping from foot to foot in his frenzy. 'I want to see her fucked – back and front like she said. Go on, Martin, fuck the dirty bitch for me—' He made his appeal with arms held wide. 'Go on, fuck her, she wants you to. I don't mind who gives her one.'

'Yes, yes,' Hortense moaned as if in agreement. 'Do it before mummy comes downstairs. Fuck me. Give me that lovely shuddery feeling I get when you make me come.'

'My God, she thinks she's a girl again,' Jessop cried in some alarm. 'You'd better know how to bring her out of it.'

'We'll see to that after I've screwed her,' Martin said, his standing cock his first priority. 'Don't worry, I'll get her back.' He cupped a heavy breast and with his other arm about her waist, hauled her on her back along the nearby couch. Standing in front of her, he threw off his clothes, his erection rearing thick and long. Hortense lay as if waiting for him, arms lifted, big breasts spread apart on her chest, knees raised and legs parted with the hairy pouch of her cunt tilted in offering.

'You bastards!' she laughed out gleefully, setting her tits jiggling in her mirth, startling both men with her outburst.

147

'What a pair of perverts. Willing to use a helpless woman in a trance for your personal entertainment. How exactly were you going to get me out of it, Martin? Count to three and snap your fingers when you'd done with me? And my dear husband only too keen to go along with it. Shame on you both!'

'So you weren't really hypnotised?' Jessop said, amazed. 'It all seemed so real, my dear. Those confessions, were they true?'

'You'd love to think so,' his wife taunted him, adding smugly, 'It was a good bit of acting, wasn't it? I enjoyed playing the little girl lost and fooling you two idiots.' She smiled at their consternation, settling back among deep cushions. 'There was method in my madness too. I began thinking what a splendid entertainment to put on for guests when Colin Cameron arranges his next party here. Martin could use his non-existent power to make me say and do all sorts of wicked things. You were very good at it,' she praised him. 'An act like that should go down well with the lecherous crowd we have here for their orgies. A real show-stopper, don't you agree?'

'It's a brilliant idea, my darling,' Jessop congratulated his wife. 'Martin would be glad to do it, he's already asked to help out at the next party.' He thought deeply, his eyes lighting up. 'He could do it with others too. Not guests, of course, but we could tutor up the professional girls we bring in on those nights. They'll do anything for their fees.'

'I'd be glad to help out,' Martin agreed, standing naked and holding his rearing cock, his eyes rivetted to Hortense's lush figure. 'You fooled me,' he told her ruefully. 'You seemed totally under my power.'

'The only thing hypnotising me is your lovely big cock,' she teased, sitting up to nurse and cradle it in her breast cleavage, then bending her head to kiss the inflamed knob.

'Oh, Mr Grimes,' she began to wail. 'Fuck me, please, before mummy comes downstairs. Give me lots of lovely comes like you do!'

'Happy to oblige,' Martin said, getting into position between her comfortable thighs. Guided by her hand, his thick stalk glided up to the hilt in a receptively moist cunt.

'When I first saw you,' he said to her face a moment prior to delivering his opening thrust, 'I thought you the sweetest, most serene, dignified lady one could meet. Though I longed to fuck you, I thought it entirely out of the question. It's lucky I'm such a rotten judge of character!'

Chapter Fourteen

BIRTHDAY BOY

Now she was out of a job and with the rent due on her expensive flat, Linda's immediate need was to secure funds. She needed ready money, lots of it – more than any salary – and there was one way to earn it quickly and easily. She was young and beautiful, attractive to men and women. A call to an escort agency led to an interview with a sweet-faced young woman and an immediate assignment. Dressed in evening wear and heavily made-up, Linda waited in her flat for the arrival of the limousine sent to collect her later that night.

This was no cheapskate outfit, she decided as a liveried chauffeur held open the door of a sleek back Lincoln Continental. Entering its spacious rear, subdued light gave the impression of a smart tuxedo-suited figure reclining in the deep upholstery. This was her date, her client, she reminded herself, and she smiled as she'd been told to do on meeting paying customers. To her delight her companion seemed slim and attractive. As she sat, Linda looked closer and was surprised to find her companion was female. With a mannish hairstyle, smoking a long thin black cigarette, the woman regarded Linda with close scrutiny.

'Very pretty, I must say,' she said, almost making it sound like a fault. 'Phoebe said when she interviewed you that you looked like a young Elizabeth Taylor. Is a secretary's wage not enough to live decently on? Maybe you're another aspiring actress making ends meet until you're discovered? Or someone's hard-up little wife perhaps? You do it for the money, that's certain. What are you?'

You surly dyke bitch, Linda thought. I could tell you what you are. 'I'm a writer,' she said. 'And of course I do it for the money. I-I wasn't informed my client would be another woman.'

'Date,' the woman snapped. 'Don't you know never to use the word client about those who pay for your company? Do you object to a date being female?'

'Not at all,' Linda said. 'Why should I?' wishing it were any other woman than the one beside her. This was the kind, she guessed, who would enjoy giving an unsatisfactory report back to the agency if not completely satisfied. The car's engine purred as they drove into the night. 'I quite like a lady being my date.'

'Do you?' mused the woman. 'We shall see. Anyway, I'm not your date. Tonight I'm your performance assessor. Do everything asked of you willingly, as if you were enjoying yourself, and there may be other calls for you. Think of the money, my dear,' she said snidely. 'You may even like the job.'

'Would that be so wrong?' Linda said calmly, accepting that the woman was another employee of the agency. 'You're not a very pleasant person, are you? You're in the business for love, I presume?'

'You could say so,' came the cool answer. 'I'm the Mona of the Mona-Lisa agency that employs you. I own it in partnership with Pheobe who interviewed you. My lover,' she said defiantly, 'so if you've any designs in that direction, forget it. I make a point of going on assignments with new girls to see how they perform. You know what that means, I presume? You do anything demanded of you sexually. That's how it is, darling. But *anything*. Are you up to that?'

'I expect I've been there before,' Linda replied, her pride not allowing her to be humble. 'What about yourself? Do you fuck men?'

'You tough little bitch,' Mona laughed sarcastically. 'You could be in for a surprise, considering what some of your dates have in mind. It's beyond your wildest imaginings – but they pay plenty for it, so go along. And I don't fuck men,' she added succinctly. 'It's not my scene. I don't have to. There's plenty of your kind to do it.'

'You really know how to put a girl at ease,' Linda said, her dislike for the woman increasing. She noted that the car was being driven along a country road. 'So what have you got in line for my kind of girl tonight?' she asked. 'Any special perversion I should know about?'

'Who knows? It's a birthday party, all stag,' Mona said. 'I'm throwing you in at the deep end with a bunch of horny men. I'm taking a chance on you, actually, for one or two of them are regulars and big spenders. Expense account executives. Therefore I insist on a little test of your capabilities, shall we say, before we arrive. I can't afford to disappoint these particular men—' her voice filled with undisguised malice '—by you being unwilling to do whatever they want.'

Sadistic lesbo cow, Linda thought, *she's taking her dislike out on me as if I posed a threat to her*. She noticed Mona tapping the glass screen between her and the driver and the car glided to a halt at the deserted roadside. 'It's rather late for some kind of a test, I'd say,' Linda retorted. 'I think you're making this test up to get at me. What if I don't pass? Would you call the whole evening off?'

'No,' Mona said easily, her mouth twisted in pleasure. She lifted the mobile telephone. 'I should merely call the office and get a reliable girl despatched and you would be finished. So, are you game? Willing to prove that pretty mouth can do more than be argumentative; or that those big tits are not just for decoration?'

'You're enjoying this,' Linda accused. 'Do as you like, then.' She determined to remain cool and aloof despite whatever indignity might be inflicted upon her. 'Get on with it, but don't expect me to respond and pretend to get aroused,' she warned. 'I'll save that for the paying customers. You do nothing for me.'

Mona laughed. 'Kneel on your elbows and knees along the seat, facing away from me with your head at the car door,' she instructed. Doing as she was told, Linda's forearms and knees dug into the soft leather upholstery. She consoled herself by repeating under her breath, 'You *need* the money, think of the money, think of the money—' as she felt her dress pulled up to the small of her back, revealing her rounded bottom, adorned with tiny tie-string black briefs. Cool hands smoothed over the raised cheeks, making Linda's resolve stiffen. The tie-string was gently tugged and her briefs fell away, leaving her vulnerable to a curved finger which stroked her sex lips and crinkled anal orifice.

'Do you like that?' Mona taunted as Linda kept her body still and showed no response. 'You will, you bitch,' the woman promised, her curled finger slipping into the warm moist folds of Linda's cunt and gently teasing her clit. 'Quite nicely lubricated already, aren't you? Now, look up while I continue back here. Surprise, surprise,' she laughed. 'We can't have your mouth unoccupied, can we?'

Before Linda's face the car door swung open and there stood the large figure of the chauffeur. His trousers were round his ankles and a lengthy flaccid cock drooped from his fist. With his free hand he pulled Linda's head forward, feeding the limp stalk between her lips as she made to utter a protest.

'Suck, suck cock, you slut!' Mona ordered sternly, using the hand not engaged in probing Linda's cunt to smack smartly at her bottom. Between her tongue and palate Linda felt the intruding prick twitch and throb, then thicken to fill her mouth with hot, live flesh. Behind her Mona's finger worked ever faster, making her give the first involuntary jerks of response. Linda sucked, bobbing her head, lost to a heightening lust, spreading her rear to take whatever Mona was prepared to give her.

She heard the chauffeur's growls, sensed the tremors of his legs, and felt the spurts as he jetted into her throat. When he withdrew from her she shuddered and took off into a climax that wracked her body as she lay prone and gasping for breath along the car seat.

'And you weren't going to respond,' Mona said contemptuously, sitting up behind Linda and revelling in the girl's sprawled posture, her legs parted and several inches of a fat dildo projecting from her cunt. She grasped the end and drew it out, holding it up as Linda turned a questioning face. 'Yes,' Mona said, still scornful. 'You took this, all of it, and didn't you just love it. We shall now proceed to your first assignment.'

'Any time you're ready,' Linda said defiantly, sitting up and adjusting her dress.

They arrived at a dark mansion set in wooded grounds. There Mona led the way into a side room where a large cardboard birthday cake, tall candles placed around the top, sat on a wheeled platform. The streamer wrapped around it proclaimed, 'Happy Birthday, Charles!'

'Who have you brought for the filling, Mona?' a man asked cheerfully as he came into the room carrying a stepladder. 'Someone tasty, I hope.' He halted in his tracks as he saw Linda. 'Good God,' he said in complete surprise. 'It's you, Linda! I wondered what you would do after being kicked out of Merlin Television. Come to this, has it?'

'Thanks very much,' Linda replied acidly, recognising

Gerald Lyle, Merlin's top TV producer. 'You put it so sweetly. I thought you at least were on my side and would find some work for me. Evidently not, you fawning slimeball.'

'What else could I be?' Gerald said candidly. 'It's my career and you, Linda, you're a never-was now! Stick to this job. Promise you may have shown at Merlin, I grant you, but Hope Mannering has given you the kiss of death. You'll never work in the media again. I can't help you. H.M. is all-powerful, remember. She'd fire me if she even suspected I wanted to help you. She might even blacklist me. I won't risk that, not even for you.'

'We're here to work, not chat about old times,' Mona complained. 'You,' she addressed Linda, 'strip off and get inside that cake. A randy birthday boy is waiting. You can talk all you want to your friend in your own time.'

Linda undressed brazenly, in anger, yet glad to note the impression her perfect body made on both the woman and the man. 'He's no friend of mine,' she said. 'He's too scared to be, the wimp.' She mounted the ladder, lifting the false icing on top, waggling her bum in contempt.

'You're even lovelier naked than I thought,' Gerald found his voice to say, looking at the swell of her breasts and the neat rounded buttocks. 'God, how I'd love to fuck you.'

'For crying out loud, let's get this show on the road,' Mona cut in. 'You, Linda, they'll be singing the birthday song when we wheel you in. Burst out of the cake, arms raised and shake those tits about. You'll be well paid for it. Shout "Happy birthday, Charles", climb out and give him a big kiss. Show him a good time, whatever he wants. Then no doubt some of the others will expect to fuck you – or watch. Masturbating before them with the dildo is always popular. Just give them what they want.'

'Everybody but *him*,' Linda said, glaring at Gerald and

156

hoisting a leg to climb into the cake, showing the enticing slit of her cunt. 'Not that creep. I'm not giving him the pleasure.'

'You'll fuck him or anyone else here,' Mona threatened. 'They're paying big money to be entertained.'

'Damn right, the vicious little bitch,' Gerald said heatedly. Linda's head reappeared from the cake to poke her tongue at him. 'I'll screw you rigid,' he promised. 'It will be all the more pleasurable for your reluctance. Time to wheel the cake in, eh, Mona? This will be like my birthday too.'

Through an eyehole in the cake Linda saw a half-circle of armchairs in an ornate lounge, and six seated men with drinks in hand awaiting her appearance. One was pulled from his chair, evidently unsure of himself as he was thrust forward, a large young man with thick spectacles. With the ragged burst of the happy birthday song, Linda popped up out of the cake, arms wide and lovely breasts wobbling. 'Happy Birthday, Charles!' she shouted, liking the look of him.

He wore an immaculately tailored evening suit, his handsome face creased in a nervous frown as if not entirely at ease with what had been arranged for him. As Linda began to descend from the ladder placed by Gerald, she slapped angrily at his hand as it sought to explore between her rear cleavage.

'Go for it, Charlie,' someone shouted as the young man was pushed close to Linda. 'Feel those tits for starters,' someone advised. 'Get out your dick and have her suck it,' another suggested. Obviously in high spirits through steady drinking, Linda thought they were acting like overgrown schoolboys. 'Come on, Charles,' said one impatiently. 'It's *your* bloody birthday. Fuck the arse off her.'

'Take out his prick and arouse him,' Mona hissed from behind her, sensing the unruly attitude of the other men while Charles stood uneasily before Linda, making no move. 'For Christ's sake get to work, girl, before this crowd turns on us. What am I paying you for?'

Linda shrugged, amused by Mona's agitation. Then she pulled down Charles's zip, delving in a hand while he stood silent and unmoving as she drew out an appreciably long limp cock. 'How nice,' she said encouragingly, feeling hands on her shoulders, pushing her down, realising Mona was trying to get her on her knees. Her eyes level with the big dick, with one hand she cupped his balls, and with the fingers of her other hand circling the stalk she drew it into her mouth. Sucking gently, she glanced up. She saw Charles shrug apologetically, his face flushed with embarrassment.

'You don't have to do that,' he said kindly. 'This is not my idea of a birthday party. So-called colleagues and friends have arranged this. I should have known what they are like. They have deliberately set out to humiliate me and make me feel a perfect ass.'

'There's one of those back here,' Gerald Lyle cried and laughed uproariously at his crude humour, as he knelt with his fingers busy at Linda's rear. She sucked with pleasure on the sweet soft prick in her mouth, getting aroused by its warmth and taste, disappointed by its refusal to grow. At the same time she fought against responding to Gerald's fondling, determined to give him no sign that she liked it. But clenching her bottom cheeks on his wrist and waggling her rear angrily encouraged him more. Charles drew away from her shamefaced, his prick leaving her lips still in its limp state. He was loudly derided for his failure to erect by the onlookers gathered around.

'Everybody's got a bloody great hard-on but the Honourable Charlie Pennman,' Gerald taunted him from behind Linda. 'Saving yourself for your high society fiancée, are you? If you don't know how to fuck *her*, we'll show you how it's done with Linda.'

'Keep out of my private life,' Charles warned, redder than

ever with embarrassment. 'I'm leaving here right now,' he added, zipping his fly with trembling hands. 'You can all go to hell!'

'My sentiments exactly,' Linda agreed, standing up and pushing Gerald from her. 'As much as I need the money, I don't like the company. Can you give me a lift back into town?'

'Just hold it,' one of the party said angrily, an erect cock in his hand. 'You can't go. We've paid for several hours. Who are we going to fuck?'

'Try her,' Linda said, turning to indicate Mona, who stood in a state of shock, hardly believing her ears. 'She's the boss of the outfit. She's the one who guarantees satisfaction. A good fucking would make a nice change for her. I'm off.'

'Not yet,' Gerald Lyle swore, taking a firm grip on Linda's wrist. 'You'll stay and entertain us like the good little whore you are.' As she jerked her arm to free herself, Gerald went over backwards, knocked flat by a well-aimed punch to the jaw from Charles.

'You had better get dressed, young lady,' he told Linda. 'I can see the party's over. I'll gladly run you back to town.'

'Don't leave me with them!' Mona screamed as she was surrounded by the men. 'I don't – don't! You know I never do.'

'You do now,' Linda said blithely, going off to retrieve her clothes. 'Count it as a performance assessment. They've paid for someone to fuck – give them their money's worth.'

She left to find Charles holding open the door of a splendid maroon Rolls parked on the gravelled drive. 'You're obviously loaded, Charles,' she teased him, getting in beside the driver's seat and smelling the newness of the soft leather upholstery, 'and an Honourable as well, so I heard that pig Gerald Lyle say. How come you got mixed up with that infantile crowd? You're really much too nice.'

'I'm a so-called honourable because my father is a so-called lord,' he said, putting the automatic gear into drive. 'It doesn't mean a thing, I earn my living. The infantile crowd are business associates – television, publishing, advertising – that I meet in the course of my work. No friends of mine, I assure you.'

'They threw a party for you,' Linda reminded him.

'Not out of kindness,' Charles stated bitterly. 'Once I was depressed and stupid enough to confide to Lyle that I have a problem.' He paused before continuing. 'You must have guessed what that is – even while being fellated by you I couldn't get an erection.'

'Stop the car,' Linda ordered as they drove under a canopy of trees. 'Are you saying that you never get a hard-on?' As Charles pulled onto the verge she reached across and squeezed his cock through his trousers. 'You *never* get this up? It's such a nice big one. I thought perhaps that in front of those people you were embarrassed, but surely – at other times you can?

'Not when it matters,' he said uncomfortably. 'Can I be frank? You seem a decent sort to be concerned about me. I've never talked this way before, except with that swine Lyle and odd psychiatrists I've consulted.' He placed a hand on Linda's as she gently stroked him. 'You don't have to do that, you know.'

'I like to,' Linda said. 'Talk all you want if it helps.'

'When they laughed at me at the party, I knew you were sympathetic and blessed you for it,' he smiled. 'Yes, I can get erections. Often just when thinking about sex. When I-I – masturbate too. But when with a girl – I don't know, it's hopeless. So I've stopped trying, I can't risk failure. Even what you are doing now, it's no use.'

'We'll see,' Linda smiled, unzipping his fly and proceeding to massage the soft flesh. 'That's why they ordered a girl for you tonight, the bastards. To shame you.'

'They had their fun at my expense,' he agreed. 'I did try, but even with someone as lovely as you – you—'

'Sucking your prick,' Linda giggled, finishing for him. 'Why not just say that? That's what I was doing – and getting to enjoy it as well. So say it. Sucking prick. Is that so difficult?' Lowering her head, she flicked the eye of his knob with her tongue tip. 'I don't find it difficult to do it. Just ask me.'

'I find it impossible to express myself,' Charles said glumly. 'I wish I could.' He gave a low moan as Linda went down on him, still gently rubbing his stalk as she enclosed the plum-shaped head within her warm lips. 'That's so *good*,' he said, his voice hoarse. 'I want you to, I need to react normally. I'm engaged to be married,' he suddenly confessed. 'What kind of husband will I be? Moira is very passionate, she'll expect satisfactory sex – she wants it now. We kiss, of course, and fondle intimately, but the fear of my not being able to complete the act always makes me break off.'

Linda ceased drawing her tongue up the underside of his prick and raised her head. 'She must complain a lot about that.'

'Persistently,' he said unhappily. 'I'm thinking of calling off the engagement. I've seen doctors and psychiatrists. What else can I do?'

'Get your Moira to do this,' Linda advised, lowering her mouth to give several hard sucks while squeezing his balls. 'Be lewd and crude, relax and tell her you're going to fuck her. It sounds like she'd appreciate that. For once don't be inhibited: suck her nipples and lick her out.' She went back to sucking him strongly, taking it deep, bobbing her head before pausing with the knob at her lips. 'I think there's life there,' she said triumphantly. 'A definite throb, it's stirring. I

161

suggest we get out and continue in the back of your car.'

He obediently joined her in the spacious rear of the Rolls. She gave him a long passionate kiss, her tongue probing his mouth. 'I'd be eternally grateful for any improvement at all,' he said. 'What must I do? I'm in your hands.'

'Feelings of inadequacy or self-inflicted modesty are not allowed for a start,' Linda warned. 'We're both going to undress completely, to be naked and unashamed. We'll take our time kissing and fondling and *talking*. We'll say whatever we'd like to do and do it. I want that for my own sake. Easy does it.' She began slipping out of her dress, looking at him meaningfully, gratified to see him throw his jacket over the front seat and begin loosening his tie. 'We'll say and do anything you want,' she reminded him, turning her shapely back to indicate he unclip her bra. 'Any hesitation and I'll take you across my knee for a spanking. What do you say to that, Mr Honourable Charles Pennman?'

'That it might be terribly exciting,' he said, his hands trembling as the bra fell away. 'Moira suggested that once herself and I wanted to, but stupidly refused. You really have the most adorable breasts,' he whispered in awe. 'So firm and delightfully tilted. So full for your slim body. Perfect breasts.'

'Tits,' Linda said firmly. 'Tonight they are tits. You've a prick and I've a cunt.' Tugging at the string of her briefs she tossed away her remaining garment, lolling back enticingly naked on the long rear seat. One hand circled the mound of a breast, the other sidled down her stomach to stroke her sex lips, her eyes fixed on Charles as he finished undressing. She admired the athletic form he uncovered.

'There's no hurry, birthday boy,' she said sweetly, 'and no great tragedy if you can't get it up. Forget that, there's so many other ways to enjoy sex. We have hands and mouths.

Tell me what you would like to do?'

'Look at you first,' Charles breathed, staring at her prone body bathed in a yellow glow from the overhead light. 'I've never seen anyone as beautiful. May I touch you?'

'I'd kill you if you don't,' Linda threatened. His hands cupped both her breasts, squeezing and lifting the orbs, plucking the taut nipples. 'Yes, yes, go on,' she encouraged. 'Do as you like, say what you like. Imagine I'm your fiancée. Use me like you're going to use her. Call me Moira – I want you to.'

'Moira, Moira,' Charles moaned, rubbing his face into the cleave of Linda's breasts. 'I want to suck you. Your nipples and your cunt,' he said fiercely. 'Eat you, all of you.' His mouth sought a nipple while Linda cupped a breast and fed it to his eager lips. Sucking greedily on each in turn while she moaned her pleasure, he left off to lower his head between her thighs. She felt his open mouth clamp over her sex and a stiff intruding tongue enter her moist cunt channel, making her writhe.

'Tongue-fuck me!' Linda begged, working her hips and grasping his head. 'Make me come, come. More, more. *Aaaghh*, yes, there! You're killing me – I've come – you've made me come!'

Her spasms subsiding, she became aware of a furious banging on the car window above her head. Turning, rising on her knees, she saw the irate face of Mona glaring in. Reaching over Linda, Charles touched the button that lowered the glass. 'Bitch, whore, slag!' the maddened woman screamed. 'Leaving me with those men! I'll see you never get agency work in London again. You'll end up on the streets where you belong!'

'I suggest you are the whore, madam,' Charles said calmly. 'As you can see we are too engaged to argue with you. Go on your odious way. In short, piss off. Depart, get the hell out.

Do I make myself clear? Get your hag-ridden face out of my car.'

Cursing, Mona walked unsteadily back to the chauffeured limousine halted nearby. Linda giggled, watching with her elbows and knees on the seat, bottom tilted and aware Charles had inserted a finger into her rear-presented cunt. 'That's what I call assertive,' she told Charles. With a backward squirm she worked her bottom cleft against his wrist. 'Now you've shown you can be so, just keep it up. And keep that up too,' she added, referring to his finger. 'That feels so good. Much more and you'll have me coming again. Oh, it's *nice*.'

'I've something that might feel nicer,' Charles said proudly. 'See what you've done for me.' Turning her head, Linda cried out in delight. An iron-hard erection reared from his crotch, thick and shiny with excitement. 'And I'm not about to waste it,' he cried. 'Stay in that position. Dog-fashion is the term, I believe. I'm going to fuck you, fuck you senseless, young woman. Whether you like it or not!'

'I shall like it,' Linda assured him joyfully, feeling the engorged knob forcing its way into her moist passage. She squealed her delight as inch after inch penetrated, calling out to him to fuck her, fuck her harder. Crouched above her, pistoning his prick into her deepest recess, withdrawing and thrusting in again, the coupling went on wantonly. Linda came with an intense shudder, still urging him on as the quickening slap of his balls on her raised bottom foretold his approaching climax. With a cry of triumph he fired his load into her in long hot spurts.

'Next time you see your Moira, give her as much,' Linda said weakly, recovering face down along the seating. 'Do let me know how you get on. I envy her that big cock. I'm sure you'll have no problem in future.'

'I certainly feel more confident now,' Charles announced,

between pressing kisses to Linda's smooth buttocks. 'Thanks to you, I'll seek her out today and find out if she's as keen to fuck as I suspect. I certainly want her to be. Want her to want this too,' he added, parting Linda's uptilted cheeks and probing his tongue into her rear-facing cleft. 'The sweet you can eat between meals without spoiling your appetite,' he muttered mischievously with his face hard into the hot damp valley of Linda's rear. 'Do you know that I'm getting another erection doing this? Just to make sure before I get in touch with Moira, don't you agree a further check on my ability is required?'

'Definitely,' Linda agreed, turning on her back and drawing him into the cradle of her open thighs. 'But never mind Moira this time, I want it too. Have this one on me!'

Chapter Fifteen

IN CAMERA

'It's got to look highly professional,' Hugh Bembridge declared, flipping through the pages of the mock-up magazine on his desk. 'And what about this title? *Mature*.' He enunciated the word as if savouring it, envisaging vast sales and money pouring in. 'We'll take a chance on it. The sooner we get the first issue onto top shelves of newsagents all over the country, the bloody better. Now we've got to work really hard to make it a success.'

'I have been,' Martin said drily. 'I've been in this office day and night.' With restraint, he refrained from asking what Bembridge meant by 'we' as it was the first time he'd shown up since Martin's interview. 'You can see for yourself. I haven't been sitting on my arse.'

Bembridge stifled a hiccup, drawing himself up to his full height.

'And I've been out on the job, Compton,' he said haughtily, which Martin did not doubt. 'Not all the work is done in this office, you know. There's dealing with the printers and distributors.' Martin wasn't fooled, he knew that work was done by Hortense. 'OK, so you've been busy,' Bembridge added grudgingly. 'The thing is,' he indicated the mock-up, 'can you keep up this standard?'

'It'll get better,' Martin said confidently. 'I've gathered

enough good articles, stories, readers' letters and picture scripts to fill several issues. We'll need photos of suitable models but I'm working on that. Hortense has sounded out prospective advertisers and got them interested.'

'That's essential,' said Bembridge. 'Adverts are the life-blood of a magazine. They're what make it pay.'

'I haven't seen any,' Martin dared put in. 'Pay, that is. Not for all the weeks I've been here.'

'Hortense deals with that,' Bembridge waved aside the issue, ignoring the fact that he had just emptied the petty cash box. 'Have faith, there's big money in a successful girlie mag. I expect a first issue that will knock their eyes out. Are you certain they'll go for your format?'

'It's different, special,' Martin enthused. 'I've studied the opposition. Good-looking mature women are shown in the best mags already. We'll feature them. Beautiful older women.'

'Not too old,' Bembridge growled. 'I want comely not homely. Well-preserved big-titted birds I don't mind, aged thirtyish to what's still considered fuckable by the readers. You've got to have good lewd pictures throughout. How are you going to manage that?'

'Several ways. We could pay an experienced photographer with his own studio and models.'

'Bloody expensive,' Bembridge frowned. 'I'm not yet Paul Raymond. What else?'

'A studio of our own.'

'Out of the question right now. Go on—'

'Use agency photographs,' Martin suggested. 'We choose what we need from prepared portfolios of art studies.'

'Not too arty,' Bembridge warned. 'Like I said, lewd and luscious. Tits, cunt and arse.'

'Nothing but the best,' Martin assured him.

'In full colour? We must have colour.'

'Certainly, but black and white is effective too, and cheaper. All as explicit as you can get. I've investigated,' Martin said. 'For a fee we can reproduce pics from a terrific selection of nudes. All beautiful models guaranteed to produce hard-ons for our readers and hook them as soon as they lift our mag down from the top shelf and glance inside.'

'I'm listening,' Bembridge said. 'Tell me more about these agencies.'

'They have books full of pictures suitable for our use. They're mostly German or Scandinavian models, but they can be captioned by us as Mrs Whatever of Bournemouth or anywhere and who's to know? We'll more than match all other mags for nude poses of the fuller figure. Like the name says, *Mature.*'

'Don't go overboard on that theme,' Bembridge advised. 'Young nubile tit and arse is still the goods.'

'I've thought of that too,' Martin said eagerly. 'Readers' Wives pics go down well. We'll have a mother and daughter section each month. Posed together and separately over several pages. Called something like "Mother's Pride" or "Family Album" in case sometimes there's more than one daughter posing. We can fake it with models until worthwhile pictures come in from actual mums and daughters. Let's offer £20 for every picture used to encourage them. Like the Readers' Letters columns, there'll be no shortage of people sending stuff in just to see it published.'

'All very well once we're a going concern,' Bembridge considered. 'You've convinced *me*, now all I've got to do is convince my rich bitch of a wife. In the meantime, how do we do all this without using any money?'

'I've talked an agency into letting us use photographs on a pay-on-publication agreement,' Martin explained. 'As fillers we'll use my drawings. The picture story of Milly Mature and her sexual adventures will take up four pages. I've drawn two

169

episodes so far. We've got lucky too. A friend I was with in art college is in the photographic business with a colleague here in London. He does family portraits and wedding albums normally, but he's offered the use of their studio and equipment for free today.' He looked at Bembridge hopefully for gratitude, getting none. 'You can't get cheaper than that.'

'What about a model? You'll need one, I presume,' Bembridge said meanly. 'Will *she* work for free?'

'Actually, yes,' Martin enjoyed saying. 'Hortense has volunteered. She'll be perfect as our first "Mature Lady of the Month" with her beautiful build.'

'How the hell would you know that?' Bembridge demanded.

'I can see the way she fills a dress,' Martin said, grinning. 'All this is going to cost you are taxi fares to and from the studio.'

'Take the bus or tube,' Bembridge ordered. 'Between the two of you I'm sure you can afford that. I'd lend you my Merc but I'm using it.'

'What a cheapskate,' Hortense observed, carrying in a mug of coffee and biscuits on a plate. 'He'll pay for nothing, not even his elevenses.' Going behind the desk to place the coffee and biscuits before him, she felt his pudgy hand slip under her skirt, going up to caress a stocking-clad thigh. 'You don't pay for that, either,' she said, walking away to stand beside Martin, and allowing him to fondle her rounded bottom. 'If it wasn't for the business parties my husband and I hold at home, we'd starve.'

'And I'd be living in Cardboard City,' Martin added.

'You're all bloody hard done by,' Bembridge moaned. 'How come I never get an invite to these shindigs you throw at home, Hortense?'

'Because you're a slob,' she said, 'and would lower the

tone. I hope your coffee chokes you.'

On the bus ride to the studio in Lambeth, Martin judged Hortense's mounting excitement as that of a highly sexed woman excited at the prospect of posing in the nude. He looked forward to that himself, but couldn't avoid voicing his concern over Bembridge's attitude to their business venture.

'Forget him,' Hortense advised cheerfully. 'We're far better off being left to get on with it. I only have anything to do with that dead loss because I've faith in you. Faith that between us we'll make a success of our magazine and make lots of money. Do you know what I'm going to do when that happens?'

'It's a nice thought,' Martin said. 'What would you do?'

'Get out of Colin Cameron's clutches for a start. He allowed Jessop and I to run that pleasure palace of his when our restaurant business failed. We were bankrupt and homeless, and he knew it. So we entertain his chosen guests as the price we have to pay.'

'I didn't think you minded that so much,' Martin wondered. 'It's just the sort of life you both enjoy, isn't it? I've never met a more highly sexed woman, and I mean that as a compliment. It's old Jessop's bag too.'

'It suits us both,' she agreed, 'but we want a place like that of our own. We have the connections now. The pleasure and profits would be all ours. I've my eye on a large old house in the country, not far from London.'

'If I get rich, put me down as your first paying guest,' Martin grinned. 'All we've got to do is create a best-selling magazine on a shoestring.'

Alighting from the bus, they found the photo studio a short walk away, the window filled with beaming portraits of newlyweds and family groups. Inside, they were as good as ignored by the good-looking black receptionist who was obviously hostile. She leaned back in her chair to announce the arrivals, then continued examining her nails, a sullen expression on her pretty face. Martin's college friend Brian emerged from behind a door, introducing his partner, Manny, a man in late middle-age who eyed Hortense shrewdly, obviously liking what he saw.

They were guided into a room with chairs, boxes of toys and a splendid rocking-horse. 'This is where we do the family stuff,' Brian explained. 'We make a living out of it but the real dough is in doing nudes and even porn when we can get suitable models. Adult stuff. Noala, our receptionist, earns extra posing for us. She's in a mood this morning because we're not using her. Come on through and see where we do the business.'

Hortense and Martin were ushered into a very different studio. It had embossed wallpaper of garish pink, framed portraits of nudes on the walls, deep carpeting of the same pink and furniture suitable for a feminine bedroom, including a large canopied bed. Behind an ornate oriental screen was a glass-enclosed shower cubicle. Overhead lights were fixed to the ceiling at angles and three cameras were set up on tripods.

'It's a perfect set-up for what I had in mind,' Martin said enthusiastically. 'Shots of Hortense in stages of undress, peeling off her bra and so on. Then naked, full-frontal and rear. Good girlie magazine pictures.'

Hortense nodded in agreement, going behind the screen as if eager to undress and exhibit herself. 'Your model doesn't seem to mind doing this kind of work,' Brian observed, an understatement if ever there was one. 'I can tell Manny is impressed with her figure too. It's just that – that—'

'She doesn't look the type,' Martin said for him. 'Too respectable and wholesome.'

'She seems too nice a person to do nudie poses, and all the better for that,' Manny agreed. 'It makes a change from some of the girls we get sent. I'd like to photograph her myself, unless you intend to.'

'Feel free, I'm strictly amateur,' Martin said. 'I'm just grateful that all this is on the house.'

'Manny's a specialist in figure portraiture,' Brian said with pride. 'He's had pictures featured in magazines worldwide.'

The men were stopped in mid-discussion by the startling appearance of Hortense. She walked from behind the screen in gauzy brief lingerie of pale mauve borrowed from the stock kept for entertaining guests at her parties. The bra overflowed with swollen creamy breast flesh, her thick nipples plainly outlined through the diaphanous fabric. A frilly suspender-belt held up sheer black stockings which encased her shapely legs. Between the fork of her rounded thighs, a miniscule triangular scrap of transparent gauze curved over her eye-catching cunt mound. The ensemble was completed by black high-heeled shoes.

'What tits,' Brian whistled softly in admiration. 'And the rest of her! She's built.'

Hortense gave a wicked twirl, waggling the moons of her bottom as if to show her rear was every bit as succulent.

'Magnificent,' Manny praised. 'This won't be work, it will be a privilege.' He adjusted a hand-held camera and addressed Hortense. 'Move around as if you were in your own bedroom, dear. Pretend you are preparing yourself for bed after an evening out. Admire yourself in the long mirror. That way I can get you front and back in one take. Look wistful, you're a beautiful woman all alone, wishing your man was with you.'

Manny snapped away, walking around Hortense, going down on his knees, then getting up on a chair. He was completely engrossed in his work. 'Now unclip your bra, love. Toss it aside and give those big boobs a shake as if glad to be free. Turn so I can get every angle. Now, out of your

173

gear in your own way, I'll move with you to suit the shots. Great! What a mover! The lady is a natural,' he enthused, seeing Hortense return to the mirror and run her hands sensually down her body from her thrusting breasts to stroke her cunt lips.

'Brian, are you worked up? Well, work that fixed camera, boy,' he shouted to his assistant. 'Now, lady,' he said to Hortense. 'Climb on the bed slowly. What a great arse! Two full cheeks with all those goodies between. Face down across the bed, dear. Now roll over slowly.'

He retreated beside Martin to grab a loaded camera. 'Where did you find such a great model?' he asked delightedly. 'An enthusiastic amateur, I'd guess, a repressed housewife who enjoys flashing her tits and fanny. Who cares? She's great! She's almost bringing herself off – way beyond girliemag stuff. I'll have to sort out the usable pics for you. We can't stop her now.'

'I don't think you could,' Martin said, his voice hoarse and a painful hard-on bulging his trouser front. In front of them Hortense sprawled across the bed, a hand clutching a tit while the other fingered her cunt. She writhed on the bed in her excitement, eyes glazed and mouth agape, further proof of her genuinely aroused state. To the amazement of her audience, she arched her back, holding one of her shoes and pushing the high heel up her cunt as she thrust against it. Each time her gasps and frenzied jerking told of an approaching climax, she would slow down before resuming, pleasuring herself as if savouring the delay, keeping herself on the verge time and time again.

'How far will this lady go, as if I couldn't guess,' Manny said wonderingly, returning for yet another loaded camera. 'I've got contacts with continental colour magazines, German and Dutch publishing firms. It's all legal over there.

Would she go with other models? You know, men *and* women?'

'If the price is right,' Martin said shrewdly, aware of the chance of much-needed cash. 'Ask her.'

'My dear,' Manny said soothingly, advancing with his camera. 'What you've done so far is great, just great. Now, if you're willing, shall we add a little something?' He smiled down at Hortense as if having only her best interest at heart, gazing at the flushed face and breasts heaving with each laboured breath. 'Under the pillow,' he advised, taking the shoe from her hand, 'you'll find something better than this. See for yourself.'

Hortense smiled wanly back, willing in her self-induced erotic trance to agree to anything. She gave a cry of delight as she reached under the pillows and brought out an oversized dildo. Flesh-coloured and rigid, it was all of a mighty twenty inches in length. At each end, perfect replicas of bulbous male knobs were moulded, making a monstrous double-headed prick.

'Oh, y-e-s,' Hortense murmured, without further delay directing one of the plum-sized ends to her cunt, easing the fat knob several inches beyond the outer swollen lips. Each forward thrust brought a heartfelt groan of pleasure from her throat, her bottom lifting to increase the depth of penetration. Seemingly lost to any awareness of the cameras clicking around the bedside, her speed of thrust began to increase as she buried more inches up herself as if needful of taking the lot. The intensity of feeling had her crowing in delight, rolling about the bed in abandon.

'She's taken half of that bloody great stalk,' Brian shouted from behind his camera tripod. 'What a greedy cunt!'

'That's crude, Brian, crude,' Manny lectured him. 'We're seeing the real thing, a one-off. Get the look on her face! Oh, I'll want to use this lady again.' He turned to Martin, all business. 'Would she allow another woman to join her? *Now*, I mean. It's worth a couple of hundred to her if she does.'

'At the moment I think you could wheel on Quasimodo to fuck her,' Martin offered promptly. 'Look at her, she's anybody's. Who do you have in mind?'

'Get Noala to haul her arse in here,' Manny ordered. 'Tell her it's showtime.' Returning with the statuesque Jamaican receptionist, still sullen and moody, Martin saw her glance with interest at Hortense.

'It's the usual money up front, honey,' Manny told her, anticipating the question. 'This is for the magazine deal that's been hanging fire for a suitable partner to work with. Clothes off, Noala, and try to look like you're enthusiastic.' He turned to Martin, shrugging. 'This is for a lesbian special, a black girl with a white one, ordered by a Hamburg publisher. They supplied the double dildo, and want it used.'

Noala gave a loud sniff of disdain, as she undressed. She folded her clothes carefully over a chair as if unaware of the men. Martin eyed her lewdly, impressed by the sleek ebony skin, elongated tits and the plump-lipped shaven haven which nestled between her shapely thighs. She glared at him contemptuously, putting up two fingers in an irate gesture. 'What's with you, creep?' she asked scathingly. 'Never seen a woman get naked before?'

'You're well worth watching,' Martin said easily. 'Pity about the sulky face, though.'

'What d'you expect?' she said snidely. 'I got a horny husband at home and two kids. I don't need to get excited over this.'

'But you need the money, honey,' Manny reminded her sharply. 'Think of that. Join the lady on the bed and earn it.'

Noala stuck out a red tongue at him and sat on the bed beside Hortense who was busily applying the twin-headed prick to her cunt. She acknowledged the black girl's arrival by reaching out to draw her close. One hand cupped a pendulous breast as her mouth sought and crushed against Noala's. Kissing her passionately, she lowered her onto the bed and then lowered her mouth to suck greedily on the girl's dark nipples. Noala stiffened, surprised by the speed and enthusiasm of the onslaught. Unsure and resisting, she tried to prise herself out from under but Hortense was intent on having her way and too driven by lust to be denied. Noala cried out in protest, shouting that she'd agreed to pose, not to be raped.

'Respond, Noala,' Manny ordered. 'At least go through the motions!' Next to Martin, working the tripod camera, Brian growled his disapproval. 'Dismal cow, this could be our best shoot ever if the bitch would only cooperate. Got the body, got the colour, and got the bloody sulks. She had a fight with her old man this morning – it makes her a bit aggressive.'

'Hortense doesn't seem to mind,' Martin said with a grin as Hortense's head dipped, her palms forcing Noala's thighs wide, and inclined the shaven cunt towards her hungry lips. The white woman's tongue homed in on the smooth ebony mound, rasping its way between the cleft and up to a bright red button of a clitty. Repeating the treatment, lapping the inner folds of flesh in long determined strokes, the invading tongue was worked in ever deeper. The black girl moaned and mewed, her protests changing to sounds of pleasure as her cunt pulsed and pouted in helpless arousal. Hortense, with her head buried between the girl's thighs, drew up Noala's legs and gripped them behind the knees to keep them high for closer access. Noala lolled back in surrender, working her hips and whimpering, her hands massaging her breasts and pinching the nipples in a delirious agony of ecstasy.

'You've got her!' Manny cackled excitedly to Hortense, his words unheard as she concentrated on licking Noala into a series of writhing spasms. 'What a turn-on! These shots will be fought over by a dozen magazines. It's perfect, the black body and the other white as porcelain. There's no need to pose you two – just carry on enjoying yourselves.'

He clicked away on close-up shots, happy to continue capturing the pair from every angle. Then Hortense suddenly sat up in front of the sprawled Jamaican girl, half of the straight dildo still buried in her cunt. Noala moaned as the tonguing was so cruelly discontinued, and looked up, her arms outstretched. Shuffling closer on her bottom, Hortense dragged Noala's legs over her upper thighs, pulling until their cunts were almost touching. Directing the protruding half of the dildo by hand, with a thrust of her hips Hortense penetrated the girl beyond the bulbous knob.

Immediately, Noala groaned and lifted her bottom, arching her back, the remainder of the double-ended dummy prick disappearing into her. Hortense fell on her back, both women lying facing the ceiling, making agitated hip movements, lifting their bottoms and squirming in their joint rapture. The ensuing rhythmic jolting at times brought their pubic mounds together, the shared stalk completely disappearing. Gasps and shudders indicated that the pair were enjoying a succession of heightened climaxes. Sated finally, their breasts rising with each intake of air, they lay in a state of collapse, still connected by the instrument of their pleasuring.

'Let's give them time to recover,' Manny said softly. 'I don't think these two are finished with each other yet.' In the silence, broken only by the heavy breathing of the women, he carefully reloaded his cameras, waiting patiently until the two females began to look around dazedly.

'That was fantastic, girls,' he informed them. 'A few more

shots and you'll be through. I want you both to turn over at the same time, keeping that thing inside you. Can you do that for me?' His voice was almost a whisper, and he made it sound like they would be doing him the greatest favour.

Hortense was the first to stir. She moved onto her side with Noala following. Finally both women were on their hands and knees, buttock to buttock, with several inches of white plastic visible between the clefts of their cheeks. With the dildo embedded in both cunt channels, they began to move their bottoms together in a grinding motion, evidently aroused once more. Their sexual excitement grew until the smack of bare backsides buffeting against each other ever faster sounded out loudly over the click of Manny's busy camera.

'Now the finishing touch,' he called over his shoulder to Martin and Brian. 'Two young studs like you won't object, I'm sure. I can see the pair of you straining in your pants, so get out of your clobber. Stand before those two horny bints with your cocks on offer. I want a happy ending.'

Martin, with an erection that seemed permanent, shed his clothes and advanced on the bed, standing close to Noala. Raising wild eyes and, seeing his rampant prick thrusting before her, she grasped the stalk and sucked gluttonously, while at her other end her bottom jerked and gyrated against Hortense's broad white arse. Across the bed, Martin saw Brian standing with his legs apart and Hortense's head bobbing as she gobbled as avidly as Noala. Manny circulated, capturing it all on film until the resulting climaxes left the two women exhausted on the bed. Martin and Brian grinned across at each other, their wilting cocks sucked dry.

'Business *after* pleasure,' Hortense announced to Martin later when asked how she would spend her £200. 'It was a pleasure making it, now it's buying much needed office equipment. *Mature* will become a reality, whatever it takes. We'll turn that money into a million.'

Chapter Sixteen

HOME COMFORTS

'What do you intend to do now?' Charles asked Linda earnestly after they had dressed and driven back to London. 'You're obviously intelligent as well as strikingly beautiful. Have you no other future except escort agency work?'

He sat on Linda's bed in her flat, watching her pack a suitcase. 'First, a shower,' she told him lightly, 'for you've made me hot and bothered with unbridled passion. Then I'll leave this obscenely overpriced flat and get away before they send some big brute to demand money I haven't got. It's called a moonlight flit.' She closed the suitcase, smiling at his concern. 'I don't suppose you've ever been in that situation?'

'I could write you a cheque for the amount,' he began, admiring the jiggle of her breasts as she shook her head. 'What you've done for me deserves a reward.'

'Forget it,' she assured him. 'I enjoyed it too, if you didn't notice.' Unconcerned, she stepped out of her evening gown, his admiring eyes fixed on her as she shed her bra and briefs to stand gloriously nude. 'Just look at your fiancée the way you are looking at me now,' she teased him. 'Like a predatory horny male. She'll like it.'

'I hope she does,' Charles said. 'I want her to be as natural and uninhibited as you. I want her to fuck and suck as eagerly. She's beautiful too. I'd expect her to go naked and unashamed on foreign holiday beaches with me, enjoying admiring looks, making me proud of her. I'd allow her lovers, men and even women, if I were there to watch and join in. It's a fantasy I have. There is no dark secret safe from you, is there?'

'It's the kind of marriage I'll have too,' Linda said. 'If you want it like that, make certain she'll do all those things for her own sake as well as yours before you marry her. Find out, for it seems you won't be happy settling for less, so what have you got to lose? Men can get stuck with women who go very cold after the honeymoon.'

'Have you a fiancé, Linda?'

'A certain Martin Compton,' Linda said wickedly. 'He doesn't know it yet, but I'll have him when I'm ready. Now are you going to join me in the shower?'

'I'd prefer if you'd do something about *this* first,' he grinned, falling back across the bed with a stiffly erect prick projecting from his fly. Wordlessly, Linda bent to wet it with her mouth before climbing over him, knees planted on either side of his hips. She lowered her crotch, holding his rigid stalk upright and guiding it into her. 'I'm getting too fond of this,' Charles joked as she squirmed down to be fully penetrated. 'I guess I'm making up for lost time—'

'Do shut up and lie still,' Linda moaned, stilling his first upward thrusting movements. 'Let me just enjoy the feel of your big cock inside me. Oh, it's heaven up me, I could sit on it all night.' She moved her hips, getting the angle of penetration she craved to intensify the pleasure, fully impaled on his length. 'God, how your Moira will love this,' she said, gently jiggling on the cylinder of hard flesh. With his balls nestling in the cushiony divide of her bum, she said, 'Don't come yet, let me ride you. I must, I must.'

Her pace increased. Despite wanting to continue the slow grinding she was compelled by the surge in her cunt to reach climax. Below her Charles gripped her hips, pulled her hard against him, pubic bone to pubic mound, eyes devouring the sight of her wildly bouncing breasts. She felt his final lunges, the spurtings as he came, and fell forward onto his chest as her own violent orgasm subsided into jerky tremors. He did not attempt to move her, but savoured the weight of her naked body while she regained her breath. 'That,' Linda announced, 'was a *fuck*. Thank you, Charley.'

'My thanks are due to you,' he said as Linda rolled aside. 'I must help you. Where will you go?'

'Home and allow my parents to pamper me,' she said. 'I'll get a morning train and be there by early afternoon.'

'I see,' Charles said thoughtfully. 'I can drive you to the train, at least.'

Dawn was approaching as they left the flat. Linda locked the door and put the keys through the letter-box. 'Goodbye to all that,' she said, laughing at his concern. 'What better way to leave than to go out with a lovely fuck. London hasn't seen the last of me, I'll be back with bells on. To Waterloo Station, my man. It has been nice knowing you.'

'I hope you'll keep in touch,' Charles said. 'I'm in the book. I want you to be at my wedding. There wouldn't be one without you.'

On the train she found in her shoulder bag a sealed envelope. She recognised it as one of her own from a drawer in her flat. Deciding Charles had placed it there while she was in the shower, she tore open the flap. Her fingers drew out a cheque for £500 attached by a paper clip to a small white card.

'Dear Linda,' she read, 'Please accept this a small contribution for the delightful way you overcame my problem. I can assure you it's much less than I've paid several eminent shrinks who did nothing for me! I'm here to help should you need a friend when returning to London. All love, C.' She reversed the card, and discovered his business details: 'Charles Pennman, Executive Director, Penn Literary Agency,' it said, with a prestige address in Grosvenor Square. *How useful*, she thought, bearing in mind the rough draft of her first novel left abandoned in her wardrobe at her parents'. Maybe he could help her after all.

On the ferry to her island home she felt it was time to get to work on the unfinished manuscript she had left behind. It would be a profitable way to spend the time and she grew keener on the idea as the bus journey to her home proceeded through lanes and villages. Her mother would welcome her return, she knew, but it was her step-brother, Norman, who answered the door. His face fell, an eager look of anticipation promptly wiped away as he regarded Linda standing there with her suitcase.

'You,' he said peevishly. 'What are you doing here?'

'I live here,' Linda reminded him sharply. 'Thanks for being so pleased to see me. What's going on? Were you expecting someone else?' She walked past him into the hall, leaving him to bring in her case. 'Mother and father are obviously out,' she teased, 'and crafty Norman's awaiting a visitor – it must be a girlfriend. You thought you had the house all to yourself. Right?'

'Why did you have to turn up now?' he complained. 'You stay away for nearly two years and suddenly breeze in and spoil my plans.' Dejected, he fell silent, sullenly regarding Linda and making her laugh at his bleak expression. It was a handsome face to be spoiled with such a dark frown, she thought, thinking her step-brother had grown from gangling youth into attractive young manhood. Amused, she felt more sympathetic towards him.

'I'll keep out of the way,' she promised. 'I'll stay in my bedroom quiet as a mouse. That's my best offer, I'm not leaving the house. If you intend to screw some girl, that's none of my business. Good luck to you.'

'You've changed,' Norman said, brightening. 'It must be your stay in London. You always used to be a rotten bitch to me.'

'And you were the little prick I couldn't stand,' Linda replied cheerfully. 'Perhaps not such a *little* prick now, I suppose. Who's the lucky girl, by the way? Becky Compton? I know you always fancied her.'

'Nearly right,' Norman said proudly, following Linda upstairs with her case, unable not to admire the swaying cheeks of her arse encased in her tight skirt. 'The name's the same. It's a dark secret; all hell would break loose if it got out. Can I trust you?'

'You're dying to tell me, anyway. What do you mean, the name's the same?' she asked.

'Compton,' Norman said furtively. 'Not the daughter, the mother. We've been at it for ages.' He preened, awaiting his step-sister's reaction. 'It's a regular thing, she's all for it. What do you say to that?'

'Good for her if she's keen, and you're supplying it,' Linda said, covering her surprise. 'After my time in London, nothing shocks me.' But she began to giggle at the thought. 'Are you really fucking Martin's mum? She always struck me as too prim and proper to enjoy sex, especially with someone so much younger. What would Martin say? You were his closest friend.'

'He once caught us at it,' Norman grinned. 'Marty was all for it, the same as you.' The doorbell rang as, encouraged by Linda's apparently liberal attitude, he was about to reveal that her own mother was also not above having a lover. There were two, in fact, that he knew of: Martin, and Linda's former tutor, Clifford Maine. The bell rang again. 'I've got to let her in,' Norman said. 'Watch from the landing, sis. Just don't make a sound and keep out of sight when I bring her upstairs.'

'Do you have her in your bedroom?' Linda said in a whispered little laugh. 'There's no half-measures with you. Leave the door open slightly.' She added, excitement fluttering in her cunt at the thought, '—I'd quite like to listen.'

'And see?' Norman taunted. 'I don't mind, you might learn a thing or two. Quietly does it, mind. She mustn't suspect anything.' He hurried down the stairs, leaving an intrigued Linda to go cautiously to the landing bannister rail. She drew back on seeing Olivia Compton appear in the hallway below. As if to demonstrate the truth of his affair, Norman immediately clasped his arms around the older woman, kissing her passionately. She returned the kiss, clinging to him, finally breaking the contact of their open mouths and sounding breathlessly excited as she teased him for his ardour.

'Let me get in,' she cried. *Having a regular supply of hard young cock has done wonders for Martin's mother*, Linda thought to herself, recalling the woman's former frosty tones.

'Don't you ever get enough?' Mrs Compton asked archly. 'It was only last night, you naughty boy. You've phoned for me every day your parents have been away. I've more to do than rush over to see you.'

'But you always do, Livvy,' Norman said smugly, loud enough for Linda to be warned. 'Let's go upstairs. We've hours before my parents return. I can't wait to get you naked on my bed.'

Boasting for my benefit, Linda thought, retreating to her bedroom. She risked a peek from behind her door. About to enter Norman's bedroom the pair had paused to kiss like young lovers, one of Norman's hands cupping an amply curved buttock cheek. After waiting for a minute or two, Linda looked out to see the bedroom door left conveniently ajar. Unable to resist, she kicked off her shoes and tip-toed across the thick landing carpet. Hardly daring to breathe, Linda crouched down to spy upon the lovemaking.

The lovers were snatching kisses as they took off their clothes. Naked, the size and shape of Olivia Compton's big breasts, the thick growth of dark hair on the bulge nestling between her dimpled thighs, made Linda stifle a gasp at such Rubenesque beauty of form. Her arousal heightening, she felt a stab of envy at her step-brother having such a partner. Jealousy, she saw him suck each of her thick nipples in turn, his hand working at the fork of her legs.

Olivia moaned out her pleasure. 'How you make me feel sexy, Norman,' she said hoarsely.

Linda approved of the rampantly erect prick Norman displayed as he fell back on the bed, his legs dangling over the edge. 'Yes! Let me watch you fuck and suck,' she encouraged them silently, her hand under her skirt, rubbing the damp crotch of her briefs. 'Go on, mount him, ride him, Olivia,' her internal voice continued. 'I can't blame you for wanting that big cock. I could take it myself.' In front of her, Olivia went down on her knees between Norman's spread legs, enveloping his prick in the cleave of her formidable breasts, holding them and moving her shoulders while he lay back groaning with pleasure.

'Do you like that, darling?' Olivia said unnecessarily in a voice hoarse with lust. 'Like your hard thing between my tits? Like it when I do this?' On *this*, she dipped her head to cover his knob with her lips and began to suck greedily, making Norman's thighs jerk and his moans increase. Bending over his loins, Olivia's cushiony buttocks pointed directly at Linda. The parted cheeks gave her an intimate view of the plump cunt and anal rosette between the lush globes of her bottom. Linda felt a strong urge to crawl forward, to kiss and tongue both orifices maddeningly, making it a threesome romp. 'Oh, Norman,' Olivia cried suddenly. 'Fuck me now, the way I like it best. Make me come!'

'Yes, put her to the cock, fuck her good!' Linda voiced silently, wishing to see her get it. Olivia rose, bending forward with her elbows on the bed, legs straddled and feet firmly planted on the carpet. Norman needed no urging. With his cock bobbing he bounded from the bed. Taking his stance behind her, with her bottom thrust out for him, he turned a grinning face towards Linda.

'Don't I always make you come, Livvy!' he announced for Linda's benefit. 'I love having you dog-fashion too. My cock in to the hilt. God, you're as juicy as ever up there. What a lovely cunt you have, what a fabulous bum.'

'You can be so crude at times, Norman dear,' Olivia croaked, gyrating her rear ecstatically as he shunted long inches of stiff prick inside her. Watching and listening, Linda knew Norman was being especially lewd for her benefit. Stroking her crotch urgently, she longed to groan out loud, to let herself go and come spectacularly, like Olivia. As Norman's belly smack-smacked her rear, she cried out, craning her neck, climaxing with her whole body, urging Norman on as he jerked and shot his volley of come deep inside her.

Sated, Olivia collapsed across the bed, her buttock cheeks twitching as her throes subsided. Norman sat beside her with a self-satisfied look on his face. Then Olivia sat up, stretching her arms and raising her large breasts. 'I really must go,' she said, fending away Norman's hands. 'I told you I have guests.' She began gathering up her clothes. 'Enough is enough, young man. I don't know why I give in to you so easily.'

'Because you love this,' Norman laughed, holding his limp dick. 'Guests or not, it didn't take you long to nip over when I called. It was worth it, wasn't it?'

'Don't make me feel worse,' Linda heard Olivia say and

decided it was time to return to her bedroom while safe to do so. 'Fancy making love with someone I've known since he was a small boy. Let's just do what we do, Norman, and leave it at that. Though you do satisfy my needs.'

Alone in her room Linda undressed, deciding to finish herself off in the privacy of a shower. Left on the verge of climaxing, her cunt palpitating in anticipation, she heard the front door being closed as she wrapped herself in a bath towel. Moments later Norman's beaming face appeared around the door.

'Did you see it all?' he said. 'See the way I made her come? Now do you believe I'm screwing her?'

'Don't kid yourself it's your irresistible charm that brings her here,' Linda scoffed, annoyed at being interrupted. 'She's a lonely older woman, mad keen on young prick – yours or anyone else's.' Norman wore just his shirt which hung open to show off his cock. 'Trying to impress me?' Linda taunted him. 'I've seen much bigger. You weren't too bad, if you must know. Of course, she'd be all for it. Hard to say how good you'd be with someone not so desperate.'

'There've been others, I've had no complaints,' he laughed. 'It turned you on watching us, didn't it? Your face is flushed. Did it make you feel like wanting some yourself? Make you need to play with your quim?'

'Mrs Compton was right,' Linda said coldly, resenting the implication. 'You *are* bloody crude. What makes you think I'd ever resort to that? Me?'

'Knowing you have diddled yourself before,' Martin grinned. 'Do you deny you kept a big black dildo in your dressing table? You made good use of that, I'll bet. But a dummy cock is not as good as the real thing, is it, Linda? Realistic as it is, it's not flesh and blood. I always wondered where the hell you got it from.'

'I should have expected a rotten pig like you to go through

my private things,' she said icily. 'I thought you'd improved. I still hate, loathe and detest you.'

'I'm glad you think so highly of me,' Norman said affably. 'Come off it, Linda. You always went through my stuff – read my dirty mags and the rest.' He sat on the bed beside her, covering her hand with his. 'We're two of a kind, we shouldn't be enemies. It runs in the family, you'd be amazed what's gone under this roof. Not just me shagging Martin's mum or you having it off with a dildo. Other things.'

'What other things?' Linda asked, pulling her hand away from his. 'Surprise me, if that's possible. Who?'

'That same outward shrine of respectability, our dear old ma and pa, pillars of propriety,' Norman began.

'I always thought them too dull to be otherwise,' Linda cut in. 'Mind you, I thought that about Olivia Compton even more. Now I've seen her naked and romping with you on your bed. What about our parents?'

'Dad for starters,' Norman said. 'He's been giving one to our daily help for years. I suspected it and hung about to catch him nipping home during the day to nail her while mum was at the office. I've seen 'em at it lots of times. The old man's no slouch, he's shagged her in every room in the house. I've seen Mrs Parsons kneeling to suck his dick in the kitchen.'

Linda compressed her lips in an amused smile. 'It doesn't surprise me,' she said. 'He's *your* father, not mine. Mind you, if he was so hot at screwing our daily I'm surprised he wasn't able to satisfy my mother.'

'Probably because she was getting her rocks off else-where,' Norman grinned. 'Yes, your sainted mother. Martin has been there frequently before he went to college and ever since when home on visits. Seems if he couldn't screw you, he went for your mum. She was at it before then too. Your old writing tutor Clifford Maine came round to dip his wick a few times. I know, because I've spied on them too.'

'No doubt you did,' Linda said drily, the information about her mother and the tutor bringing back her own past. She hitched up the towel swathed about her, realising it had slipped to expose the swell of her breasts down to her nipples. Glancing down she saw her step-brother's prick regaining stiffness and length, poking out of the opened shirt. 'You're exciting yourself,' she said, annoyed with herself for feeling aroused at the sight. 'Put that dirty thing away. Better still, get out of my room.'

'Do you really want me to?' Norman said calculatingly. He lifted her hand and curled her fingers around his rigid stalk. He was delighted to observe she maintained her grip. 'What's gone on in this house, you could write a book about,' he hinted slyly.

With his tool hot and thick in her hand, its pulsing throb exciting her despite a determination not to respond, she said, 'I can imagine how you and Martin would revel in discussing fucking each other's mothers.' Lovely face flushed and her voice strained, she struggled to appear unaffected. With an effort she released his cock from her hand. 'No,' she murmured as if unsure of herself. 'No, not with you.'

'Why not?' Norman insisted, lowering her across the bed and pulling the towel from around her. He kissed her mouth before she could turn her face away, then went down to flick each stiff nipple with his tongue tip and probed a finger between her parted sex lips. He was encouraged by her stifled moan, a stiffening of her body and an involuntary tilting of her pelvis. Lower still, he replaced the exploratory finger with his tongue, delving into her recess, concentrating on ensuring her arousal to the point of no return.

'*Please*, no,' Linda breathed. 'God, no – not with you,' she went on weakly, at the same time parting her legs, her bottom writhing. 'You filthy beast, Norman. You're seducing me. I don't want to – I won't.'

'Won't?' he said harshly, raising his head. 'You're juiced up and dying for it.' He poised himself between the cradle of her thighs, nudging the knob of his prick against her swollen pouting sex lips. Below him she lay wide-eyed and silent, as if accepting her fate. 'You want my cock, don't you?' Norman said. 'You need it badly. Say you do. Tell me!'

'Yes, I want it,' she complied, sobbing out the plea. With a forward movement of his flanks he had his prick up her to the balls. Thus skewered, she lifted her hips to receive its full length, pulling him into her, her heels drumming on his back. His excitement increased with her reaction, their bellies smacking as she met his incoming thrusts.

'You bastard, making me like this!' she croaked out as he fucked her to the first of several strong climaxes. At last Norman jetted his load in the dying moments of her final orgasm and she pushed him off as he slumped on top of her.

'Get off me,' she ordered, recovering. 'You won't ever do that to me again, I promise. Don't get any ideas. It was a one-off and you can think yourself bloody lucky.'

'Oh, I do,' Norman said proudly, looking down at Linda and thinking what gorgeous tits she had as they heaved and panted. 'Two in one day. My best mate's mother and now my step-sister – both coming on my cock. Just like it happens in the book.'

Linda frowned, showing reluctant interest. 'What book?' she asked, disbelieving. 'Do you mean one you've written? Don't make me laugh.'

'*Your* book, actually,' Norman grinned, moving aside as if expecting to be struck. 'You think you're the only literary genius around? It wasn't finished, so Martin and I have done you a good turn.'

'You found it in my wardrobe and you'd no right to touch it,' Linda screamed in fury. 'What did you and Martin do to it? I hate both of you.'

'Cool it, Linda,' Norman urged, holding her wrists to prevent a flurry of blows. 'Marty and I had some fun with it, that's all, during his vacations. *Your* precious manuscript is still as it was, unfinished. We read it and saw it was all about families like us – sexy – so we added other chapters in our own version and came up with a classic ending. At least Martin did. He's good.'

'It will be a load of rubbish, I've no doubt,' Linda said, still fuming, covering herself with her bath towel. 'All I can ever remember you two reading were nudist publications and girlie mags.'

'You can read it if you like,' Norman teased. 'There's still a lot of your original work in it. We loved the bit about the girl sneaking off to screw her teacher. I think we improved it no end – I'll bet you'll agree when you see it.'

'I've no time to read novels by good authors, never mind trash written by you and Martin,' she said spitefully. 'In future, leave my private things alone. Now get out of my room. I need to wash away your disgusting sweat. Don't you ever try anything with me again.'

As she showered she reluctantly admitted to herself that Norman had fucked her spectacularly, though she was still resentful that her unfinished novel had been interfered with as a joke. Returning to her room she found a thick cardboard folder on her bed. Several hundred neatly typed pages were tucked inside. *Families* had been the working title of her book. Now she saw the title page read as *Relative Affairs*. She had to admit that was better. The same page bore her name as the author.

Curiosity got the better of her as she scanned the opening paragraph. 'It was not that kind of family, she was not that kind of girl,' it began. 'So Lynn supposed, despite the recurring dreams . . .'

It was not the way she had written the beginning but, intrigued, she lay across the bed, cupping her chin in her palms and reading on.

Chapter Seventeen

GETTING THERE

Hortense replaced the receiver, dialled and made another call, then she went through to Martin, working at his drawing board in the outer office. He glanced at his watch, saw it was after nine at night. 'Don't tell me. Jessop's phoned to say it's time we quit for the day and went home,' he joked. 'The special dinner he's cooked for us is spoiling. Or wouldn't he dare?'

'No, he wouldn't,' Hortense replied. 'I've just had a call from some girl with a foreign accent. She said she's in Hugh's flat and he's passed out. In a drunken stupor, I'd guess, but they're getting worried because they can't rouse him.'

'*They're* worried?' Martin queried, amused.

'Two of them at least,' Hortense supposed. 'Bembridge always was greedy. The girl who phoned sounded calm enough but she thinks he's in a bad way. She's found his business card and phoned here. Lucky we were working late.'

'Tonight and every night,' Martin laughed. 'We bust a gut getting the magazine out while laughing boy entertains lady friends. What do you intend doing about him?'

'Not a thing, I'm leaving it to you,' Hortense said. 'I've phoned for a taxi to take you to his place. Kick out those girls and get him to bed.'

'What if I kick *him* out and take the girls to bed?' Martin suggested. He saw by the look Hortense gave him that she was not amused. 'Only kidding,' he assured her. 'As if I'd fuck anyone else.'

He alighted at Bembridge's apartment building none too pleased with his errand of mercy, having been looking forward to one of Jessop's culinary masterpieces and then taking the chef's wife to bed. He went up in the lift, impressed by the luxury of the place; it was owned he knew by Bembridge's wife, a mystery woman he had never seen. As his finger touched the bell, the door swung open – opened as if whoever was inside was impatient for his arrival. A young Chinese girl, her pretty face heavily painted, stood in front of him patently very concerned. She wore a bra which barely covered pointed pear-shaped breasts and a miniscule triangle of the same white lacy material at the fork of her slender thighs.

'He's on the floor, we couldn't lift him back on the bed after he fell off,' she explained, leading Martin in. Bembridge sprawled on the thick carpet like a beached whale, wearing nothing but a suspender-belt and fishnet stockings, his large belly jutting. Sitting on the bed directly above him was a gorgeously curved Asian girl. Completely naked and seemingly at ease, with a drink in her hand, she repeatedly prodded Bembridge with her toe. 'I think your friend is dead,' she announced, her calm manner the opposite of the Chinese girl's fear and anxiety. 'He doesn't look too good.'

'Your estimate is a little generous, but otherwise correct,' Martin had to admit. 'Not a pretty sight to say the least. Old Hugh went out happy, no doubt. You girls were too much for him.'

'We do nothing to him,' the Chinese girl protested, gingerly stepping around the prone figure. 'No fuck, no suck yet. Only drink with him. Have drink before make sex.'

'*We'll* drink his health then,' Martin decided, going to the laden sideboard, refilling the girls' glasses and pouring a malt whisky for himself. 'He looks better dead than he did alive. Cheers.'

The Chinese girl screamed and leapt in the air as the supposed corpse let out a long loud belch, struggling to sit up and then collapsing again, his eyes rolling back to the whites. 'It's his ghost,' screeched the terrified Chinese girl. 'His ghost is rising!'

'Don't be stupid, that's only a drunken fat man,' said the Asian girl angrily, resuming poking Bembridge with her foot. 'He drank too much before we came here and hasn't paid us.' She turned to Martin aggressively. 'You. What are you going to do about it?'

'As you're so concerned,' Martin said, 'I'm calling for an ambulance.' He dialled the emergency number. 'There's evidently life in him yet. Just what were you two doing here, as if I need to ask?' Martin spoke briefly to the operator, replacing the phone.

'We're from the Mona-Lisa Agency,' the Chinese girl said, still trembling. 'I am Mai Wun and my friend is Surgit Kuar. Mr Bembridge send for us.'

'And he never paid our fee,' the Asian girl reminded Martin. 'We must have money to take back with us. It was agreed.'

'Wouldn't you say this was a special case for skipping the payment?' Martin argued, kneeling beside Hugh Bembridge, the girls watching with interest as he pressed an ear to the chest of the recumbent form. 'No fuck, no suck, remember?' he repeated Mai Wun's words. 'No pay fee. Don't look at me, I'm always skint.'

'He ordered two girls and we came,' Surgit insisted emphatically. 'Two to do lesbian show, to let him spank Mai Wun over his knee, also for me to cane his behind before we fuck with him.'

197

'The poor bastard would hate missing out on that lot,' Martin said with genuine sympathy. 'I can't get a heart beat, but then I never thought he had a heart. Either of you two care to try the kiss of life on him? Halfway down might be more effective in his case. That should rouse him.'

'No money, no nothing,' said the sullen Asian beauty. 'If we return to the agency without the agreed fee, Mona will accuse us of keeping it. You bloody kiss him.'

'Looks like it's curtains for poor old Bembridge then,' Martin decided. 'Let's hope the ambulance gets here soon. God, he's going cold, the least we can do is cover him.' From his kneeling position he tugged at the duvet Surgit was sitting on, making her rise from the bed, her large breasts jiggling and revealing the black mass of hair between her ample thighs before she sat back on the bed. Pulling the duvet up to Bembridge's chin, Martin investigated the male clothing strewn beside the bed. In the inside jacket pocket he found a bulging wallet and an unposted letter. The trousers yielded keys as well as loose coins and a handkerchief.

Watched suspiciously by Surgit, Martin retained the wallet, letter and keys. 'It's okay,' he assured her. 'I work for the guy and will keep these safe for him.' A glance in the wallet showed a thick sheaf of new banknotes: fifties, twenties and tens as well as credit cards. 'He couldn't pay me, but the mingy sod was loaded,' he said aloud to himself. 'There must be at least a grand in here.'

'You pay us then,' the insistent Surgit urged him. 'Someone must. Otherwise it will be no commission for us and a wasted night. I will write you a receipt. It is £150 for each girl.'

'You pair must be very good,' Martin said as the chimes at the door announcing the arrival of the ambulance crew. Mai Wun let them in, a burly female paramedic the size of a Sumo wrestler, followed by her male driver pushing a wheelchair of the collapsible kind.

'I can see it's all been happening here,' the ambulance woman said, going immediately to the prone Bembridge and drawing back the duvet to attend to him. Martin supplied Bembridge's details and the other paramedic wrote them down on his clipboard. 'Probable heart attack while drinking and taking on these two bimbos,' said the woman as she rose to her feet and put away a stethoscope. 'He looks about as good as I would in those suspenders and fishnets. Let's have him in the vehicle and off to hospital.'

'Do I pack a case for him?' Martin asked.

'Your friend won't need a thing for some time, if ever,' she said, lifting the deadweight Bembridge with ease and sitting him in the wheelchair. 'Do you wish to accompany him to hospital – or one of his young ladies?' she added with the glimmer of a smile.

'I don't think so,' Martin grinned in return, following them out to the lift. 'I'll phone in the morning to see how he's making out. He's got a wife too,' he remembered. 'When I find out where she is I'll inform her, of course.'

Returning to the bedroom he saw the two girls gathering up their clothes. 'Whoa!' he said. 'Are you tired of my company?' He took the wallet from his pocket and counted out some crisp notes. 'A hundred and fifty each, but if you want the dough you have to earn it. Fair's fair. On the bed, ladies, and I'll be with you as soon as I've made a phone call. Make yourselves ready.'

He studied the letter he had found and read the address: 'Mrs Bonita Bembridge, Westbury Court Clinic, Roehampton.' Dialling Hortense, he briefly explained it was a hospital job for the unfortunate Hugh. 'I've found a letter to his wife. I won't contact her tonight as she's evidently in some sort of hospital – a clinic, the address says. I'll wait until morning.'

'Where are you now?' Hortense enquired. Her tone

softened, its implication seductive. 'Will you be home tonight? I'm speaking on my bedside phone in a lonely bed, wearing nothing but a dab of perfume.'

Glancing back, Martin saw Surgit and Mai naked together on the bed, kissing and fondling passionately, the Chinese girl's slim paper-white form contrasting with the dark-brown Asian's heavier build. *It's no act that*, Martin decided, *it's their thing and they've started without me.* Pausing with the telephone in hand, he watched in fascination as Surgit fed her big rounded teats to Mai's lips, her wrist working as she finger-fucked the writhing girl underneath.

'Are you still there?' Hortense demanded impatiently. 'I was looking forward to being laid tonight especially. I want you here, Martin. What are you doing now?'

'Standing by a sick bed,' he said, watching Surgit's head between Mai's spread thighs, tonguing hungrily at her cunt. 'I don't know if I can get away.' The Asian girl rose up on her hands and knees, with her back hollowed and a hand between the plump buttock cheeks busily pleasuring herself. Mai's croaks and cries at the intensity of her licking out reached Hortense at the other end of the line.

'My God, someone must be in agony there,' she said. 'I suppose you'll have to stay if Hugh is liable to expire. He wouldn't do as much for you.'

'Someone has to do it,' Martin sighed, impressed by the ample curves of Surgit's raised bottom. 'I'm just going to have to face it.' Replacing the receiver, he loosened his tie in preparation for stripping off. Moments later, bare to the skin and with an erection at full stretch, he padded to the foot of the bed. Kneeling on the thick carpet, he went in face first, his palms spreading the smooth dark-brown cheeks. Surgit's initial squeal of surprise turned to one of pleasure as he licked at the fingers titillating her quim and she waggled her arse to encourage him.

Her sweet copious juices drenched his mouth and chin. The cunt he probed with his searching tongue proved a musky, sopping cavern of soft folds of twitching flesh. 'Fuck me,' he heard the girl moan against Mai's cunt. 'Fuck me hard, whoever you are. Put it up me quick!' He'd never met one readier to be given the dick, Martin decided, eager to fulfil her wish. He rose over her back and found himself looking into the seemingly agonised face of the Chinese girl. He gave her a friendly wink as his engorged prick slid into Surgit's cunt.

The expression 'like a hot knife through butter' came to mind as the first push took him in to the hilt, his balls lodging comfortably in the deep valley of her cushiony arse. Hard up Surgit's hot slippery recess, shunting his big cock effortlessly into its depth, Martin considered it too wide and slack for full pleasure. He was suddenly surprised as Surgit expertly tightened up. He felt the fleshy walls of her pussy clamp around his shaft in a vice-like grip then just as suddenly they relaxed again. Once more the strong inner muscles contracted, closing around his shaft like a fist, making him feel he was being milked. The process was repeated and on each momentary release he thrust forward to her cervix, bringing a series of strangled groans from her throat.

He realised Surgit was *good*, that he was being delightfully manipulated by a genius at fucking. 'You divine witch,' he murmured, his flanks pistoning as she balled her behind into his belly, his hands full of her soft, heavy tit.

'Oh yes, fuck, fuck me!' she was screaming, her gyrations mounting as she accomplished several orgasms. Proud of servicing such a feisty girl so effectively as she collapsed over Mai, Martin felt his balls gripped by a small hand, drawing his still erect stander from the Asian girl's cunt. Mai was looking up at him appealingly. 'You fuck me now,' she said politely. 'Fuck like you did Surgit.'

He pushed the limp form of Surgit forward as Mai tilted her pelvis and directed his prick to her cunt. Tight as she was, aided by her juices and Surgit's saliva, Martin forced a passage and fucked her. Through sheer willpower he held back the hot load surging in his balls until she squealed in orgasm. His chest lay on Surgit's bottom as his flanks heaved and Mai squeaked her pleasure, the intensity of the coupling mounting until both were shouting out in their climaxes. Finally, Martin flooded her quim, revelling in the spasms as Mai convulsed below him.

He awoke with daylight lighting the room through the curtains, the two naked females either side of him deep in sleep after the night's exertions. He rose, noting it was past nine by his watch, and phoned the hospital to be informed Bembridge's condition was stable. Next he called Hortense at the office, reminding himself it was the first time in weeks he had missed being there with her.

'I knew it would be a long night for both of us,' she commiserated, the sly humour in her voice evident. 'I thought of you being there. You wouldn't have got much sleep, you poor boy.'

'True,' Martin admitted. 'I did what I had to do.' Across the room he saw Surgit getting out of bed. As she yawned and stretched her weighty tits were hoisted enticingly. Mai, too, was stirring. Her neat, sharply pointed breasts appeared above the duvet as she sat up. Her nipples were a bright red, still stiff from the combined sucking of Surgit and Martin. She slipped out of the bed, following Surgit's ample bare bottom into the adjoining bathroom. Standing nude, with a hard-on, Martin was impatient to join the girls and replace the phone. 'I'm going to clean up and seek out Mrs Bembridge,' he told Hortense. 'I'll use Hugh's car as it's parked here at the hospital. Tell you all the details when I see you.'

Seconds later, bounding into the bathroom, he was inside

the glass screen of the shower cubicle and under the warm spray with Surgit and Mai. 'Make room,' he ordered, laughing as they squealed and tried to push him out. A swipe with his hand at Surgit's sudsy bottom and one to Mai's smaller rear led to an exchange of long kisses and a grope of their tits. He felt two different hands at his crotch, Surgit squeezing his balls and Mai's slim fingers curled about his prick. 'He has a black man's cock,' the Chinese girl giggled, slipping down on her knees beside Surgit. Two mouths shared the stalk as Martin stood and let them have their way. He looked down at their two heads bobbing, their mouths sucking, and decided it a perfect way to start a day.

It was a pleasure to drive the Mercedes to Westbury Court Clinic. The imposing mansion stood behind high wrought-iron gates and a tree-lined driveway ran through secluded wooded grounds. The reception area was filled with potted plants and the sound of soft classical music. A receptionist dressed as a nursing sister sat behind a large desk. 'Do you have any food or alcoholic beverage or tobacco?' she enquired as he went up to her. 'Those things may not be brought in. Whom do you wish to visit?'

Before Martin could answer, one of the telephones on her desk rang. 'Mrs Bembridge says you are to go right up to her room,' she said, replacing the phone. 'I'll call a nurse to show you to her suite.' Martin followed the nurse up the stairs, passing a number of men and women dressed in towelling robes. The nurse knocked on a double door in a deeply carpeted corridor and then left Martin to enter alone.

Inside, a woman sat in a gilt chair having her blonde hair combed and set by an effeminate-looking fellow; a girl sat beside the woman manicuring her nails. There was a familiar look about the pampered blonde that puzzled Martin – had they met before? She was in her thirties, her face attractively round and even-featured. Voluptuous too, Martin could tell from the upper half of the robe she wore. Suddenly he remembered the night before he had left home for college, when he had put this same woman in a taxi to be taken home, too drunk to stay awake to complete sucking him off.

'You're not my husband,' said Bonita Bembridge. 'When I saw the Merc driving up I thought it was him. Who are you and what do you want?'

'Mr Bembridge is in St. Jude's hospital,' Martin explained. 'His condition is stable this morning and I've some valuables of his that I felt you should take care of. I'm Martin Compton and work in his publishing house. I've a letter for you, giving this address.'

'And when did he write this?' she asked as she was handed the letter. 'After he was taken ill?'

'It must have been before,' Martin said. 'It was on him when I found him, along with his wallet containing a large amount of money and his keys.' He gave them to her and, without a glance, she put them on the manicurist's table. 'I used his car to get here—'

'*My* car,' Bonita Bembridge said succinctly. 'Hugh doesn't own the shirt on his back. That letter will be begging me for more money to keep his publishing business solvent. You work on this magazine he's producing so what do you do with it all? You must have plush offices, champagne lunches and bottomless expense accounts.'

'The crafty sod,' Martin couldn't help saying. 'We work in an office in a condemned building, producing the magazine on a shoestring. I haven't been paid a single bean since I started and neither has Hortense. And there's at least a grand in that wallet.'

'Go,' she said to the hairdresser and manicurist. 'Leave us.' As the door closed behind them she looked at Martin, her generous lips forming an amused smile. 'That's my

Hugh, the no-good slob. The only reason I gave him regular sums was so his staff could be paid their salaries. All twelve of you.'

'Only two,' Martin corrected her. 'Mind you, we've got a product that will return your investment handsomely. We're ready for the first edition of *Mature* to be printed. It's a sure bestseller.'

'What's stopping you then?' she asked, still amused.

'The printers have this curious hang-up about being paid,' Martin grinned. 'They've dealt with your husband before.'

'This isn't the first time you've proved your honesty with me, is it?' she said, her smile now mischievous as a bejewelled hand indicated the wallet. 'We've met before. At a disco or dance, I dimly remember, and I was the worse for drink. Whatever we were up to, afterwards you put me in a taxi with my handbag. It was a while ago but I do recollect part of it. Just what were we up to, by the way?'

'Do you really want to know?' Martin said. 'It might shock you.'

'Nothing shocks me, young man,' she laughed. 'Not knowing is annoying. I recall you took me somewhere – under the stage where a noisy group were playing. Then it seems I passed out. I insist on knowing what went on.'

'Before you conked out,' Martin said hesitantly, 'you – you were fellating me.'

Bonita Bembridge laughed softly, the big breasts beneath her robe jiggling alluringly. 'Such a pretentious word,' she said, 'for having a prick in the mouth and sucking it off. I'm considered very good at it. Did I prove satisfactory to you?'

As always, such openly suggestive talk by a woman produced the stirrings of an erection Martin did not attempt to conceal. 'You passed out just when it was getting good,' he told her. 'Very good. Would you care to continue where we left off?'

'Cheeky boy,' she teased, 'and I thought you were more interested in getting your old magazine published. My jacuzzi will be ready now, so join me in a hot tub and we'll talk business – and whatever else may come up. You may find me generous if you get me in the right mood. Let's find out how persuasive you really are.'

Later, driving back to the office in the Mercedes, having been told to use the car as his own and with a cheque that would pay the printers, Martin looked back on a highly successful morning. It was business with pleasure, he recalled joyfully, especially while watching the voluptuous Bonita shed her robe and join him naked in the jacuzzi. Such tits, ripe handfuls for him to gorge upon, and a cunt that was begging for his prick. Later she had sucked him off to prove her expertise and he had returned the favour by going down on her and making her come again.

The lunch served in her suite had amazed him. Prime steak and sautéed potatoes, a selection of sweets. 'I'm not a patient here,' she said when he expressed surprise at the food. 'I used to be and I liked it so much I bought the place and now I live here.' He had fucked her across the bed after lunch and promised to visit regularly to keep her informed of the magazine's progress.

Hortense was working at her desk when he got back. He waved the cheque under her nose as he walked in.

'How did you manage this?' Hortense said excitedly, examining the cheque and hugging him, overjoyed by the windfall. 'She certainly came across. Did you have to go down on your bended knees?'

'I certainly did,' Martin replied, recalling Bonita's spread thighs as he tongued her. 'Now let's tell the printer it's all systems go!'

Chapter Eighteen

RUDE AWAKENINGS

Linda read through the pages of her revised novel well into the evening. Unable to put it aside, she had to concede that it read well. Her original work had been turned into a veritable page-turner. Considerable skill and talent had been used to combine her writing with another hand, that of Martin's, she had no doubt, with Norman providing the parts that included his particular adventures.

The families depicted were plainly recognisable as her own and the Comptons, here brought vividly to life. Sex reared its head throughout the unfolding story as the individuals featured sought to satisfy each other's lusts. The surprise ending was cleverly conceived, a highly creditable twist that Linda wished she had thought up herself. She finished the last word, feeling that, like Alice going through the looking-glass, she had actually entered the book. Norman appeared at her bedroom door as she laid the manuscript aside. She returned his grin with a glare, aggrieved that such compulsive reading was not all her own achievement.

'I couldn't wait any longer for our revered parents to return,' he said cheerfully. 'I've been out to get a Chinese. I know you used to love that stuff. Get dressed and I'll see you downstairs.'

He hadn't said a word about what she thought of the

revised book, Linda reflected as he left. No doubt he was waiting for her to make some comment but she had no intention of praising it. In the kitchen she found the table laid and chilled wine with the food. Norman even held her chair for her as she sat down. Grudgingly she had to admit he had improved in her absence. The sex between them had been comparable to any she had experienced. As if reading her thoughts, he raised the matter as she silently began to eat.

'Still mad at me for screwing you?' he enquired, watching her tackling her food with relish. 'I'm not, I thought it great. You seem none the worse for it.'

'You caught me unawares,' she retorted haughtily. 'It certainly won't happen again. I can't understand why I let you.'

'You didn't let me so much as join in wholeheartedly,' Norman reminded her with a grin. 'Admit it, Linda. You really went at it, jerking your arse, loving every inch up you. You went wild.'

'Only because it was unexpected,' she said casually. 'It must have been that. You forced me. For years we've been brother and sister. What you did was – was almost incest.'

'Did that turn you on?' he laughed mockingly. 'But we're not brother and sister, so what harm has been done? I've thought about fucking you before now.'

'That doesn't surprise me,' Linda sneered. 'It's all included in that awful book you and Martin have concocted. What dirty minds the pair of you have. And it's obvious who you've written about. You've hardly changed the names.'

'You started it,' Norman pointed out. 'The two families, and the names you chose for them, are all your own ideas. Martin and I simply added the other things you wouldn't know about.'

'And didn't wish to know,' Linda said emphatically. 'You two had no right. You've ruined my book.'

'Have we?' Norman challenged. 'When I peeked into your room you couldn't put it down. You should thank Martin for improving your novel. It's worth publishing.'

'It's rubbish,' Linda said maliciously. 'Fancy revealing those things about our families. No one escapes, even that woman Martin called Aunt Joyce. Did they really have an affair?'

'He screwed her rotten,' Norman grinned, 'as well as having your mother. But you wrote some lurid stuff too, like the girl being fucked by her boss. Was that Hugh Bembridge and you?'

'It's author's licence to add spice to the story,' she lied. 'No doubt you fucked Becky Compton, not just her mother. I can believe that.'

Further argument was abruptly ended by the arrival of their parents. While hugging her mother Linda could think only of Marion allowing Martin to bed her. Her step-father's kiss of welcome reminded her he was servicing the plump daily help. 'The house hasn't changed,' Linda said, tempting fate. 'Does Mrs Parsons still clean?'

'Yes, and I think she's got a lover,' Marion Simon said, unable to resist a jibe at her husband. She had no intention of revealing anything about their previous night's stay at Joyce Long's house or what had been uncovered, but had to get her dig in. 'I don't know what he sees in her with that huge bust and bottom. I presume he manages to satisfy her, whoever he is.' She looked hard at her husband, making him swallow nervously.

'What do you think, dad?' Linda laughed. 'Do you suspect Mrs Parsons of having a bit on the side? I wonder who he is?'

'How would I know?' he said, trying to sound casual. 'I don't think she'd be unfaithful to that husband of hers.'

'I've so much to catch up with,' Linda said, turning to her mother. 'What news of Martin Compton since he graduated

209

from art school?' she asked innocently. 'We've completely lost touch.'

'You were never very nice to that boy,' Marion Simon said, her face remaining unaffected by the reference to her lover. *Full marks for handling that with such aplomb*, Linda had to concede. 'He always asks how you are on his visits home,' her mother continued. 'Never misses coming to see us. Norman could tell you more if you're really interested. They telephone each other regularly.'

'Marty's doing okay,' Norman said. 'He called only yesterday. He's in London, working for a magazine publisher. Claims he's the art director, writer, editor, the whole bag of beans. I thought he was bullshitting but he actually offered me a job on the staff. He put a woman director of the company on the line to verify it.'

'There's a job going in publishing?' Linda said, her interest aroused. 'And you weren't interested?'

'Norman's going to university,' his father put in proudly. 'What with you working in television, Linda, your mother and I are grateful both our children have done so well. We never miss the programmes you help to make. One actually had your name on the credits as a researcher. No doubt there'll be more.'

'No doubt,' Linda said, ignoring the fact that she and Merlin had parted company, not wishing to dwell on that subject. 'It's a pity you both weren't here when I arrived. I have to return tomorrow.'

'So soon?' her mother complained.

'I've seen you all, that's why I came,' Linda said. 'It was a spur of the moment thing. I must get back to London – there's so much to do.' There was indeed, she slyly considered, planning her next move. A job going in the publishing concern Martin was involved with was too good a chance to pass up. He would surely put in a good word for her – she was certain he must still fancy her. She was also calculating what Charles Pennman, the literary agent, might think of her revised novel. It could be that he would consider it worthy of publication. Hadn't his note offered to help her in any way on her return to London?

She covered a genuine yawn with her hand, tired from the previous night spent with Charles, the journey home and the strenuous sex with Norman. Excusing herself, she announced she was ready for bed. She was about to fall asleep, when her mother appeared to tuck her in, wanting to talk. 'I do worry about you in London on your own,' Marion Simon confessed, as if leading up to more. 'It must be full of temptations for a pretty young girl. All those media people and their parties. The literary crowd especially, I believe, have loose morals.'

'How would you know, mum?' Linda laughed. 'What literary people have you met? Name one.'

'Your tutor Clifford Maine,' she said. 'His latest book is on sale now.' She hesitated, as if reluctant to say more. 'That man tried to seduce *me* when we met to discuss your lessons. The beastly lecher made it obvious what he wanted.'

'He really tried to seduce you?' Linda feigned great surprise, inwardly amused by her mother's outrage considering she had gone to Clifford willingly. 'I'll bet you put him in his place.'

'Of course,' she said naturally. 'I never much liked the coarse brute but you were so keen to be taught by him.'

'So, what you've always wondered,' Linda smiled innocently, 'is whether he tried to seduce your daughter as well. Of course not, mummy. Now I'd really like to sleep. It's been a tiring day.'

She felt her mother kiss her brow, snuggling down and happily considering her prospects. Missing London already, she couldn't wait to get back. Charles's cheque for £500 would cushion her return and this time she would make good. Sleep followed, until she stirred as if in an erotic dream, highly aroused and undulating her bottom and hips to the pleasurable feeling in her cunt. For long moments she responded, deep in a trance, suddenly coming to with open eyes to see the dim light of dawn through the curtains. Beside her in the gloom, sitting up on her bed, Norman had an arm under the duvet, a finger insidiously working away in the moist folds of her crevice.

She held his wrist, stopping its movement, sitting up and using her other hand to draw the duvet up over her bare breasts. 'What,' she hissed fiercely despite the excited throb in her sex, 'just what the hell do you think you're doing?'

'Trying to work you up for another jump before you leave,' whispered Norman candidly. 'I woke with this magnificent hard-on.' He leaned back to reveal his rearing cock. 'It's a pity to waste it.'

'You must be mad!' Linda objected with all the force she could command. 'How could you think such a thing? With our parents next door – how could you?'

'We'll do it quietly,' Norman grinned, 'very quietly. One of those long slow lovely fucks that won't disturb the neighbours. Come on, Linda, your pussy's sopping, I can feel it.'

'You really know how to smooth-talk a girl,' Linda told him nastily. 'Take your hand away and get out of my room.'

'Please,' Norman said more seriously. 'You look lovely with that dark hair falling to your shoulders. And what nice shoulders they are.' He caressed one gently, moving his hand down her arm to draw the duvet away from her breasts. With pleasure he heard her intake of breath. 'God, you're beautiful,' he observed. 'Not just your face, but all over. Your tits – breasts – are gorgeous.' The finger inside her cunt recommenced its titillation and she responded with a low anguished

212

moan, giving an involuntary squirm of her pelvis. To her hoarse 'Don't, Norman, *please*,' he insisted that she did want him to fuck her.

'N-n-no!' she moaned as his lips crushed her mouth. 'Don't start that. Talk to me instead. Tell me more about Martin. I'd like to see him when I go back to London—' Her voice wavered as he kissed her neck and lowered his mouth to the curve of her breasts. 'Do you have his address?'

'A telephone number,' Norman mumbled into her cleavage, 'is all I've got. I'll give it to you before you leave.' He dragged the duvet aside, enthralled by her silvery nakedness in the early light. 'God,' he muttered, head lowering further as he parted her thighs.

Her whines and whimpers and the way she lifted her bottom as he licked her told him her resistance was spent. 'Do, do that, yes,' he heard and her fingers parted the outer lips to offer him the delicate pink flesh beyond the inner lips, the moist folds yielding to his tongue. Moving over her, he heard the pounding of her heart, as he covered the cushiony ripeness of her breasts.

'N-n-not *there*,' she begged as he unerringly embedded his prick hard into her.

'Yes, *there*,' he replied determinedly. 'You wanted it, you've got it! Now *fuck*!'

With the feel of a male body on her and a hard cylinder of flesh pounding her cunt, ripples of intense pleasure surged from her swollen clitty to her belly and breasts. She squirmed below him, ankles crossed behind Norman's back, her hands pulling at his flanks to haul him closer.

'Go on, go on, I tell you!' she ordered, wanting every inch of his thick, glistening cock. At her urging he renewed his thrusts. In their throes they pummelled the mattress, bellies smacking, sweat bonding naked flesh, crying out their pleasure, heedless of all else.

Mrs Simon, lying awake beside her sleeping husband, heard the sounds from her daughter's bedroom with disbelief. She got up and padded along the landing carpet, a shaken woman. She opened Linda's door wide enough to look inside and saw her worst fears confirmed. She witnessed the rapid rise and fall of Norman's haunches as he fucked her daughter. From the foot of the bed, she saw how Linda's bottom tilted to take his prick and how it eased out, wet and thick, to plunge in again. *It's all in*, she observed, made weak at the sight, *all in to the root*. Her step-son's balls bounced into the cheeks of her daughter's bottom as they fucked non-stop.

Rooted to the spot, despite her despair, Marion Simon realised that her shock was increased by the sexual excitement now churning in her belly. She remained transfixed until the frenzied coupling ended, then she stole away, getting back into bed beside her sleeping husband. Her thoughts raced in turmoil and the sight of the young couples' sexual prowess remained vivid in her mind's eye. She lay prone, her hands cupping her breasts, squeezing them tightly as if wishing to ease her conscience through pain. Her nipples dug into her palms, hard as flints, further evidence of her high arousal. Automatically, one hand went between her thighs, stroking her moist outer lips. Unable to resist, a finger probed inside, contributing its physical presence to the urgent throb in her cunt.

'Linda and Norman, Norman and Linda,' she muttered incredulously as if to her slumbering husband. 'I couldn't believe it, but I *saw* them. What Norman was doing to her – well! – it looked so *good* the way he was doing it. My God, he was going up her, so thick and long, making her go wild. And she was just loving it, my Linda with your Norman!' Her hand left her cunt, going around her husband's waist as she sat up over his curved back, reaching into his pyjama trousers to clasp a limp, fully relaxed prick.

'They were fucking, the pair of them. Fucking,' she said hoarsely in his ear. 'I stood and watched, *wanted* to see them fuck. I saw it all, couldn't stop. Our kids. Norman was so good at it too – so help me, it made *me* want him. I wished it was me! Isn't that just awful? To think of him fucking me?' She moaned almost wistfully at the wicked thought, starting to stroke the soft dick in her grasp, feeling it respond and grow fat.

Mr Simon grunted in sleep, turning on his back. The throb and heat in her hand made her lust unbearable. She drew back the covers and lowered her face. Mouth poised, she engulfed the swollen cock's helmet with her lips, head bobbing, sucking greedily on the stalk now stiffly erect in her grip. With hollowed cheeks she suctioned, as extra inches of cock were drawn deep into her throat. Slurping and gobbling noisily, her free hand resumed pleasuring her pulsating cunt.

'What – what?' her husband groaned, eyes opening to see his wife's bobbing head. 'Oh you divine bitch, yes!' he urged, now aware what had woken him so delightfully. Grasping her shoulders he bucked his hips to fuck her mouth, giving a croak of ecstasy as he inundated her throat with jets of hot emission. Marion swallowed, gulping as she convulsed in a self-induced orgasm. She rolled apart from him, regaining composure to see her husband beaming down gratefully for the treat.

'What brought that on?' he asked good-humouredly. 'Not that I'm complaining. Were you having a vivid dream, dear?'

'Too vivid,' she said worriedly. 'If only you knew.' Marion Simon pulled the duvet over herself, shaking. Thank goodness her step-son was leaving for university, she thought, wondering how long she could resist going to his bed now she had witnessed his prowess.

'Too bad Linda has to return to London,' her husband

said, turning away from her. 'And I'll be away all week at a boring conference in Harrowgate. At least Norman will be here as company for you. Try to make his last few days at home a bit special, won't you, dear? I'm sure you'll think of something . . .'

Chapter Nineteen

PARTY PEOPLE

The night Linda began and ended her short career as an escort girl was a time of celebration for the publishers of *Mature*. Fresh from his shower, standing naked while shaving, Martin saw Hortense's reflection in the brightly lit mirror as she entered the bathroom. Her intention was plain from the wicked smile on her face as she advanced on him. 'Your party guests will be arriving soon, Mrs Jessop,' he told her with mock severity. 'I suggest you try to control your obvious lust. Is this any way for a married lady to behave?'

'It's *exactly* the way you like married ladies or any other kind to behave, you lecherous young man,' she charged. Martin watched her mirrored image with admiration as she shrugged her bathrobe from her shoulders, uncovering her magnificent breasts. She wobbling them seductively as the robe slithered over her broad hips to the floor. Then she posed, tilting her breasts in cupped hands, brazenly jerking her thatched mound in Martin's direction. 'Let's fuck,' she said simply.

'There isn't time,' Martin replied, relishing her invitation and fully intending to oblige. 'I'm due in Wimbledon to bring a fresh body to tonight's celebratory bash, remember? It's time I left to collect Auntie Joyce.'

'We'll *make* time,' Hortense declared. He felt a pair of big pliant tits press into his back and a plump cunt prominence rub salaciously against his arse cheeks. 'This Joyce you claim to have fucked so frequently can wait her turn. As for the guests, Jessop will receive them. *We* made the magazine a success. It's *our* party and we'll fuck if we want to. Like right now, Martin.'

'If you put it that way,' he agreed, 'we'll start the proceedings with a bang. Great, isn't it? Already there are two reprints of the magazine's first issue and advertisers clamouring to buy space.' Her hand circled his waist, grasping his cock, her firm tits massaging his shoulder blades and the crisp coarse hair on her cunt scratching his rear. '*Nice* prick,' he heard her mutter throatily as she rubbed his tool and felt it stiffen and stretch in her hand. 'Give it to me, Martin dear. Fuck me with that nice big prick.'

'How you love a good prick,' he teased her, gyrating his arse against her thrusting crotch. 'You love it in your hand, mouth, between your tits, up your cunt, even up your bum. I bet you wish you had one.'

'Never!' Hortense laughed. 'With one of these,' she pointed out, rising on her toes to squirm her cunt harder against his bottom, 'I can get as many of those as I want. I'll take yours now!'

Martin twisted her around, balancing her ample buttocks on the rim of the washbasin. With her back to the mirror, thighs parting and legs lifting to circle his waist, she directed his knob to rub against the outer lips of her quim. With one thrust forward, he penetrated deeply into warm fleshy folds oily with arousal. 'You've been playing with yourself,' he accused as he fucked her slowly and deliberately. Rising on tiptoe to give her full measure, withdrawing almost clear of her clinging pussy lips, he exulted in the soft moans and sighs this produced. Tormenting her, calmly enjoying working her into a frenzy, he awaited her plea to be fucked *harder, faster*.

His prick had never felt so rigid as it shunted in and out of her cunt, her inner muscles gripping it as if afraid she would never fuck again. Her squirming and jerking threatened to tear the washbasin off the wall.

'Damn you, give it to me,' Martin heard her shout. Her ankles locked about his middle as she increased her pace of thrust. 'Fuck me harder, faster!' she yelled. 'Fuck it up me, make me come! Yes, *aaagh*, I'm there, there! It's *coming*!'

Martin, helpless to prevent the spunk surging from his balls in response to her excitement, worked his flanks to match her heaves, jetting his load as she cried out loudly in her throes. He stepped back at once, withdrawing his prick as she attempted to retain it, her features contorted as the final spasms shuddered through her damp body. 'You beast, Martin,' she complained. 'I wanted to come again. Once is never enough.'

'Then let me, dear,' Jessop said, entering the bathroom, his eyes glued to Hortense's gaping cunt. She remained lolling with her back hard against the mirror, her breasts heaving from her exertions, thighs widely parted. 'I'd be glad to oblige.' He went down on his knees before her, her sex, at eye-level, still gaping from Martin's girth, his lips drawn to the spot he craved. With tongue extended, the tip gave a tentative lick to the glistening crevice. A forward movement of his head had his open mouth clamped over his wife's cunt with his tongue probing deeply. Martin turned to leave them to it, pleased for Jessop as his tonguing had Hortense moaning and crying, her pelvis lifting in fucking motions.

Once dressed, Martin went downstairs, the tortured groans of Jessop licking out his wife growing fainter. In the lounge he came across Manny, the photographer, taking pictures of the splendid buffet decoratively laid out. 'Hortense's old man certainly lays a good spread,' Manny said, snapping away. 'He fussed about, moving the champagne glasses with a ruler to get them exact. I take it he doesn't mind who fucks her either.'

'He gets off on it,' Martin said, 'but don't knock him for that. In their own way they're an ideal couple.'

'Talented too,' Manny said. 'Look at the cake he's baked. A perfect replica in icing of the cover of your magazine. That's got to be included in your featured spread of *Mature*'s celebration party.'

Martin agreed. 'I've planned six colour pages to cover the event. *Playboy* features their own parties so why shouldn't we? Once it swings tonight, Manny, get all the gaiety, the balloons and streamers, but most of all plenty of pics of tit and arse. Let our readers see we're where they'd like to be, attending a raunchy romp.

'We'll need a few female bodies for that,' the photographer said. 'Brian is bringing Noala to add colour. Hortense is already known in your mag and has a great body. Who else have you lined up?'

'Two friendly whores I know, a Chinese and Asian girl,' Martin said. 'They're paid performers, but they'll enjoy doing lesbian poses.'

'Don't want anything too posed,' Manny advised. 'I want shots of it all happening naturally, with everybody stripped and making out like it was a great party. You and Brian will be joining the ladies, no doubt. We must have a few male bodies circulating. I'll get you from discreet angles, of course. We can't show erect willies.'

'Then you'd better shoot us from the waist up,' Martin laughed. 'Jessop will be in it, serving the guests in his frilly apron. Besides that, two other mature females of very photogenic proportions are coming to bare all. I'm leaving right now to fetch one of them.'

'Do they know what they're in for?' Manny asked. 'I

presume they'll go along with anything. Who haven't you screwed?'

'I could name one I'd like to,' Martin said, thinking of Linda Simon. 'But you won't be disappointed with the two I've invited once you've seen their big tits. Bonny Bembridge will arrive in her chauffeured limo. She sank money in *Mature* to get us published and fucks like it was going out of fashion. The one I'm fetching I've always called Aunt Joyce. We've been at it for years, man and boy. Just make sure you've got plenty of film.'

It promises to be a memorable evening, Martin thought happily as he drove to Wimbledon. He intended to fuck as many of the women present as he could, creating a record for himself. Parking the Mercedes in front of Joyce's house his headlights lit up another car. Not visitors, he hoped, finding Joyce at the front door, holding a finger to her lips for quiet and ushering him into the hallway.

'I've been watching out for you, I heard your car,' she whispered. 'John and Marion Simon are in my lounge. They've been antique-hunting in London and dropped in unexpectedly yesterday. I had to ask them to stay and they're still here, drinking and arguing.'

'So you can't attend our sexy shindig?' Martin said disappointedly, keeping his voice low as Joyce ushered him upstairs. 'You'll miss a great night.'

'Perhaps not,' Joyce smiled mischievously, guiding him into her bedroom. 'Perhaps they'd like to come along and discover a few things about sexual freedom. They've had affairs and different lovers but won't admit it to each other. I think it's time they shared their experiences. The marriage is rocky and dull. Your party could be what saves it. Invite them. They're an attractive couple.'

While she spoke, standing face to face with Martin, she drew her fingers and palm over his crotch, cupping his balls

221

in her hand and giving them a suggestive squeeze. 'I don't know about asking Marion Simon and her old man to the party,' he said, the heat in his balls spreading to his cock. 'It's a fuck and suck do. Anything goes. Would they go along with that?'

'Why not?' Joyce asked, a knowing smile on her attractive face. 'Neither are exactly celibate, except with each other by their own accounts. We've been drinking all evening and a few home truths about the Simon marriage have been revealed. They don't fuck anymore, except with others, I happen to know.' She giggled as she stroked Martin's engorged stalk through his trousers. 'Has she taken this lovely big prick often?'

'I've had my leg over Marion a time or two,' Martin admitted. 'Did she tell you about it?'

'When her husband went off to bed after a row last night,' Joyce said smugly. 'She slept with me rather than him. We made love. Perhaps expecting to shock me, she boasted of having had both men and women lovers. And guess who she claimed was the best ride of all? Young Martin Compton from the Island.'

'So what did you say – what's new?' Martin grinned, sharing her amusement. 'He's fucked me too?'

'I didn't want to spoil her big moment,' Joyce said merrily. 'I never speak with my mouth full, anyway. I happened to be going down on her. Having worked her up nicely, she mumbled on about how you were built so hugely, and she couldn't resist your big prick. She said she would love to take it up her cunt tonight.'

'Taking Marion to the party would be okay,' Martin agreed, as Joyce lowered his zip and withdrew his rigid cock. 'She'd go down well, if you'd excuse the pun. But I'm not so sure about John seeing his wife cavorting naked in a crowd. I don't know him all that well.'

222

'I do,' Joyce said slyly. 'Intimately. You weren't the only one who fucked me on my Island holidays, young man. John Simon wouldn't object to going to your orgy, just his unfaithful wife. I brought up the subject this evening. He was all for attending. She refused out of spite, didn't like to think of her husband enjoying himself.'

'In that case,' Martin decided, indicating the stiff prick held in her clasp and being gently rubbed, 'since you've brought this up, I suggest that we use it. How about a quickie here before I go back to the party. I'll sneak downstairs afterwards.'

'You'll sneak nowhere, young man' Joyce informed him. 'I'm sending the objectionable Marion Simon up to you. Much as I'd like you to use that thing on me, I've got it hard for *her*. Get her going and I'll return with her husband. That should break the ice.'

'He might just break my neck,' Martin protested. 'It's crazy. Where did you get such an idea?'

'From John himself,' Joyce said deviously. 'His wife was at the hairdresser's this afternoon and he had me, of course. Then we cooked up the whole scene, knowing you were coming. He said he's longed to see his wife at it with another man or woman, so we'll let him. It works both ways. She'll be taking the cock that she craves and he can see it all happening.'

'It could cause a bloody riot,' Martin objected. 'Are you certain?'

'It will work,' Joyce said confidently. 'Marion's been primed, she's randy and tipsy. If she's caught on the job, she'll be made to admit what an adulterous wife she is. Letting their hair down could be the saving of their relationship, a form of marriage-counselling. They could hardly refuse to go to your party after we're through with them, could they?'

Left alone, Martin was not so sure. The presence of Marion and John Simon would add to the numbers for the magazine feature, but he didn't share Joyce's confidence. He lolled back across the bed, his prick poking solidly upright from his open fly, awaiting Marion's entrance. She came into the bedroom and stopped in her tracks at the sight before her.

'Martin!' she cried and sank to her knees before his outstretched legs, clasping the big erection in her right hand. 'Joyce said there was a surprise waiting for me. Did you come specially for me?'

'I didn't know you were here,' Martin said, watching her open lips encircle his knob. 'I came to take Joyce to a celebration party. You can suck and fuck all you want there. I'm inviting you and John.'

'Never mind him,' Marion said curtly, her tongue extending to lick the thick stalk in her grasp. 'How I've missed this big brute. I've masturbated often, thinking of it fucking me. Fuck me with it right now, Martin. You want it and I want it.' Giving a final long suck and drawing her teeth along his length, she stood and hitched up the skirt of her dress. 'I'm going to impale myself on *that*,' she warned. 'Stay right where you are.'

'What if your husband comes up?' Martin said, admiring the white thighs on view as she pulled down her knickers. 'I'd love you to ride me, but it's hardly the time and the place. What would he have to say?'

'I don't care,' she said savagely. 'I want to be fucked and I don't care who knows about it. He deserves a wife that has to get her satisfaction elsewhere.' She kicked her briefs off her feet and drew her dress over her head, casting it aside. Fumbling behind her back, she unclipped her bra and released her superbly formed breasts. 'You usually do all this for me, Martin,' she reminded him tipsily, standing full-frontal before him. 'Now you undress too. When did you ever turn down a chance to fuck me?'

'True,' he admitted, taking off his clothes and hoping Joyce's scheme would not end in fiasco, his rampant tool urging him on. Standing together, skin to skin, they embraced, her hard nipples burning into his chest, his upright prick pressed against her belly. Mouths fused and tongues searching, they fell back across the bed with Martin underneath as she positioned herself over his crotch. Desperately seeking the prick she craved, Marion directed it to her cunt, bearing down to receive full penetration. It slid right up and the sensation of taking the whole thick stem inside her made her groan with pleasure.

She climaxed almost with her first grinding motions, a hair-trigger orgasm that jolted her body and bounced her tits. Crying out for him to continue, she bucked her bottom and shifted her pelvis to vary the angle of penetration. Her anguished cries were loud as she ordered him to fuck her harder, riding madly as a second and third come shook her torso. Martin, aware that Joyce and Marion's husband had entered the room, was relieved when she toppled off him and sprawled on her back, her breasts heaving and cunt parted, glistening pinkly.

'What a randy cow,' John Simon announced calmly, walking up to the bedside and peeling off his shirt. 'She hasn't fucked me like that for ages. It's my turn to give her one, I think, don't you?'

'Yes, why should they be the only ones having fun,' Joyce said meaningfully. 'Fuck her, John, she obviously wants more.' She eyed Martin's prick, seeing it still mightily erect. 'He can fuck me alongside.'

'Just what is going on?' Marion demanded, sobering somewhat. 'So what if you caught us fucking, I don't care. I want Martin to fuck me again, so damn you both. Do it, Martin. Never mind them.'

225

'Go ahead, Martin,' her husband said. 'No doubt you've had her dozens of times. I'll wait my turn. I know you're not the only one that's been between my wife's thighs.'

'You know nothing!' Marion screeched. 'Not a damned thing.'

'But we'd like to know, Marion dear,' Joyce said soothingly. Naked herself, she stood looking down between Marion's spread legs. 'None of us should have secrets. What have you to hide now, lying there still tingling from taking Martin's beautiful cock? We're all adult people.' She leaned forward, letting her fingers trail over Marion's pouting cleft, inserting a tip and stroking the engorged clitoris.

'My, you're sopping in there,' Joyce said sweetly as Marion groaned and flinched. 'I don't blame any man, or woman, wanting to do naughty things to this delightful thing. You husband doesn't care as long as it makes you happy.' She turned to Martin and John. 'Don't just lie beside the lovely lady, you two. Kiss her, fondle those gorgeous big tits, suck one each. Show you *appreciate* her while I play with her pretty nest. Now, isn't that nice for you, Marion? Just lie back and confess all your wicked secrets.'

'You bitch!' Marion groaned under the triple assault on her body. 'If this is intended to make me reveal secrets to my husband, it won't work. N-n-no—' Despite her resolve, she moaned ecstatically as the two men lying beside her held a large breast each, kissing the mounds, closing in on her taut nipples and sucking avidly. 'I won't have it,' she protested weakly. 'It's outrageous.'

'Outrageous pleasure for a promiscuous woman, I'd say,' Joyce murmured, lowering herself between Marion's spread legs and pressing kisses to her upper thighs. She trailed her tongue up the swollen sex-lips, lapping like a cat, sensing Marion's reaction by the barely suppressed writhing of her pelvis. 'You like this, don't you?' Joyce purred. 'Like the two men making free with your big tits and suckling you. Like your sweet pussy licked too. Do I see you holding a stiff prick in each hand now, Marion dear? Martin's is a monster, isn't it? I'm sure you want *that* right up you, don't you, darling?'

'You bitch!' Marion repeated in her agony, Joyce's tongue expertly increasing her state of arousal. 'You *know* I want it, want Martin to fuck me again. Leave us alone please!'

'No one fucks you just yet,' Joyce ordered. 'We want you to talk first, remember? Confession is good for the soul and makes good listening. We all should have nothing to hide. Martin has fucked me, and so has your husband. And I've had all of you.'

'I don't care who's had you,' Marion wailed, her body writhing in her urge to get relief. 'Just bring me off, somebody *please*. I'll tell you what you want! Martin, help me. Fuck me, do it! He's the only one, I swear, the only other one I've ever let have me.'

'She's lying,' her husband said over his wife's sprawled body. 'Some nights she used to go off in her car and return bright-eyed and flushed. I used to picture her with some man, naked along the back seat. I always suspected it was Linda's tutor, Clifford Maine. Was he fucking you?'

'Yes, he was,' Marion admitted. 'He and anyone else who paid me attention, damn you. Hugh Bembridge too, if you must know. Linda worked for him and I suspected they were lovers. He used to fuck me, and there were others you don't even know about.'

'You've been very busy, I'm proud of you,' John said, 'The kind of wife I've always wanted. I can see I'll have to be more attentive.'

'You can be as attentive as you like later at the party. But I've got to get back there,' Martin said, sitting up. 'I take it you'll all be coming with me? It'll finish off what we've started here, I guarantee.'

227

'Let's go, Marion,' John urged his wife. 'Let's put some life back into our marriage. If you want to fuck Martin or anyone else that's fine by me. I intend to fuck you myself.'

'It seems a pity we've all got to get dressed again,' Joyce smiled, rising from between Marion's thighs. 'I take it that will only be temporary, Martin? It *is* a birthday-suit party, isn't it?'

'It will be everybody's birthday,' Martin promised. 'Too good to miss. You will be coming with us, Marion, won't you?'

'Provided that's a statement of fact,' she laughed, sitting up. 'I've been desperate for a good come with you dirty devils having your way with me. In fact I've never felt more like coming.'

On arrival at the Jessop's house, Martin led his friends in to find Manny loading his camera in the doorway of the lounge. Before them a throng of naked people were engaged in frantic sexual activities, including a black man fucking Bonita Bembridge strenuously across the buffet table.

'I like the look of the women you've brought,' Manny said, eyeing Joyce and Marion. 'The more the merrier. I'm afraid we started without you – Hortense thought you'd got lost. I've got some great shots, many of 'em only usable in foreign publications, but the sale of those will pay for this party. As you can see, a good time is being had by all.'

'Quite,' Martin agreed. 'Who's the big black stud bonking Mrs Bembridge? I don't remember inviting him.'

'That's Noala's hubby,' Manny said. 'She brought him along as an extra cock. He's proved very popular with the ladies. Quite a table-ender he's giving that woman, isn't he? You've got some catching up to do. Brian is about pooped out already.'

'I'm here to give my all,' Martin said, 'and I've brought

good reinforcements. What do you think, girls?' he asked Joyce and Marion, his arm around their waists. 'Shall we join the others?'

'Try and stop us,' the women said almost together. In front of them Hortense arose, glowing and naked, from the arms of Surgit the buxom Asian girl. She stepped over the prone forms of Noala and Mai Wun as she greeted the arrivals. 'Welcome to our celebration party,' she said. 'You can see how it is, girls. No doubt Martin filled you in.'

'Not yet,' Marion said. 'But he's going to. He's good at that, as I'm sure we all know.'

'None better,' Hortense agreed. 'Martin's going to have a busy time tonight. I'm glad to see you've brought another nice man to help out. Won't you introduce us?'

'My husband, John,' Marion said pleasantly. 'I'd be obliged if you'd show him some rather more really exotic ways of pleasing a woman. He's keen but he needs bringing out. I'm sure you could liberate him.'

'You've brought him to the right place,' Hortense smiled, 'and he should be grateful for having such an understanding wife. Come along, John,' she said, taking him by the hand and leading him off to where Surgit lay naked across the huge couch. 'Let's find out just how liberated you can be with two eager women. Your wife insists and so do Surgit and I.'

'He's happy,' Martin said, watching John being divested of his clothes by the two naked females on the couch. 'That leaves me as the only one you've got, ladies. What do you intend to do with me?' He hugged Marion and Joyce to him. 'Decide which one wants it first. You can't both have me together.'

'But we can,' Marion said disarmingly. 'Joyce and I discussed what we'd like to do with you last evening. One astride your big cock and the other sitting over your face. That way we can kiss and our hands will be free to fondle our boobs while having you at both ends.'

'On the floor, Martin,' Joyce said, leading him to an empty floor space before the fireplace. 'You can come up for air when we change ends. For once, you can find out what it is to be used.'

'I know I shall regret this in the morning,' Martin vowed. 'If I survive that long. But what a way to go. I'm all yours!'

Chapter Twenty

HOW TO HANDLE A WOMAN

On the train to London, Linda felt supremely confident. Her shoulder bag contained the generous cheque Charles had given her for services rendered, plus another £100 her mother had insisted she take. Her suitcase contained the thick manuscript of *Family Affairs* which she intended to submit for experts to judge its worth, and there was the job with Martin's publishing firm which she considered as good as hers.

She alighted at Wimbledon station with yet another scheme in mind, a bed for the night without having to spend any of her nest-egg. Using a pay-phone on the railway platform, she first called Martin's number. Hortense's voice replied, 'Bembridge Publications, can I help you?' Linda took the professionally polite voice to be that of a mere receptionist. 'I wish to speak to Mr Martin Compton,' she said authoritatively. 'Put me through to his office. This is important.'

'Important or not, Mr Compton is having an early lunch right now,' Hortense replied, trying to contain the amusement in her voice. She was over the desk, phone in hand, legs straggled and skirt rucked over her waist. Behind her in the desk chair, Martin had drawn down her panties, palms parting her bottom cheeks, kissing and lapping at the succulent cunt revealed in the great divide.

'Do you know when he'll be in?' Linda asked.

'Very soon, I hope,' Hortense said, struggling to prevent a low moan as his tongue flicked her clitty. 'I want him in right now. No doubt he'll come before long – I'm expecting his entrance any minute.'

With creditable restraint, Hortense stifled a gasp as she felt long inches of fat tool eased up her receptive cunt channel. Holding the phone firmly, she sensuously gyrated her arse back against Martin's stomach, savouring the bar of flesh inside her. 'Something has just come up,' she said to Linda as Martin began a gentle fucking motion behind her. 'Who shall I say was calling? If you leave your number, he'll call you back.'

'I've no number yet,' Linda replied, growing annoyed. 'I've just arrived in London. I'll call again. Tell him it's Linda Simon from his home town. A very old friend,' she elaborated. She paused, deciding to chance her luck. 'I'm really after a job at your office. I heard there's one going for an experienced writer and thought Martin might put in a good word for me.'

'Where did you hear about a job?' Hortense said, her interest aroused while enjoying a very lewd slow fucking, made all the more pleasurable by conversing on the telephone. 'We haven't advertised for anyone.'

'The job was offered to my brother,' Linda said. 'But he's going to Cambridge so I thought I'd offer myself. I suppose you're just the receptionist and wouldn't know about any vacancy.'

'I'm a director and shareholder as it happens,' Linda heard to her chagrin. Hortense hollowed her back as Martin shunted his prick into her, content to prolong the pulsing feeling in her cunt until the conversation was over, then she would let herself go. 'It was me who spoke to your brother,' she added. 'Martin might well recommend you, young lady, but I shall need to interview you. I've something urgent to attend to right now, so I'll give you our address. I'll be here all day tomorrow. I'll look forward to meeting you.'

After she put the phone down, Linda leafed through the telephone directory until she found the place she was looking for. A short taxi ride brought her to a small flower shop. Outside it, perched on a stepladder watering hanging baskets, she recognised Joyce Long, the comfortably built friend of the Compton family. Linda approached, regarding the woman, thinking how Martin must have enjoyed fucking so curvaceous a body. She too must have loved his huge stiff young prick up her. Linda paused at the foot of the ladder. Joyce glanced down, recognising with surprise and pleasure a familiar face from the Island.

'Linda Simon!' she exclaimed delightedly. 'How you've grown – what a lovely young woman you are now. It must be several years since I last saw you. Have you just arrived from home?'

'This morning. Your friend Mrs Compton sends her regards and tells you not to make it too long before you visit her again,' Linda lied blatantly. 'I'm only in Wimbledon because I've an interview in London tomorrow. I've a friend here I thought could put me up for the night.'

'And you took time to call and pass on Olivia's message,' Joyce said, peeling off rubber gloves as she got off the stepladder. 'How very kind. Where does your friend live? I could drive you over there. My partner Margaret can look after the shop.'

'I've already called there,' Linda said as if annoyed at herself. 'I should have phoned first, of course. She's a writer like myself, and a neighbour said she's away on an assignment. In Africa,' she added for effect. 'Now I have to find a

233

place to stay tonight at least. Would you know of a reasonable bed and breakfast?'

'No need for that,' Joyce said immediately. 'I've a guest bedroom in my house. You're more than welcome to stay. It's almost time to close the shop anyway. I'll get my coat and drive you home, my dear.'

Linda congratulated herself on her guile as Joyce drove into a smart suburb. She had never before taken much notice of the comely spinster, considering her of little interest. Now, noting the handsome face, the burnished red hair and the large firm breasts, she realised how Martin must have relished bedding her. *My* Martin, Linda thought feeling oddly resentful, deciding she would need to do something to even the score. A seduction was favourite, looking across at the attractive mature single woman and wondering if she had ever known lesbian love.

In Joyce's comfortable dining room they ate chicken salad and shared a bottle of wine. Shown to her bedroom later, Linda undressed and remained nude under a silken robe that clung to the curves of her figure. She heard Joyce locking up and ascending the stairs, waiting a few moments before setting her plan in motion. A tentative knock on the bedroom door of her host and Linda walked in. Joyce was caught naked beside her bed, about to put on her nightdress. She turned to Linda expressing surprise. 'Is there something you need, dear?' she asked, apparently unflustered at being seen nude. 'Do you want an extra pillow? I can fetch you one.'

'I'm not ready to sleep,' Linda said. 'Not the way I feel. Would it shock you to be told I find you very attractive? Leave off your nightdress, Joyce. Please let me look at you.'

'What a strange thing for you to say,' Joyce said guardedly. 'Why would you want that?' She draped her nightgown over a chair, turning to Linda quite naturally. 'Another woman

234

and an older one? Why do you want to look at me like that, Linda?'

'Because of your lovely body,' Linda said, making her voice sound huskily sensuous. 'Because your big breasts are so firm and enticing to me. I want to admire them, kiss them if you'd let me,' she stressed, walking to Joyce. 'They look so beautifully full and heavy, yet still uplifted.'

'I've always thought them too big,' Joyce smiled easily. 'I'm glad you like them.'

'And all the rest of you,' Linda said, one hand reaching out to rove lightly across Joyce's tits. 'Such a figure, so shapely – your hips and thighs. That bush of hair around your vagina too. I could kiss you there, I bet you'd taste sweet.'

'Such flattery,' Joyce said. 'You're attempting to seduce me, young lady. Is this just another conquest?'

'I mean every word,' Linda said, lightly kissing Joyce's nipples in turn, noting they had stiffened. 'You like this too, I know. I hope I mature as beautifully as you when I'm older. Let's compare ourselves.'

Slipping out of her robe to reveal her nakedness, she moved against the older woman, nipple to nipple, nudging her pubic mound into Joyce's. With arms around each other, their mouths fused in a long kiss, they fell across the bed. 'You're sweet, and no doubt you've done this before,' Joyce said between kisses. 'So have I, to give in to you so easily. But you're so young, what made you think I'd let you?'

'Something I heard about you being so sexy,' Linda purred maliciously, her mouth poised over Joyce's nipples, feeling the body beneath her stiffen. 'Martin loved playing with these big tits when you went to his bed,' she teased. 'Did you lie back and let him suck them? Like this?' She mouthed each nipple in turn, enjoying Joyce's apprehension. 'How stiff and thick your teats get. This makes you excited, doesn't it? What about Martin's huge stiff cock – you must have gone wild with that shoved up your cunt.'

'How do you know about us?' Joyce said coldly. 'Did Martin tell you?'

'His mother doesn't know – yet,' Linda said deviously. 'That's the main thing. She'd never forgive her best friend for seducing her son.' Her hand slipped down, cupping Joyce's forested cunt mound, slipping a finger into the warm folds of flesh. 'We won't tell her, will we, Aunt Joyce? Did Martin call you auntie when fucking you? Tonight it's my turn. Then we'll both have a secret to keep, won't we?'

To her surprise, Joyce gave a scornful laugh. 'You cunning little bitch,' she said, thinking of the uninhibited sexual high jinks at Hortense Jessop's celebration party – Linda's mother included. 'You came here to have me, using blackmail if thought necessary, to get your own revenge on me for daring to sleep with Martin Compton. So you think he's your private property, do you?'

'When I finally decide to have him,' Linda retorted. 'Anyway, he would never have gone for an older woman like you if I'd let him have his way with me. Just as I'm having my way with you. I'm getting you all aroused, Auntie Joyce,' she sneered. 'Your face is flushed and your big tits swollen. Your cunt is juicy too. I'll bet now that you want me to make you come. Who needs blackmail with you, you horny spinster!'

Unresisting, Joyce let Linda lie across her, cunt against cunt, belly to belly, breasts flattened. 'You don't want me to stop, I can tell,' Linda said tauntingly in Joyce's face while working her hips. 'I want to hear you say "Don't stop".'

'Then you'd better make it good,' Joyce warned, her voice changing to the authoritative tones of experience. 'You little cow, do you think you invented sex between women? What do you imagine single females like myself do with no man available? Grow up! Make me come over and over again if you're so clever. Other women I've slept with can.' Her words made Linda cease thrusting and she sat up with an annoyed frown. 'What's stopping you?' Joyce demanded. 'You were eager enough to have your way with me. Is there no fun in it if I'm not shocked?'

'I've changed my mind,' Linda said petulently. 'You aren't my type. Let's forget the whole thing.'

'But *I* don't want to,' Joyce threatened. She held Linda's wrist as the girl made to get off the bed. 'You'll stay and have sex with me. You might learn something. That's an order, little girl.'

'Let go of me!' Linda shrieked. 'You can't force me!' Twisting and turning in fury, she was helpless in the grip of the bigger and stronger woman. Her anger increased as she was turned over and pinned down across Joyce's knees, facing the carpet. 'You bitch! Fuck you,' she swore in her rage. 'How dare you?'

'The more you struggle the worse it will be,' Joyce promised cheerfully. 'Bitch, fuck – what language from a young lady. My, what a pretty little bottom you have. Such a neat bum. I quite don't know whether to kiss it or spank it. I think I'll do both.'

'You won't!' Linda cried, striving to free herself from the relentless hold. With legs kicking and hot tears of humiliation brimming her eyes, she realised she had met her match. 'You old witch,' she sobbed. 'Let me up. I've never been treated like this. I won't have it.'

'But you will,' Joyce said grimly. 'And it's high time you did, you spoiled brat. Must I make you lie still?' Stretching out a hand, she reached for the handle of a wooden hairbrush on the cabinet beside her bed. With the same sweep of her arm she brought its oval-shaped back smartly down across the agitated girl's bottom. Stung by the sudden blow, startled by its resounding *thwack*, Linda howled in pain and fury, clenching her cheeks. A further flurry of smacks made her concede and she lay still across Joyce's cushiony lap as the spanking proceeded, her moons reddened and twitching. When the punishment ceased, she moaned almost pleasurably, buttock cheeks relaxing and parting.

'No more,' she begged contritely. '*Please* don't spank me any more. My poor bottom feels on fire. I know I deserved what I got, I swear I've learned my lesson.'

'I don't think you have,' Joyce said kindly. No longer pinned down, Linda made no attempt to move, lying obediently as if awaiting permission to rise. 'You must learn never to start what you won't finish.' She felt a speculative jiggle of Linda's crotch against a knee. 'That bottom-warming heated you right through to your naughty little puss and excited you, didn't it, my sweet? I can see it pouting so prettily pink below me.' Joyce slipped a finger into Linda's wet quim and the girl moaned gratefully, bottom gyrating in responsive motions.

'Don't stop, please,' Linda whined. 'I know I've been a bad girl, but now I want *you* to make me come. Do dirty things to me, give me a good come. I – I'll do the same for you – Oh, please make me come!'

'Of course, dear,' Joyce assured the girl across her lap. 'I've the very thing for you – an old friend.' She reversed the hairbrush in her hand, holding the oval end with its bristles. For a moment she caressed Linda's swollen outer sex lips with the rounded tip of the brush handle before sliding several inches into her cunt. She was rewarded by hearing a groan of relief and pleasure as Linda accepted its penetration, working her bottom and tilting it to receive more. At each backward thrust Joyce tantalisingly withdrew the handle, making Linda scream with frustration as she jerked in her frenzy to lodge the object deep within her.

'Fuck me, fuck me with it, whatever it is!' Linda howled. 'Harder, faster – don't take it out! It's heaven, I love it.'

238

'You certainly do, you horny little thing,' Joyce teased, making Linda thrust her bottom harder as she sought the desired depth. 'What a greedy girl you are. You must learn to make it last. You young people have a lot to learn. If you allow the intensity to build slowly, your final spasms will be all the better. Grip the brush handle with your pussy lips, dear. Use your vaginal muscles to milk it, like you do with the real thing. As I did with your Martin,' she added archly. 'The dear boy did so love to fuck his Aunt Joyce.'

Her irony went unnoticed by Linda who was worked up into such a state of arousal that all she could think of was taking the prick-shaped article up her cunt. 'A brush handle,' she groaned, bucking her hips wildly. 'I don't care what it is, ram it in, damn you! I can't take much more of this. Fuck me for God's sake!'

Joyce relented, the pert bottom across her knees bouncing up to match the thrust that she gave to bury the full length into Linda. The girl moaned out her pleasure, hips and bottom undulating as Joyce shunted the smooth cylinder of wood, rotating it as she went in, aware that Linda was climaxing again and again.

At long last her spasms decreased, leaving her limp and gasping across Joyce's lap. When she had recovered suffi-ciently, she sat up and straddled Joyce's knees belly to belly. They kissed lingeringly, their breasts crushed together in the embrace. Linda took the brush from Joyce's hand, regarding it with a smile.

'Fucked by a brush handle,' she said in wonder, 'and it felt so *good*. That's a first for me.'

'I said it was an old friend,' Joyce said, pleased. 'There were no sex aids like vibrators and dildoes for single girls in my early days. We had to improvise. Human nature and sexual needs being the same as now, we made do with big carrots, straight bananas, even medium-sized cucumbers. One day years ago, I spotted this brush in a shop. I had to have it. Since then I have thought of purchasing a dummy penis, they look so realistic, but I've never done so.'

'That would be like being unfaithful,' Linda giggled. 'Do you think the brush was deliberately manufactured to be used as a cock? I mean, given its shape? Even the carved end is a rounded knob.'

'I've always thought so,' Joyce smiled, kissing Linda fondly. 'It's done sterling service for me – and my girl-friends.'

'It certainly works,' Linda laughed.

'Come to bed with me, my dear,' Joyce said. 'There are other ways too. Many more lovely ways for two women to make love.'

'I can't wait for you to show me,' Linda agreed, bending her head to flick her tongue over Joyce's thick nipples. 'And perhaps one or two of my own I could show you. I always thought of you as a frigid spinster. How wrong can one be? Tell me, was Martin a good fuck? Did he make you come when you went to his bed?'

'Martin's a naughty boy,' Joyce recalled with evident pleasure. 'A very well-endowed naughty boy. It wasn't all me, our affair. He visited here while he was at college, too. He couldn't fuck me enough with that lovely big stiff cock. In every room, in the bath, even once while I was cooking at the stove. You know what he's like. I'm sure he used to fuck you when you went together.'

'He tried hard enough but I always kept him at bay,' Linda said wistfully. 'I thought that he would want me all the more. I'll be seeing him again tomorrow. Who knows? I may give him a treat.'

'Give *yourself* a treat, young lady,' Joyce advised saucily, 'for that thing of his is not only enormous but he knows how to use it. I can confirm that. Bring him here with you sometime. I like a good threesome.'

'Joyce, you're amazing,' Linda giggled, climbing into bed. 'In his absence it will have to be the hairbrush, I suppose. Bring it with you – I'm sure we'll find a use for it in the night.'

Chapter Twenty-One

THREE'S COMPANY

The cheap plastic notice on the paint-peeled door told Linda she had found Bembridge Publications. She was hugely unimpressed by its outward appearance. It's hardly upmarket, she thought, recalling the plush offices of Merlin Television, spitefully pleased Martin's supposedly prestigious employment looked such a back-street operation. She nevertheless felt a flutter of excitement at the prospect of meeting the young man she believed was still besotted by her beauty of face and figure. She had teased him and kept him frustrated in the past – it might be rewarding to continue like that. She liked the idea of him dancing attendance on her while they were working together, hopeful of sexual favours he had always been denied.

Martin came out of the door as she made to press the bell. Looking very much the keen young executive in his business suit, he carried a briefcase and car keys. For a moment she found herself at a loss to speak, her stomach fluttering and a strange affection for him weakening her knees.

'Hello, Martin,' she found voice to say feebly.

'Hi, Linda,' he replied easily. 'Trying for a job, are you? Can't stop, got business.' He strode on as if all the years they had known each other counted for nothing. He jumped into a Mercedes saloon parked at the pavement and drove off without a second look.

'And up yours too!' Linda said after the departing car, angry at herself for the emotion she had felt on seeing him. '*Love*, I don't fall in love,' she muttered to herself. 'Not like that, not with him! Get a grip on yourself, Linda Simon.' Furious, she walked into the office.

Her initial impression that the place was shabby had been too generous, she decided, looking around the empty outer office. Two desks jostled for space and there was a tilted drawing board, overflowing paper-filled shelves and an old wardrobe doubling as a cupboard. In the inner office Hortense Jessop looked up from her desk as Linda entered.

'You must be the girl who telephoned yesterday,' she said. 'Linda, isn't it? Lift those page proofs off that chair and sit down. We're in a bit of a muddle here at present.'

'I noticed,' Linda said meanly, still smarting from her brief meeting with Martin. 'Who did your office decor – Charles Dickens?' In front of her the pleasant-faced woman set her lips in a thin smile.

'Very droll,' she said. 'You do want the job, I assume? I was told you were clever but could be awkward. A beautiful bitch was how my managing editor and fellow director described you. Martin did not exaggerate. I can see you're aware what a lovely girl you are. You gave him a hard time, I believe.'

'He wanted more than I thought proper to give,' Linda said, making it her defence, even lowering her eyes. 'He was always after – you know—'

'And you're not that kind of girl,' Hortense smiled knowingly. 'You missed out. Martin is going places. He's worth having.'

'I think I know him better than you,' Linda said haughtily.

244

'In which way do you mean? As a steady boyfriend?'

'That and the undoubted fact Martin comes well equipped,' Hortense said wrily. 'He's a huge talent. But then you never let him prove it. We have another mutual acquaintance too, of course. Hugh Bembridge. He started this publishing company. You were once in his employ as a journalist on a weekly newspaper. The *Island Investigator*, I believe.'

'Bembridge Publications!' Linda said, brightening. 'I never thought it was the same person. We're old friends. So Hugh is the owner of all this, is he?'

'Not any more,' Hortense said, watching Linda's reaction. 'Drink and loose women finally did for him. He's resident in a clinic for the foreseeable future. Tough, but he had a good run, didn't he? He used to talk about you quite a lot.'

'Nothing good, I suppose,' Linda said uneasily.

'On the contrary,' Hortense assured her. 'Everything good. What a promising writer you were. Obliging too. *Very* obliging.'

'What do you mean by that?' Linda asked, her face colouring. 'What did he say?'

'Boast would be more correct,' Hortense said levelly. 'Hugh was a kiss-and-tell man. More than that, a fuck and describe all the lurid details man. He said you and he were on intimate terms, to put it mildly. With such a lovely girl as you it would be expected of him. He can't help himself. All females are fair game.'

'Does that in any way affect my chance of employment here?' Linda said coldly. 'Otherwise I'd say it was none of your bloody business.'

'Actually it improves your chances,' Hortense answered. From her desk drawer she brought out a magazine and passed it across. 'That's what we publish. A so-called girlie mag, made as prurient as we dare without falling foul of the law. That's the first issue of *Mature* and the sales returns are most encouraging. Would it be below your literary ambitions to work on such a publication? And another similar we have in mind?'

'I think I'd find it fun,' Linda said. 'What makes you think that I wouldn't?'

'I never did,' Hortense stated. 'The things you got up to with Hugh Bembridge must have given you an education. You were quite a naughty girl I understand.'

'We fucked and did lots of other things while I worked for him,' Linda said boldly. 'You're obviously aware of that.'

'Useful experience you can put in your writing for us,' Hortense explained. 'Martin's envisaged a monthly series about a pretty girl reporter. How her various assignments and her determination to get an interview leads her to sexual adventures. With men, women, couples, whatever – including her randy editor. Good, lewd excesses.'

'I get the picture,' Linda agreed.

'And would you pose for the cameras?' Hortense asked. 'It would be nice to include photographs of you to go with the text. You know, a revealing shot of you nude behind your word-processor. With large round spectacles and a wig, your own mother wouldn't know you. Posing would mean extra money, of course. It could be your own feature.'

'We could have the girl journalist investigating the hostess agencies,' Linda enthused, remembering her own foray into that world and other experiences. 'She would be a strip-tease artiste or a strippogram girl. There's no end of situations I could write about.'

'That's exactly what we're after,' Hortense praised. 'We have in mind a local nudist club you could join to help research a story, using a fictitious club to spice it up. We need an Agony Aunt too, but one with a difference. We could have Aunt Linda's Lust Line, maybe.' She passed

Linda a handwritten letter. 'Take a look at that.'

'My wife's furry pussy is driving me bonkers,' Linda read. 'Only I'm not bonking and it's a real pussy. She lavishes all her love upon this darned cat and there's none left for me nowadays. It gets the kisses and cuddles and sleeps in our bed, while I haven't had a kind word, let alone a good fuck, for over a year. What can I do? Yours, Harold, East Grinstead.'

'A genuine letter from a reader of *Mature*,' Hortense said. 'How would you reply to that?'

'By telling him not to be such a wimp,' Linda laughed. 'I'd strongly suggest he kick the cat out of the bed. Then he should put his wife across his knee and spank her bottom until she agrees to anything – particularly a resumption of their marital sex.'

'You wouldn't advise seeking professional help? Guidance from a marriage counsellor?'

'Not if it's to be my column.'

'Here's another,' Hortense said, scanning a typed page. 'It's from a man who suspects his wife of having a lesbian relationship with her best friend. She's still having regular sex with her husband but he's dying to know if she's having an affair with this other woman. He says that they're very close. They kiss fondly in front of him and hold hands. He doesn't know what to think. How would you advise?'

'His wife is still screwing him,' Linda said, 'and no doubt doing other wifely duties like cooking and cleaning. So he should be kind and allow her a little variation in probably a mundane life. He's intrigued, I bet he likes the idea. If so, I'd suggest he encourage them to come out and let him watch. Men pay to see women making love. It could be that it would lead to a threesome with him included.'

'I'd say you're hired,' Hortense smiled. She watched Linda looking through the magazine she held. 'What do you think of it?'

'It's very professional. Good art paper. I like the title.'

'Martin thought of it,' Hortense said. 'Also the layout, the typography, a good deal of the printed content. The splendid art-work too. He drew the picture stories. He draws the naked female form to perfection. Such breasts and figures.'

'So I see,' Linda had to say, studying the line drawings depicting the sexual misadventures of 'Millie Mature'. She giggled, holding up the page. 'I know this woman. The sod has used his mother's friend Joyce as his model. It's her actually. I saw her only this morning.'

'Keep looking,' Hortense smiled. 'At first we had to work on a shoestring. Tell me what you think of our Mature Lady of the Month.'

'This – this is *you*!' Linda said, finding the first of several colour pages featuring the woman in front of her. Hortense was pictured in a transparent mauve suspender-belt, sheer stockings and high-heeled shoes. Over the page she posed full-frontal, giving a mouth-watering view of her big bulging breasts, each forward-thrusting orb surmounted with a thick uptilted nipple.

Glancing at Hortense sitting casually behind her desk then looking back at the explicit photographs, Linda felt an involuntary stirring in her cunt. It was a definite pulsing throb that always triggered copious lubrication and certain arousal. She gazed fixedly at the plump hairy mound so invitingly thrust out as if on offer, nestling between smoothly rounded thighs.

'I think you're beautiful,' Linda said hoarsely. 'My God, these pictures take one's breath away. Who was the photographer? He's caught your lovely figure so erotically.'

'Manny is very good, we've used him extensively,' Hortense said. 'Think what he could do with your lovely young figure, my dear. Thank you for your kind words about mine. Ripely mature, I suppose. But readers have

248

demanded more "Lydia from Carlisle", as she's captioned.'

'I don't wonder,' Linda said weakly, crossing her legs and grinding her upper thighs together as surreptitiously as she dared. Turning the pages, Hortense was portrayed in many seductive poses: on her back with her large breasts lolling and legs spread; kneeling on all fours away from the camera, rounded buttock cheeks parted to reveal a tight pink anal orifice and the downward hang of her split cunt bulge. The churning in Linda's lower belly and moist cunt increased, her face flushed as she looked at the last picture in the series. Hortense lay across a bed as if comatose, a sly smile on her lovely face, with several types of vibrators around her on the bedcover.

'The glazed look in your eyes,' Linda said throatily, the throb in her cunt becoming more insistent. 'Did – did you actually use one of that selection of sex toys strewn around you?'

'I didn't need to,' Hortense answered calmly. 'I've nothing against using them, of course; they can be quite effective. It was a sales gimmick, part of an agreement with the people who advertise their vibrators in our pages. If you think it looks like I'd just had an orgasm,' she smiled, 'I'd had several. Martin had just fucked me, and he's very good at it. That too was photographed, though not for our magazine use, of course. It was for continental publications and I've no shame in admitting it. At the time we were desperate for cash to start up *Mature*. We did several contracted assignments, Martin and I, and with others. He was a very sought-after model.'

'I've no doubt,' Linda said drily, recalling the one time she had seen Martin's superior endowment. 'I suppose he has a flat near here. As an old friend I hoped he could put me up for the night.'

'He stays in my home,' Hortense said, smiling at Linda's

frown. 'And so can you, my dear, I've loads of room. It's close to these old offices, not that we'll be here much longer now that we're a success.' She was thinking what an addition Linda would make to her parties as she made the suggestion. 'You'll like it there. It will give Martin a surprise when he gets back from his business trip tomorrow. It's almost time for dinner anyway, so I'll drive you home now. What did you do with yourself today? I thought you weren't coming to the interview.'

'I stayed overnight in Wimbledon,' Linda explained. 'It was almost lunchtime before I got away from my friend. Then I delivered the manuscript of a novel I've written to a literary agency. The man I'd hoped to give it to wasn't there so I left a note for him, giving this address and telephone number if he wanted to get in touch about it. I had no other place I could think of.'

'A novelist indeed,' said Hortense. 'You clever girl.'

At the large house Hortense took her to Linda was met by the fawning Jessop. She was shown her bedroom and then wined and dined with him acting as waiter. Later, unpacking her case in her room after more wine and discussions with Hortense, she decided luck had been with her. She didn't even have to run her own bath, enjoying the luxury of having it done for her by the little man she was surprised to learn was Hortense's husband. Lying in the scented suds she had no idea he was watching her on the house's closed circuit television and, in her euphoric mood, she wouldn't have cared anyway.

Her offhand treatment by Martin was the one aggravating feature of a day that had gone splendidly to plan. The manuscript of her book was lodged with Charles Pennman's literary agency and an interesting post at Bembridge Publication was hers. Getting the offer of a place to stay at Hortense's had been a bonus. Resentment at both Martin and herself for the schoolgirlish rush of affection she'd experienced on seeing him made her determined he would suffer. How dare he give her the brush-off? Living in the same house and working together would be easy meat – she the tempting meat and the ever-randy Martin unable to resist the dish. Cheered by the thought, she soaped her breasts until she was fondling them, pinching at the stiffening nipples. One hand went under the scented bathwater and her cunt tilted to the probing fingers, Hortense's ripe nakedness in mind.

Watching her movements in front of the closed-circuit screen in his bedroom, Jessop stroked his engorged prick, growling his pleasure at the sight of the young woman unashamedly masturbating. His wife's entrance went unnoticed until she was beside him, sharing the scene with wry amusement. The bath was shown full-length from above, as was Linda as she lay back, jerking her hips in the final throes of making herself come. The frantic working of the wrist and hand at her raised cunt was clearly visible above the sudsy water.

'Jessop, you filthy beast,' Hortense scolded her husband. 'Fancy spying on our young guest! You deserve a good strap on your bottom.'

'I know I do!' Jessop agreed eagerly in excitement. 'I do, I do! Only first let me fuck you, my love.' He turned proudly to show her the erection in his hand. 'Lie on the bed, dear, don't let's waste this,' he begged. 'Then you can beat the wickedness out of me.'

'Most certainly not,' Hortense refused him sternly. 'I shall do neither. It would be like rewarding your disgusting conduct. And cease what you are doing to yourself this instant!' To increase his agitation, she switched off the television. Well aware of the charge her husband got from being so denied, she added scathingly, 'No more watching

251

TV for dirty little boys who can't behave. Go to your bed! You can lie there and think about your shameful conduct. Goodnight!'

Back in her room, Linda heard the soft tap at her door and welcomed Hortense's appearance, dropping the towel swathed about her to let the other woman see her naked beauty. 'How very lovely you are,' Hortense said, advancing. 'So pink and glowing. Did you enjoy your bath, my dear?' She reached forward a hand to gently glide across Linda's breasts, letting her palm rub against the still taut nipples, cupping one as if to test its mass and weight. 'How big and shapely they are, my dear, for such a slim young thing. I find them delightful. Do you mind my admiring you?'

'N-no, no,' Linda said, made breathless by the woman's nearness and the suddenness of her advances. 'I didn't know about you. You have a husband and you said that Martin had had you. I didn't know whether you made love with women too.'

'Sometimes,' Hortense smiled, lowering her hand between Linda's thighs, finding them obligingly parted for her and trailing two fingers seductively over moist cunt lips. 'Especially with a young beauty like you. My husband has his own special pleasures, as I have my own. Martin has fucked me for business and because he's so very satisfactory to sleep with. May I sleep with you tonight?'

'Oh yes,' Linda agreed a moment before their mouths fused together in a lingering kiss, tongues entwined. Then she felt herself lowered across the bed, Hortense kneeling before her and between the spread legs. The fingers toying within her cunt made her arch her pelvis to the delightful shuddery feeling, writhing her hips and bottom. 'Your tongue,' she begged hoarsely. 'Lick me out, tongue-fuck me, Hortense. Do that, please, and I'll do it to you. I will, I promise. I'd love to.'

'Bembridge did not exaggerate,' Hortense said. 'You *are* a hot little piece, aren't you?'

Linda felt the increased weight on the bed beside her and then Hortense was lifting her as she found herself drawn on top of the other woman, head to toe. Directly below her face was the plump split mound of Hortense's cunt that she had found so erotically tempting in the magazine pictures. With a heartfelt moan she covered it with her mouth, sucking in the fleshy lips, lapping and licking greedily and then forcing in a stiffened tongue. At her nether end she felt her buttock cheeks pulled apart. A warm wet tongue trailed over her pouting cleft, going on to flick the tip over her wrinkled bottom hole.

'Oh, God, yes!' Linda groaned, gobbling Hortense's gaping cunt, driven in her lust to explore the deepest recess of the pungently juicy quim.

The lewd scene did not go unobserved. Jessop was watching with mounting excitement in front of the screen in his room. Aroused beyond reason at the sight of these two delectably naked females eating each other's cunts in the *soixante-neuf* position, he scampered across the landing to get in on the act.

An inner voice told him to tread warily as he reached the door, and he entered soundlessly then stood rooted to the spot by the greed and urgency with which the two women were gorging on cunt. Lost to all but the wanton sight before him, his lust unstoppable, Jessop climbed up on the bed. He crouched on his knees before his wife's head, his rampant cock poised before the uptilted moons of Linda's pert bottom. With a croak that was meant as an apology for his rash action, looking down over Linda's gyrating arse and seeing his wife's face, tongue extended, he muttered 'Just this once, my dear, I can't help meself.'

The contact of his inflamed knob to her rear orifice and its

sudden entrance made Linda stiffen and gasp. 'Wha-what?'
she cried full into Hortense's cunt. Further taut inches eased
into her back passage and the surprised utterance tailed off
into a long '*Mmmmm – ooh*,' of pleasure. 'Oh, y-e-s,
whoever you are,' she encouraged, waggling her behind and
loving the hot intruder jammed up her behind. 'Do it, do it!
It feels so *good* in there. Go on, push, push – all of it!
Hortense,' she groaned in her ecstasy, 'someone is up my
bum, buggering me, fucking my bottom hole. Has Martin
returned?'

Hortense, engrossed in enjoying Linda's succulence,
opened her eyes to see two spindly thighs either side of her
head. Above her the stalk of a stiffened prick she recognised
as her husband's was pistoning in to the hilt, burying itself in
Linda's arsehole. Each forward thrust stretched the serrated
ring, with an accompanying squeal of pleasure from the girl
on the receiving end. Jessop's balls, swinging weightily,
brushed Hortense's nose as he energetically shafted Linda's
rear, bum-tailing her with a will that was being fully appreciated.

'Jessop!' His wife berated him for such unheard-of impul-
siveness. 'How dare you! What do you think you are doing?'

'Shagging a great piece of arse,' he gurgled in delight,
made reckless by lust. His hands gripped Linda's dangling
breasts as he buffeted her rear end. 'Lick my balls, dearest.
Lick my balls!'

'Keep licking me too!' Linda cried out, momentarily lifting
her face from Hortense's cunt. Delirious with the prick tight
up her anal passage, she bucked and jerked, coming strongly
as she felt the long spurts of Jessop's hot fluid drench her
innards. Beneath them Hortense convulsed in heaving
spasms and shudders, brought off by Linda's mouth and
tongue. Cries and moans accompanied the trio of climaxes
until the intensity passed and left them sprawled limp and

sated in a tangled heap on the rumpled bed.

Jessop was the first to rise, cautiously padding from the room as if realising the enormity of his behaviour. Hortense stretched out her hand to caress Linda's smooth buttock cheeks as the girl recovered, lying face down, arsehole still twitching and leaking her fucker's emission. 'You and your husband,' she giggled in response, 'are quite a pair. Do you always include your house guests in your romps?'

'We do actually,' Hortense said. 'We hold special group-sex parties here. Does that shock you? I must admit that I didn't expect Jessop to join in just now.' She laughed. 'He got quite above himself.'

'He actually got above me,' Linda reminded her mischievously.

'So I noticed,' Hortense returned. 'And you didn't seem to mind at all. All the same, Jessop didn't ask our permission to join in, did he?' She slipped from the bed, breasts and buttock cheeks jiggling, crossing to the wardrobe and returning with a bamboo cane. 'I keep one of these in every bedroom,' she explained, smiling, 'and know how to use it on guests who need a dominant female to keep them in hand. Which reminds me, it was quite disgraceful of Jessop to bugger you like that. He'll pay for it.'

'Don't tell me you feel he should be punished?' Linda laughed.

'He'd be sadly disappointed if I didn't,' Hortense said, swishing the thin cane through the air. 'Come along with me. He'll be skulking in there, fearing the worst, bless him. We can't have him doing just what he likes now, can we?'

'Definitely not,' Linda agreed wickedly. 'Lead on. I'd like to do the same to Martin – for practically ignoring me this morning. And,' she added thoughtfully, 'for not trying hard enough to have me, even though I wouldn't let him. Martin seems to have fucked everyone else, including you and my own mother. I intend to marry him, you know.'

'Then start out as you intend to finish,' Hortense said meaningfully, handing Linda the cane. 'Keep him guessing. Be his wife, his mistress, his whore. Take the cane and get some practice in by using it on my husband. You'll find you'll get to like it.'

'I guess I owe him one for fucking me up the bum,' Linda considered, giving the cane a good swish. 'I'll do it. Poor Jessop. If I thrash him extra hard it's because he'll be sitting in for Martin until it's his turn.'

Chapter Twenty-Two

SITTING ON A GOLD MINE

Working with Linda and living in the same house, forcibly recalled to Martin her exceptional beauty. His initial attempts to flatter and cajole her into his bed proved worse than fruitless, seeming only to increase her determination to keep him at a distance. Doing her work on the magazine quite brilliantly but giving him no personal encouragement, he had to conclude she was the same stand-offish and superior prick-teaser he'd found so frustrating in his youth. Playing so hard to get while working together and sleeping under the same roof made it all the more aggravating.

Two can play that game, he decided, sure of the perverse pleasure it gave her to keep him at arm's length. So he pretended complete indifference to her indifference, all the time convinced her act was as false as his. Nevertheless he was determined not to reveal his desire which was increasing daily. He consoled himself he had all the sexual outlets he could handle with Hortense, Bonita Bembridge and the models he employed for magazine shoots. Unaware that Linda visited Jessop's bed for sexual satisfaction, Martin was sure she would crack in time. It was not easy for him but, like Linda herself, he waited for the other to make the first move.

The little bitch made it harder and harder for him as the weeks flew by. She had such marvellous tits and an arse that he longed to make free with. He knew she was angling to push him over the edge.

Passing her open bedroom door he was unable to stop himself looking in. Linda stood by the bed, wearing nothing but miniscule lacy briefs, about to position the cups of her bra over her flawless breasts. He groaned in despair at such a display of tantalising beauty. In their cat-and-mouse game, he had to admit ruefully, she was armed with all the superior weapons.

'Don't just stand gawping, Martin,' she said severely. 'Make yourself useful and hook me up.' She turned her back to him and he struggled to keep his hands from trembling as she let him fasten the bra. Before his downward gaze was the seductive sweep of her narrowing waist, curving out to the rounds of shapely buttocks barely concealed by their scant covering. Wordlessly he turned to leave, shaken but reluctantly congratulating himself on finding the willpower to resist her. As an added touch he closed her door firmly, then expelled a long breath at the effort.

Hortense came up the stairs to the landing, smiling knowingly at the sight of him leaving Linda's room. 'And about time,' she said. 'You two are made for each other. Did you fuck her?'

'No,' I didn't,' Martin said angrily. 'I'm going to fuck you.' Taking her wrist firmly, he led her into his bedroom. Hurriedly he pushed her across the bed, roughly drawing off her briefs and casting them aside. He unzipped and penetrated her without further preliminaries, fucking her strenuously and seeking only to relieve himself, uncaring of her pleasure.

Being Hortense, she threw her legs around his waist in response to his heaves and had an orgasm as Martin loosed his bottled-up venom into her. Rolling off her and gasping in lungfuls of air, he attempted to make an apology. 'I don't know what came over me,' he said, for once ashamed of his treatment of a woman. 'I didn't mean to use you like that.'

'I quite like being used,' Hortense silenced him. 'I rather enjoy being dragged off and thrown across a bed occasionally. But it wasn't me you were thinking of, was it, young man? What did Linda do to light such a fire in you?'

'The cow was standing almost naked when I passed her room,' he admitted. 'Deliberately, of course, the ball-breaking bitch.'

'You should have sauntered in and screwed her,' Hortense advised, laughing delightedly, 'instead of grabbing me as a substitute. I'm sure it's what you both want. Neither of you will give an inch.'

'I'd like to give her all my inches,' Martin laughed bitterly. 'But who needs her anyway, with the best ride of all here beside me? The trouble is, blast it, I'm stuck on her. I always was and it is worse now I see her all the time.'

'Just tell her that,' Hortense said. 'She's waiting for you to make the first move, so swallow your pride. I know she fancies taking that big cock of yours. Linda is a horny little piece on the quiet.'

'Don't know where she's getting it then,' Martin grumbled. 'Not from me. She works late, then stays in her room writing. She must play with herself for relief.'

He wondered why Hortense suddenly chuckled and stared at her face. 'You're not the only one in this house,' she said pointedly. 'She's slipped into my room before now, every time you've been away and aren't in my bed. We used my double dildo and everything else. She's very keen.'

'You've done more than I have with her then,' Martin said.

'So has someone else,' Hortense teased. 'Horny little

259

Linda has another source of pleasure here. She goes to my husband's room when the urge takes her. You look quite shocked.'

'You mean Jessop is giving her one?' he gasped. 'No wonder I'm shocked. Are you sure?'

'Absolutely,' she smiled at his concern. 'You sleep like a log beside me once you've had your fill. I've heard noises from Jessop's room and knew she was there and what for. Linda likes her vice versa, if you know what I mean. Jessop is only too happy to oblige.'

'The old arse-bandit,' Martin swore. 'I didn't know he had it in him.'

'It's in her it goes,' Hortense corrected. 'Right up her sweet little bottom. She got the taste for it while the three of us were in bed one night. Now she goes back for more.'

'The dirty little slut,' Martin grumbled. 'Fuck her.'

'You fuck everyone else,' Hortense reminded him, 'including the girl's mother. Don't take it badly. She feels safe with Jessop, it's purely physical enjoyment. With you she'd feel it's a commitment – as it will be when you finally get it together. You should be happy to want such an adventurous and sexy girl.'

'I wouldn't want a frigid one,' Martin had to agree. 'She could let me in there as well as others, just the same. I'd still want to marry her.'

'She's the only kind of wife your sort should have,' Hortense said wisely. 'Stay where you are, I'll prove to you how suitable she'd be.' She slipped off the bed, switching on the television set across the room. 'Are you sitting comfortably?' she smiled. 'Get a load of this, Martin – the young woman who's keeping you at arm's length.'

He saw the darkened screen flash alive, to show Jessop sitting up in bed. Seen from the hidden camera above, his face was a picture of delight as Linda approached. She advanced towards his bed, shrugging off her dressing gown, revealing herself gorgeously nude.

'Closed circuit in every room,' Hortense reminded Martin. 'I was determined to video one of her nocturnal visits. I popped in here to tape it.'

'Why didn't you include me?' Martin complained.

'Because you were in my bed, sound asleep after making a beast of yourself with me,' she laughed. 'So you can't resent Linda going elsewhere. She's quite beautiful, isn't she? Such breasts and silky thighs. Worth having for keeps, young man, no matter what. It's my husband she's gone to and I don't object.'

Wide-eyed, Martin watched Linda stretch out face down across the bed, her delightfully pert buttocks tilted in offering. Jessop got out from under the duvet to press kisses of homage to the rounded cheeks. He parted them widely, delving into the cleave with a long extended tongue. Linda's initial soft sighs were clearly heard, her bottom rotating as her pleasure mounted. Taking his time, Jessop tongued her thoroughly, rasping his licking and lapping tongue from cunt to arsehole, now using the tip to probe at both orifices.

'Well done, Jessop,' Hortense said proudly. 'I taught him to do that to me. Now she'll want the same from you one day. It arouses her tremendously and your girl loves it. Now she wants more from him. Listen carefully.'

The mumbling from Linda's lips was barely audible as she spoke for the first time. 'Do it, Jessop,' she insisted in her strangled tone. 'Do what you do to me. Up my bum. Do it now, please.'

On the screen before them Jessop rose on his knees behind the raised posterior. Bolt upright and swollen with his lust, he guided his prick to Linda's crinkled rear entrance and pressed it home. Frowning his resentment, Martin saw the bulbous knob depress the anal ring which yielded before the

261

invading stalk and allowed inch after inch to disappear. At once its presence produced pleasurable groans from Linda's throat. Martin felt the pounding of his heart as her pierced bottom rotated and thrust, the white globes lifting to receive the big cock. Half-in, up to his balls, Jessop easing his tool out, wet and thick, then the sliding continued, the stretching of her rear hole. Quivering in her delirium, Linda craned her neck and whimpered at each stroke.

'What a horny cow,' Martin swore, jealous feelings mounting as the wantonness of the coupling increased. 'Taking it like that – strolling in and cocking up her arse without a word. I know what I'd like to do to her.'

'Exactly what Jessop is doing, I should imagine,' Hortense said, 'and it should make you admit how much you want her. Swallow your pride and tell her. We females like to be told we're wanted.' She indicated the screen where with back dipped and buttocks jerking, head lolling and hair flying about her face, Linda cried out for more, *harder*, *deeper*. 'Think of you making her like that,' Martin was told.

'I bloody well am,' he admitted ruefully, seeing Linda's final convulsions as she fell forward and Jessop's limp cock was withdrawn. Face down, buttocks twitching involuntarily, she lay until she was somewhat recovered, then rose shakily to pick up her discarded dressing gown and walk unsteadily from the room. 'She might have thanked him,' Martin said sarcastically as Hortense switched off the tape.

'No need,' Hortense said flatly. 'They use each other, that's all, and your jealousy is unwarranted. She got what she wanted and went off savouring the feel of a prick up her naughty bottom, giddy with the nice glowing aftermath and a pleasant itch in her back passage. I know, I've been there. How could you begrudge her that?'

Working at the office later, the images of the video engaging his thoughts, he found it impossible to concentrate. He knew for certain he desired Linda more than he had ever wanted any female. Refusing an invitation to join Hortense for lunch, needing to be alone to consider how to win her without conceding defeat, some visitors arrived. A man and an extremely pretty girl stood before his desk, both immaculately dressed and waiting for him to emerge from his reverie.

'We did ring,' said the man, adjusting his spectacles and speaking in a refined voice. 'I also telephoned earlier to try to make an appointment with Miss Simon, if she's available.'

'You must have spoken to Hortense,' Martin said, his interest now aroused at the mention of Linda. 'Miss Simon is out on an assignment, she must have missed your call. Can I help? I'm an associate of hers, Martin Compton. Do you know her?'

'Charles does – intimately,' the young woman purred wickedly. 'Raves about her obliging nature and beauty. I want to see for myself.'

'Be quiet, Moira,' the young man said sternly. He produced a business card, handing it to Martin. 'Charles Pennman,' he introduced himself. 'Miss Simon submitted a novel to my literary agency and I wish to see her about it.'

'I knew she'd written a book,' Martin said, noting the sly smile on Moira's face and admiring her full breasts and shapely figure. 'I'm surprised to hear she's trying to get it published. Don't tell me you think it shows promise?'

'The girl is sitting on a gold mine, so my fiancé would have me believe,' Moira said, her manner still mischievous. 'He should know.'

'Several publishers want the book,' Charles cut in to silence her. 'Television companies have been shown copies of the manuscript; they're talking about producing a big budget series. Will you see Miss Simon today sometime?'

'This evening,' Martin said. 'We live at the same address.'

'Under the same roof,' Moira observed succinctly. 'How cosy. Are you lovers?'

'Ignore my fiancée,' Charles advised. 'We've been celebrating her birthday with a champagne lunch. She has no right to ask that.'

'Happy birthday,' Martin said, giving her an appreciative look. 'It wouldn't be gentlemanly to say we were lovers, would it?'

'Then you do fuck her,' Moira said delightedly. 'You look like you'd be very good at it, I'm sure. Charles has fucked her too, did you know? He goes on about how marvellously sexy she is, how good in bed. Oh, I say, do you mind? Have I put my foot in it?'

'Everybody's fucked Linda,' Martin said casually, covering his mortification apparently at being the only one not to have. 'Good for you, Charles. As we're being frank, your fiancée is well worth fucking too. If that's all, I'll tell Linda to get in touch.'

'As soon as possible,' Charles said. 'It's wonderful news.'

'Then let's make it a double celebration at Charles' apartment tonight,' Moira suggested brightly, her intent obvious as she gave Martin the eye. 'My birthday and Linda's book.'

'It could prove interesting,' Charles approved, noting the looks Martin was getting from his fiancée. 'Come along and bring Linda.'

On returning from his work Martin knocked on Linda's bedroom door and found Linda working on her notes after the day's investigation of a Brighton club. 'It's exactly right for *Mature*,' she said enthusiastically. 'A bar where only young studs and older ladies are allowed in. Toy boys and randy vintage women getting it together in the afternoon. The husbands haven't got a clue what their wives are up to. I've got the story and pictures.'

'Charles Pennman called at the office,' Martin said. 'We've been invited to his apartment tonight. It's his fiancée's birthday.' Then added nonchalantly, 'Oh, and he's got news about your book.'

'You saw Charles?' Linda exclaimed, her interest aroused. 'Did he think *Family Affairs* was any good?'

'Publishers are clamouring for it,' Martin grinned. 'No kidding. The TV people too. You'll hear all about it later. Would you object to me escorting you? I'd like to see how the other half lives. His fiancée, Moira, seems right out of the top drawer, a real looker.'

Martin parked the Mercedes outside the Belgravia apartment and ushered Linda up the steps, thinking he had never seen her look lovelier. Wearing an off-the-shoulder gown and filling it very effectively, she was a vision of beauty. He felt proud to accompany her and wished she had dressed up for him alone. They were led into an ornate lounge by a butler. A side table had been set with a buffet meal and there was champagne on ice. Of their host there was no sign as the manservant bowed and left the room.

'This guy Pennman isn't short of the readies,' Martin observed cynically. 'Just what is he to you, Linda?'

'My literary agent,' she said sharply. 'What are you implying? I sent him my book and it seems he likes it.'

'Much more than that,' Charles said emphatically, joining them and clad in a towelling bathrobe. 'Forgive me for receiving you like this. My fiancée and I fell among friends who insisted on toasting her birthday. We finally escaped and were about to revive ourselves in the sauna. Moira is in there now, sobering up, I hope. We've had quite a day.'

'And my novel?' Linda was impatient to learn. 'Martin says publishers and television people are interested.'

'Which means a double celebration tonight,' Charles said, taking Linda in his arms. 'How absolutely beautiful you are,' he told her effusely. 'So good to see you again and be the bearer of exciting news.' Holding her close he kissed her, lightly at first but then lingeringly, deeply, a lover's kiss. As Martin watched his resentment grew, certain by the passionate way she returned the kiss that she was doing it to deliberately annoy him. What's more, she was succeeding.

'She's quite a girl, isn't she?' Charles said, still with Linda's breasts flattened to his chest as their mouths parted. 'Such a find, gorgeous *and* talented. She'll be right up there with the bestselling women novelists. Her work is so creative, with passages of real literary merit too. It's a marvellous first novel.'

'Fucking her had nothing to do with it, I suppose?' Martin suggested meanly, annoyed by their obvious intimacy. 'A girl's got to use all her assets – everyone fucks Linda.'

'Except *you*,' she said furiously, 'and you never will! Don't talk to me about who fucks who, you bastard. You fuck Hortense and anyone else who's available – even my mother.'

'I don't take Jessop's cock up my arse,' Martin retorted, his anger flaring. 'Or let a fatso like Hugh Bembridge screw me.'

'You fuck his wife,' Linda charged. 'That makes us even.'

'Please, please!' Charles intervened, laughing. 'Much as I find this talk fascinating, fucking Linda, delightful as that is, could not in any way influence my opinion of her work. I suggest you both sweat off your aggression with Moira and I in the sauna. She suggested you join us when my servant said you had arrived. She'll be waiting for us.'

Glaring at each other, Linda and Martin were led down basement steps to a swimming pool with a wooden hut at one end behind a diving board. They were shown into separate cubicles and Martin stripped, wrapping himself in a huge white fluffy towel. He waited outside with Charles until

Linda appeared, similarly wrapped in a towel. In the sauna, Martin saw Moira through a steamy heat haze lying belly down on a cushioned bench along the wall.

The resentment he had felt at Linda's familiarity with Charles was dispelled by the sight of the agent's fiancée. Beaded with perspiration and glowing pink, Moira's back narrowed to flaring hips and curved out to enticingly rounded buttock cheeks and long shapely legs. 'Towels and robes are taboo in here,' she said pointedly, rolling over on her back. 'What's there to hide? You're welcome to see all I've got.'

And it shouldn't be hidden, Martin decided, admiring her large rounded breasts glistening with sweat, the thick nipples and dense bush of fair hair surrounding the lips of her cunt. He hung his towel on one of several pegs behind the door and turned, already semi-erect, to give her a good look. Charles, he noted with pleasure, without the spectacles and robe was athletically built but unable to match him in the prick department.

As ever, Linda nude was a glorious prospect. Ignoring Martin, she sat beside Charles as Moira sat up to make room for them. He clasped an arm around both young women and they cuddled up to him, breasts pressed to his sides. Tilting their faces, he kissed them in turn while their hands fondled his balls and cock.

Martin sat on the bench opposite, resisting the urge to cross over and join in. The heat of the sauna made rivulets of sweat course down his chest to his crotch. He saw Linda glance at him smugly as she stroked Charles's prick while he was fed one of Moira's nipples. In reply, Martin stuck two fingers of scorn up to show his contempt. His prick, however, had a will of its own. It responded by erecting to its full thickness and length, rearing magnificently from between his thighs as if to signal it needed attention. The others were too busy to notice.

267

Charles was lying back full length along the bench, with both girls giving him the treatment. Moira bent to suck avidly on his engorged stalk, her head bobbing as she deep-throated. Linda, still gloating at Martin, squatted over Charles's face, stifling his moans as she squirmed her cunt over his nose and mouth.

Thoroughly pissed off, Martin made sarcastic remarks. 'You can fuck and suck all you want, you sods,' he shouted, his frustration mounting. He lolled back against the log wall to show off his huge stander to best advantage. 'Don't mind me. Why don't you fuck one of them, Charles?'

'Yes, I want to see you fuck Linda,' Moira announced, removing her mouth from his prick. 'Fuck her like you've told me about, Charles darling. I've got you big and stiff.'

As if to taunt Martin further, Linda lay on her back along the bench, widening her thighs and drawing up her knees as Charles stood over her. Moira's hand directed his prick to Linda's quim and his first thrust buried its length in to the balls. 'Yes, oh yes!' Martin heard Linda's gasp of pleasure, seeing her buck her hips wantonly as he fucked her energetically. Even in her throes her eyes sought Martin's, with a look that plainly stated 'Charles is screwing me and don't you wish it were you?' Martin retorted heatedly, 'Bitch! You don't know what you're missing.'

Moira, on her knees beside them, watching every inch of cock being shunted in and out of Linda's cunt, turned on hearing Martin's raised voice. For the first time she saw his erect state, the monstrous stalk rising level with his navel. 'I can see what's she's missing,' she said brazenly, crawling across to kneel up between his legs. One cupped hand nursed Martin's balls while the other clasped his prick's girth, her fingers unable to span its thick mass. 'My God,' she said in wonder. 'It's quite unbelievably huge, isn't it? What a shame for this to go to waste. Don't you think I ought to be allowed to try it out for size? I've never seen such a big one.'

'Suck it and it will grow even bigger for you,' Martin growled, still peeved by the way Linda was responding to the prick up her. 'Then you can sit on it facing your fiancé. That way we can watch him fucking Linda. You enjoy seeing them fuck, don't you?'

'And you're letting her annoy you,' Moira announced, lowering her lips to his prick. 'Grow up. You don't own her yet, do you? She's doing it to show what you're missing too, Martin. Lord, I don't think I can get this thing in my mouth.'

'You can try,' Martin said, relenting. He sighed his pleasure as her warm mouth covered the top of his stem, sucking greedily, going on to stir the molten fire in his balls. He lifted her up before he lost control to such expert cocksucking. Moira twisted around, her back to his chest, thighs parted as her hand sought his prick. Guiding it, she squirmed down to embed herself fully, a gasp escaping her lips as the upright bar of flesh penetrated deeper than she had experienced. Their bodies slippery in the heat of the sauna, she moaned and worked her arse in quickening jerky motions as her initial climax came. She fell back on his chest, riding for seconds.

Martin delighted in the soft buttock flesh bouncing in his lap and the sensation of his prick sliding up and down in a tight moist cunt channel. His hands cupped her big tits, thumbs flicking at the taut nipples, content to let her do the work, enjoying her whinnying at the utter pleasure she received. From his vantage point, chin resting on Moira's shoulder, he saw that Linda and Charles had finished. They both sat up to watch as Moira pleasured herself so shamelessly on his stalk. Linda's eyes, he noted with mounting elation, smouldered with anger and resentment. To add to her anguish, Moira began flopping about even more wildly on Martin's prick, her cries growing lewder and louder as she lost all control of herself.

'Charles, Charles,' Moira howled, out of her mind as the continuing tremors wracked her body and she shuddered to climax after climax. 'Martin is fucking *me*. He's fucking *your* fiancée and she loves it! I can feel his hard thing in my cunt. Right up to my stomach. The brute is making me come and come—' Her writhing told of yet another sapping orgasm but still she wanted more. 'I want you both, darling,' she screeched. 'Fuck my tits and my mouth while I sit on Martin's big prick. Please!'

It was Linda who crossed to Moira and unceremoniously dragged her off Martin's lap. With a sweep of her hand she smacked Martin hard across the face before demanding that Charles drive her home. With a last glare at Martin she left the sauna.

'What the devil was that about?' Martin asked as Charles prepared to go after Linda. 'We were all at it. What got into her?'

'It was what *didn't* get into her – that big prick of yours,' Moira advised, laughing. 'The only cure is to fuck her with it. When are you two going to get it together? Obviously you should!'

'You tell me,' Martin said ruefully. 'After tonight, maybe never.'

Chapter Twenty-Three

HELL HATH NO FURY . . .

Charles waited until the plates were removed and he and Martin were alone in an enclosed corner of the restaurant. Now he broached the subject on his mind. 'With Linda absent it's a chance to discuss the business her book will accrue. I haven't been able to change her mind about the television rights. Perhaps, as an old friend, you could?'

'Old friend?' Martin said wistfully. 'She doesn't pass the time of day with me since that session in your sauna. How could I help you?'

'As her collaborator then?' Charles suggested. 'She did once hint you had a hand in the writing. If so, you can claim a legal interest in the book and a share of proceeds.'

'It's her book,' Martin said, smiling thoughtfully. 'Her own idea and creative work. I may have read the rough and offered advice, but what she wants for her novel is her own business.' He sat back, pleased to give her the credit, replete with a splendid lunch in luxurious surroundings. 'She's quite a girl, isn't she?'

'A bestselling prospect who must capitalise on her success,' Charles pointed out. 'The expected worldwide sales has made the novel sought after by every major television company. She insists Merlin TV makes the series. They in turn would give their eye-teeth for the contract.'

271

'They've turned out excellent programmes in the past,' Martin said. 'Linda worked for them at one time. She knows their set-up and the production staff. I'm sure she must think they're the best people to handle it.'

'They fired her and she left under a cloud,' Charles returned. 'I made a discreet enquiry and I was told bluntly she's poison in their eyes. It beats me why she's so insistent they get the book. She must have a kind heart.'

'Or more likely an evil one,' Martin grinned. 'Who knows what's in her devious mind? Maybe it's pay-back time.'

'Perhaps,' Charles agreed, 'but without Linda's novel they're in deep trouble at Merlin. Recent programmes have not had wide sales. There's talk that Hope Mannering, their chairperson and head of all production, is due for the chop. Takeover bids are being mooted. It's hardly the time to gift them a prime series, I'd say. Apart from that the money they can offer can't match Hollywood rates.'

They were interrupted by Charles' fiancée, Moira, drawing back the curtain and entering the cubicle. 'Business, business,' she complained jokingly. 'There must be a more interesting subject. Isn't it lovely and private in here?' She got down on her knees, raising the table-cloth as if about to crawl under. 'I take it you two have eaten?' she said impishly. 'My turn now, I think, gentlemen.'

'Moira,' Charles said severely as Moira disappeared under the table. He fell silent a moment later as he felt his zip drawn down and a cool hand withdraw his prick. A glance at Martin's grinning face told him that he too was getting the same treatment. With a lengthening cock in each hand, Moira kissed the bulbous knobs in turn before sucking gently on each one, bringing them to full erection. The feel of pricks swelling and filling her mouth increased her suction until both men shot their loads.

'Now I want to be fucked,' Moira announced blithely,

rising from under the table, licking her lips. 'By both of you, right now. Let's hurry back to the apartment, Charles dear.'

'I'd say this horny fiancée of mine won't be satisfied until we've both laid her,' Charles conceded. 'An afternoon threesome on our waterbed seems a reasonable request. After we've seen to that, however, please try to talk Linda out of going to Merlin TV, Martin. It doesn't make good business sense.'

Nor did it to Martin, although he didn't think she would listen to him. The afternoon had quickly lengthened into evening before he left Charles Pennman's apartment, the time spent helping to satisfy the insatiable Moira. They had fucked and sucked her in all possible permutations as the eager society girl revelled in having two men at the same time.

Back at the Jessops' house later, he went up to Linda's room, hesitating before knocking. 'It's me, Martin,' he called through the door. 'It's a business matter.'

'Come in if you must,' Linda said, sounding almost friendly. 'That is if you don't object to seeing me about to shower.' Martin pushed open her door to see her wrapped in a bathrobe, looking particularly desirable.

'God, but you're beautiful,' he said, struck by the deep cleavage of her perfect breasts revealed in the open neck of her robe. 'I swear you get lovelier each day.'

'Is that all you've got to say – I thought it was business,' she replied haughtily. 'Lucky for you I've had a very useful meeting today. It's put me in a good mood. Right now I can even put up with you.'

'Whatever it was, I'm glad to hear it,' Martin said. 'You look like the cat who got the cream. Who was the lucky man?'

'Lucky *woman*,' Linda said teasingly, watching Martin's reaction. 'I looked up Louise, a girl I once worked with at

Merlin television. She has no reason to thank them for the way they've treated her. I'm now in the position to do her a good turn, to help her get her own back.'

'You're doing the whole of Merlin TV a good turn in giving them your book, according to Charles Pennman,' Martin said. 'I saw him today and he truly believes it's not a good deal. You can do better with other TV companies. He begged me to try to change your mind.'

'And what did you say to that?' she asked quietly.

'That it's none of my business, the book is yours to do with as you wish,' he answered sincerely. 'Right now, looking as you do, I only know how much I long to make love to you.'

'I'm sure you do,' Linda laughed, pleased by his admission. 'On the subject of fucking, was that bitch Moira there when you were with Charles? Did you fuck her, Martin?'

'Of course not,' Martin lied. 'That was a one-off, a heat of the moment thing in that damned sauna. I'm sorry it happened. She just about raped me. With you it would be different. Won't you – please. Don't you feel like it?'

'I might have done,' Linda said, enjoying his obvious anguish, 'but I've already been quite nicely satisfied. With Louise, remember? We worked out a plan of revenge, had a glass or two of wine and it just happened. We had a lovely time in bed.'

'That I would have liked to have witnessed,' Martin admitted ruefully, 'or even offered to help out. But what about Merlin television? What's in your wicked little mind? It can't be to ruin them, unless you aim to withdraw the offer at the last moment?'

'They'll get the contract on *my* terms,' Linda said delightedly. 'Tomorrow all will be revealed. I'm keeping a promise I once made to myself. Believe me, it couldn't happen to a nastier bunch.'

★ ★ ★

274

The following morning, in the outer office of Merlin Television's executive suite, Giles French looked up in surprise to see Louise entering his domain without her usual respectful knock.

'Just what punishable misdemeanour have you committed now, girlie?' he asked sarcastically. 'Are you due for another bottom warming? I believe you're acquired a liking for the way the blessed Hope Mannering spanks your bum.'

'Believe what you like,' Louise returned forcefully, finding being bold easier than she'd envisaged. 'She's not going to hurt or humiliate me any more.'

'Brave words, Louise,' Gerald Lyle, Merlin's senior television producer said scornfully. He rose from the chair he had occupied, clutching a bulging briefcase. 'I'm going in to see the lady boss so I'll pass on your message of defiance. I'll be bearing bad tidings of our poor ratings – are you sure you want me to add to her misery by telling her you are no longer willing to be put across her knee?'

'Go ahead and tell her,' Louise said cheerfully. 'Tell her she's a sadistic bitch and she's never going to lay a hand on me ever again. I mean it.'

'That should make her quite distraught,' Giles said, his humour having a bitter edge. 'It's one of Ms Mannering's sole pleasures these dark days. Would you deprive her of relieving her ill temper on your sweet little arse?' He looked at Louise, suddenly frowning, his humour gone. 'My, my the worm really has turned. What the hell are you doing here if you haven't been summoned to the royal presence? Tread carefully, girl, all our jobs are on the line these days.'

'It will take a miracle to save us,' Gerald Lyle put in glumly.

'It could be that miracle is about to happen,' Louise said smugly. 'Outside this office are two people Hope Mannering had better see. Get her out here and I'll call them in.'

'No one, but no one, sees H.M. without an appointment,' Giles said stuffily. 'Certainly not on the say-so of a junior researcher.'

'Then she'll miss the chance of signing up a bestselling novel for a TV series,' Louise warned. 'Can she afford that?'

'Just what is going on out here?' Hope Mannering demanded, emerging from her inner office. 'I've heard all this and can't believe my ears. Have you gone mad, Louise?'

'I've never been more serious,' Louise said, going to the door and ushering Linda and Charles into the office. 'I think you'd be wise to hear what's on offer.'

It was with the utmost pleasure that Linda saw the look of utter surprise on the three faces before her. Gerald Lyle stared as if in shock while Giles leapt up from his seat. 'You!' a furious Hope Mannering stuttered. 'You treacherous whore, are you in on this fiasco?'

'Hardly a fiasco, madam, if it means your company will get a plum series to produce,' Charles spoke up, seriously businesslike. 'I refer to my client's novel. You know her as Linda Simon. She is the author of *Family Affairs*, the latest publishing sensation.' He allowed himself a smile at her consternation. 'Did I forget to mention that during our negotiations? Of course, I used her pen name.'

'Pen name, any name, I refuse to agree to anything that involves that disloyal bitch!' Hope Mannering screeched. 'As for Louise, she's fired as from now. Get out of here, all of you!'

'You can't fire me, I quit,' Louise said. 'I've been offered a better job with the magazine company Linda works for. Do you really think we should leave?'

'No!' Giles French spoke up defiantly. 'Look. H.M., our careers are more important than personal feelings right now. Yours as head of Merlin TV, Gerald's and mine and all your employees. A hit series based on a bestseller would put

Merlin back in the big league.'

Gerald Lyle backed him up. 'Whatever you've got against Linda, H.M., forget it. You're not alone in this.'

'I'll do as I think fit,' Hope Mannering said haughtily. 'I am still the boss here.'

'Not for much longer, I think, if you turn down Linda's offer,' Charles advised calmly. 'Merlin's in trouble. The shareholders are out for your blood. I suggest you agree to my client's demands. Do so and the contract can be signed before we leave. You have her promise.'

'You must agree!' both Giles and Gerald said urgently. 'Give her whatever she asks. You can't do otherwise.'

'What is it she's asking?' Hope Mannering said nervously.

'For a little of my own back,' Linda said menacingly. 'And not just you, either, you dyke bitch, but your two sleazeball mates here who turned against me when I was down. What's more, Louise has a score to settle. Let us proceed to your inner sanctum, where you keep a bed to interview young girls. Do we agree, or shall Mr Pennman tear up the contract he's brought with him?'

'I go under duress,' Hope complained bitterly, leading the way into her private room, followed dutifully by Giles and Gerald. They stood together and awaited their fate as Linda, Louise and Charles confronted them.

'To start with, the three of you strip,' Linda ordered. 'Take everything off. That should be easy enough for you three, knowing how keen you are to see others naked.'

The three undressed hesitantly, at last standing nude and vulnerable before Linda and Louise. Hope's wide mouth was twisted in anger and her eyes blazed behind her large spectacles. 'Bend over the bed, bottom up,' Linda told her. 'Have you got the cane, Louise?'

'I know where she keeps it,' Louise said grimly, holding up the whippy length of bamboo. 'The heartless cow made me fetch it every time she punished me. I'm going to enjoy this.'

'No!' Hope cried fearfully. 'I refuse to be a party to this.' She flinched her buttock cheeks as the first crack of the cane hit home. Moaning, whimpering, she buried her face in the pillows as each stroke landed. At last Linda demanded that she turn and sit up. She did with her hair tumbling about her face and eyes brimming with tears of humiliation. 'I hope you are quite satisfied, you bitches!' she spat out.

'There's more,' Linda assured Hope, pushing Giles and Gerald in front of her. They stood apprehensive, awkward in their naked state, both cocks drooping. 'Suck!' she was commanded. 'Suck them both. Make them hard and erect so they can fuck you. Big and stiff so you'll know what's up you.'

'I don't, you know I don't,' Hope appealed, her resistance gone at the thought. 'I *never* have sex with men. Please don't make me.'

'I said suck,' Linda insisted. 'You may even get a taste for it. Start on Giles, it will be something new for him as well to have a woman.'

'For the company's sake, do as the vindictive bitch says,' Giles said impatiently. 'It's not my bag either, dear, but if that's what she wants, do it!'

With a groan of dismay, Hope obeyed, reaching for the proffered prick, handling it distastefully as she lowered her head. It felt long, thick and hot and it was already twitching in her grasp as she took it in her mouth. As she sucked she felt the shaft swelling and heard Giles' low moan of disbelief at gaining such a rapid erection. He reached for her head, pulling it to him as her suction increased. The warming of her bottom had spread through to her cunt and lower belly, triggering unsolicited arousal, moistening the inner folds of her sex. Now helpless to resist, she gorged greedily on the prick filling her mouth between tongue and palate.

'I'd hardly call that punishing them,' Charles observed humorously. 'She's positively eating him and he's buckling at the knees and thrusting his hips. Even their friend Gerald's got a big hard-on watching them. It's bloody well having an effect on me too. See, Gerald has pushed in, wanting his share. Now she's switched to sucking him.'

'She'll hate herself for this later,' Linda said hopefully, the sight of Hope Mannering avidly sucking cock was having its effect on her as she felt wetness soaking her briefs. 'This isn't turning out the way I thought it would but it's even better. Believe me, Mannering is a tyrant who treats all her underlings with utter contempt. Just look at her cocksucking that pair. Now she'll be reminded of this episode every time she sees those two. I think I'll have Gerald fuck her for good measure.'

On hearing her, Gerald turned his head, nodding agreement. 'I've always wanted to fuck sense into the arrogant bitch,' he growled, drawing his prick from her lips and pushing her down onto the bed. At his first thrust forward he penetrated to the balls, her legs splayed and her protesting scream silenced as he clamped his mouth over hers. The watching group fell silent as they saw Hope respond helplessly, clasping Gerald to her, whimpering in her pleasure and matching his deep thrusts. As if to prove she was still a dominant figure, she rolled Gerald over until he was below her, falling across him with her breasts pressed to his chest, working her pelvis as if she were fucking him. Her broad buttocks lifted and fell with each thrust, enticing Giles to move forward behind her with his erect cock poised almost between the deep cleft of her arse. He looked at Linda appealingly.

'Go on then,' Linda urged, responding to his silent plea. 'Bugger her. Sandwich her between you and Gerald. Give it to her.'

'Yes!' Louise said eagerly. 'Do it, Giles. She's had me there with her strap-on dildo. Pay her back for what she's done to me.' Laughing, she added, 'I'll fetch the lubricating jelly. She always made me do that, but this time it will be a pleasure.'

'There's no need,' Giles growled. 'The bitch deserves cold turkey.' He parted her broad cheeks, inserting a finger into the puckered hole. 'I've felt tighter,' he announced, curving his body over her, letting his prick trail up and down her rear entrance. Hope groaned, stiffened, then twitched and wriggled her bottom. 'If you must,' she whined, still impaled on Gerald's stalk. 'You bastards, making me do this. Go ahead then, fuck me from both ends, fuck my cunt and my arse. Do it to me!'

As she spoke, Giles slid a couple of inches into her hole. Hope gasped and, a moment later, took his full length into her back passage. She arched her back, meeting each lunge of Giles's tool with a matching thrust of her bottom before pushing down to engulf Gerald's cock. Gabbling incoherently, climax after climax shook her body as both men jerked and flooded both her passages with their come.

'We'll give them time to recover,' Linda said, satisfied at last. 'Then we'll finalise the contract. After this exhibition, I know just the man I want to fuck me.'

Martin returned home late and was greeted by Hortense in the lounge. 'I stayed at the printers,' he said, 'and saw the new issue of *Mature* to bed. If I say so myself, it's the best yet.' She smiled as he undid the buttons of her blouse, removing it to admire the fullness of her breasts in her overflowing bra. He pulled it off and feasted his eyes on the plump mounds, weighty enough in their mass to have an enticing droop, the nipples proud and erect. Undressing her was always a special pleasure. To his surprise, she held his hands and stopped him going on. Her smile was mischievous.

'Go up to your room,' she advised. 'You'll find all you really want up there. You've waited long enough.'

Shrugging, Martin obeyed. He entered his room and stopped dead in amazement at the sight of Linda lying gorgeously nude on his bed.

'Will you marry me, Martin,' she asked teasingly, 'and make an honest woman of me? Or do I have to go on bended knees?'

'Later perhaps,' Martin grinned, 'when we've tried every other position.' He shed his jacket and yanked at his tie. 'I thought you'd never ask. Hortense said I'd find all I really want waiting for me. She was right.'

'Then hurry up,' Linda said, holding out her arms to him in invitation. 'Make love to me.'

'Like I never did before,' Martin vowed solemnly.

'Well, not with me,' Linda giggled. 'Just with my mother and everyone else. Now it's my turn!'

A selection of Erotica from Headline

BLUE HEAVENS	Nick Bancroft	£4.99	☐
MAID	Dagmar Brand	£4.99	☐
EROS IN AUTUMN	Anonymous	£4.99	☐
EROTICON THRILLS	Anonymous	£4.99	☐
IN THE GROOVE	Lesley Asquith	£4.99	☐
THE CALL OF THE FLESH	Faye Rossignol	£4.99	☐
SWEET VIBRATIONS	Jeff Charles	£4.99	☐
UNDER THE WHIP	Nick Aymes	£4.99	☐
RETURN TO THE CASTING COUCH	Becky Bell	£4.99	☐
MAIDS IN HEAVEN	Samantha Austen	£4.99	☐
CLOSE UP	Felice Ash	£4.99	☐
TOUCH ME, FEEL ME	Rosanna Challis	£4.99	☐

All Headline books are available at your local bookshop or newsagent, or can be ordered direct from the publisher. Just tick the titles you want and fill in the form below. Prices and availability subject to change without notice.

Headline Book Publishing, Cash Sales Department, Bookpoint, 39 Milton Park, Abingdon, OXON, OX14 4TD, UK. If you have a credit card you may order by telephone – 01235 400400.

Please enclose a cheque or postal order made payable to Bookpoint Ltd to the value of the cover price and allow the following for postage and packing:

UK & BFPO: £1.00 for the first book, 50p for the second book and 30p for each additional book ordered up to a maximum charge of £3.00.
OVERSEAS & EIRE: £2.00 for the first book, £1.00 for the second book and 50p for each additional book.

Name ....

Address ....

....

....

If you would prefer to pay by credit card, please complete:
Please debit my Visa/Access/Diner's Card/American Express (delete as applicable) card no:

Signature .... Expiry Date ....